Grim

Richard Lowe

The Writing King

Grim

Table of Contents

See books by Richard Lowe at
https://masterofworlds.com

Get free publishing insights and industry updates at
https://thewritingking.substack.com

For ghostwriting and book coaching services see
https://thewritingking.com

Hunter on the Ice

He is to my left when we spread across the ice. He has always been to my left. We have run together since we were boys at the edge of the group, too small to hunt, old enough to watch. I do not think of him with a name. He is just him, the specific him, the one whose throwing arm I know the way I know my own.

Eight of us. Four pairs. We build the fire small on the bank above the frozen lake, small enough that the smoke will not carry to the animal before we are ready, and we pass the ochre around in a piece of folded hide and mark each other in pairs the way we always mark each other before a hunt.

My pair presses his palm against my chest and leaves the red there, over my heart, and I do the same to him, and we look at each other. Nothing needed saying. We have done this enough times that the doing is the saying.

The youngest gets the ochre on his chin instead of his cheek. The man beside him fixes it without making a thing of it. The youngest does not know yet that this is kindness. He will learn. He is still learning most things.

Then the dance. The same as always, the steps worn into us the way a path wears into ground. I lead because I lead everything. When it ends I can feel the group in my chest. We are ready.

The mammoth is on the far side of the lake. I found it yesterday, old male, moving alone, slow with age and anger. I watched it for a long time before I came back to the group. I have been reading animals as long as I have been reading ice. I know where this animal will go and how fast and what it will do when it feels threatened.

Before we spread, I saw something at the far edge of the ice. A dark mark, too straight to be shadow, too large to be a crack. I made a note of it and did not think about it again. The mammoth moves the way I said it would move. I am right about this. I am right about everything until the moment my left foot goes through.

Not the deep ice, the edge ice, where the shore meets the lake, where I have crossed a thousand times and where the thickness is less than I read it this morning. I read it wrong this morning. This has never happened to me before.

The cold arrives before I have time to be surprised by it. It is total, not cold the way the air is cold but cold the way the water is cold, which is every surface of the body at once, every boundary between the inside and the outside going the same direction at the same time.

My pair shouts my name. I hear it. I hear everything clearly. I cannot make my arms do what arms do in this situation. I have told others. I told a young man last winter. The instructions are correct. My arms do not receive them.

The cold takes the breath. Not the way cold air takes the breath but the way the body stops agreeing to breathe when the cold is this complete. I am aware of my pair on the ice above me. I am aware of the sound the ice makes when someone is moving on it carefully. I am aware that I read the ice wrong this morning.

I was the best reader in the group.

* * *

We spread across the ice the way we always spread, pairs on each flank, my pair and I at the front. The ice says solid under my feet, solid, solid, the old familiar language of it coming up through my soles and I trust it the way I trust my own hands.

I am running when my left foot goes through.

Not far. Ankle deep, no more, and I am out before the cold has finished arriving, the weight transferred, one stride broken into two wrong ones. Less than a breath. But I am running and the mammoth is already turning and a broken stride at this distance is everything.

I stumble. Not down, not fully, but enough. The spear leaves my hand off-balance, the throw already decided by the body before the stumble, going wide of where I needed it.

The mammoth is on top of me.

The tusk finds me in the side. The impact is not like anything I have a comparison for, the force of it transferring through me in less than a breath, and then I am on the ice and the animal is past me and the sky is above me the color of old bone.

I breathe. The air goes in but not far enough, stops somewhere in the middle of my chest where something is no longer the right shape. I try again. Same result. My hand finds my side and what it finds there is wet and hot and the wrong temperature for the outside of a body.

I know what this is. I have put my hands on animals with this kind of damage. I know exactly what my hand is telling me and I lie still with it because lying still is the only thing left that I can choose.

The cold from the wet foot moves through me. It meets the damage in the middle and the two things together change the quality of the pain, make it distant. Distant is the last thing before gone.

My group finishes the hunt without me. I can hear it happening. The calls between them, the sounds of the animal going down, the sounds of a kill made well. They did it. The meat will carry the children through the worst of the winter. I was right about the animal.

I was wrong about the ice.

My pair is beside me before the sounds have stopped. I look at his face and his face tells me what my body already knows. He puts his hand over the red mark on my chest, his palm exactly where I pressed it by the fire in the dark, and holds it there. I feel the warmth of his hand and I hold onto it. The warmth is the realest thing left.

I want to tell him something. Something about the ice and the one step and his hand on my chest and the children who will eat this winter. I look at him. I think he reads me the way I read ice. I think he gets most of it.

They make the decision. I watch it happen in the group the way decisions happen, each person reading the others, the conclusion arriving in all of them at once. The wounded do not stop winter. The dead do not stop winter. The living have to move. I would make the same decision. I have made the same decision.

My pair is last. He stands over me and I watch him memorize me, the way you memorize the safe crossing.

The sky is the color of old bone.

I stop.

Then I am above the body. Looking down at the hunter on the ice beside the hole he fell through, my pair kneeling over him, his hand on my chest over the red ochre mark, the mammoth somewhere beyond the tree line with the group still on it.

I watch my pair for a while. The way his face works through the calculation. The way he looks at me and then at the mammoth and then at me again.

I do not feel the cold anymore.

* * *

I do not disappear.

This is the first wrong thing and I have no word for wrong in this way. I have a word for the ice that will not hold, for the animal that does not behave as animals behave, for the weather that does not match what the sky promised. This is not those kinds of wrong. This is wrong in a way I have no word for because nothing in my life or the lives of anyone I have known has made this word necessary.

I am still here.

I stopped. I felt myself stop. The breathing, the cold, the hand on my chest, the sky, and then none of those things, and I was certain that was the end of it because everything I have ever known about dying tells me that is the end of it. The animals I have killed. The people I have sat with. The ones who went before me. They stopped and they were gone. That is what stopping means.

I stopped and I am not gone.

No body remained. There is no cold. There is no sky. There is only the knowing that I am still here, without anything to be here in, without any of the things that here has always required.

I have no word for this. I have no thought that reaches this. I have the animal response to the thing that should not be, the full-body flinch of the creature confronted with the impossible, except I have no body to flinch with and so the response goes nowhere and I am left holding it, this wordless wrongness, this impossible continuing.

The group is gone. I feel them leave the way I feel weather move on, the warmth of them receding, and then there is nothing in any direction that is them. I am alone. The mammoth is dead on the ice somewhere near me but I cannot feel where near is anymore. The ice is under me but I cannot feel under.

They come before the light is full.

I know them. Spotted, heavy, moving in the way of their kind, reading the air with their faces. I have hunted around them all my life, given them their space. Three of them, the largest I have felt, and I feel them the way I now feel everything, not with eyes, without eyes, with what is left of the thing that has always read the world.

The largest turns toward where I am.

It reads me the way I read ice. I can feel it deciding.

It comes for me last, after the others have begun carrying pieces of the mammoth back to wherever their young are waiting. It takes its time. It has nowhere else to be.

I feel it find me. I feel the weight of it over what I was. I feel what it does to what the cold left behind, the tearing, the working through of frozen muscle and crusted hide, the sounds of it that I have heard before from a distance and am hearing now from inside. I am present for all of it.

Each thing it takes I feel taken. Each place it opens I feel opened. The cold had shut most of the pain down but this brings something back, something that is not quite pain because pain requires a body and I have no body, something that is the memory of pain playing against whatever I have become instead of nerves.

It is not cruel. It feeds its young the way we fed our children today with the mammoth. The world does not distinguish. I understand this. The understanding does not reach the part of me that is having this happen.

What it takes it takes. What it leaves it leaves on the ice, scattered, smaller than I was.

I am still in what it leaves.

* * *

Winter holds what is left of me in the ice. I am aware of the holding. I am aware of everything the way I have been aware of everything since I stopped. The wrong kind of aware. The kind that has no body to stop and no eyes to close and no sleep to fall into.

The thaw comes. I know the thaw. I have read the signs of it all my life, the sound of ice releasing, the smell of water moving under where it had been still. The thaw comes and what the ice releases the water takes, and pieces of what I was move with the water, and I am in those pieces, still in them, aware in the moving.

The warm season brings the small things. They work through what the ice left behind. I am present for their working. I had a word for dead. This is not that word.

The cold returns. I feel it enter what remains of me, feel the water in the last solid pieces of me expand and crack the way water always cracks what contains it. Pieces separate. I feel the separating.

More seasons. More thaws. What I was spreads across the lakebed and the bank and the low ground where the water goes when the ice releases it. I am in the ground. I am in the roots of things that grow in the ground. I am in the things that eat those things.

None of it is me. All of it was me. I am aware in all of it at once in a way that has no comparison in anything I lived through while I was living.

I think about my pair. I think about his hand on my chest, the red ochre, his palm over my heart in the dark before the hunt. I think about him memorizing me. I think about the youngest hunter, who could not watch, and whether someone has taught him to watch by now. I think about these things across the long dissolution and I do not stop thinking about them and this is the only thing that is still only mine.

* * *

Something comes when the last of me is gone.

The birds stop moving. I feel them stop the way I now feel everything, not with eyes, without eyes, but with what replaced eyes. A fox near the bank of what the lake has become sits down and faces toward where I am most concentrated and does not move. The animals read something the way I read ice, something that should not be here, something that fits no shape they have a name for.

I read it too.

Vast. Patient. The attention of something that has been doing whatever it does for longer than I can hold as a thought. It stands where nothing stood. It does something I cannot see with eyes I do not have.

And then it is interested in me specifically and the interest of it lands on what I have become and I feel it the way I felt the spotted hunters reading me on the ice, the decision being made, except this one is different, this one is not about hunger, this one is something I have no category for at all.

I have been afraid many times. I have felt the full-body knowledge of the thing that will kill me, the bear, the water, the cold, the wrong step. I know what afraid is in the body.

I have no body and I know what this is.

The vastness does something with what I have become. I cannot see what. I cannot understand what. The fox moves. The birds move. The thing that was here is not here anymore.

I am not here anymore either.

The Watcher on the Hill

I pressed myself against the rough stone, dust grinding between my teeth like meal. The air reeked of iron and parched earth, but beneath lay something fouler. The copper-sweet stench of blood mingled with the sharp bite of fear-sweat and loosened bowels.

My pulse hammered against my throat. I had followed whispers through Jerusalem's twisting streets to this accursed place, drawn by something I could not name: a pull that had grown stronger with each step up the barren slope.

The hill of Golgotha stretched before me: wind-scoured, the three crosses clawing at the darkening sky like the fingers of buried giants.

Upon the center beam hung Yeshua of Nazareth. His flesh was torn parchment, bone showing white through the ruin of muscle that spasmed with each desperate breath. To either side, lesser men (thieves, iron-pinned and bleeding) writhed and sagged, their moans carried on the wind like the cries of dying beasts. One had soiled himself; the stench mixed with blood-copper and the sickly-sweet smell of festering wounds. The sound of wood groaning under human weight filled the spaces between their gasps.

One Roman remained. He leaned against his spear and spat into the dust. That was his job and he was doing it. I crouched behind my outcropping, watching, waiting. Something had compelled me to witness this, though I knew not what.

Others stood on the hill. Not mourners, mourners stayed at the base of the slope or kept close. A child, perhaps six years old, sat apart from all of them, building something small in the dust with her hands. Nobody watched her. Not soldiers, these stood at different points along the ridge with no apparent purpose, no formation, no duty I could read. Three that I could count from where I crouched, perhaps four.

They faced the center cross the way you face something that requires your full attention. They did not speak to each other. They did not move. I registered them and could not place them in any category I had and turned my attention back to the center cross, which was why I had come.

From my hiding place the labored breathing of the crucified reached me, the occasional moan of agony, the creak of wood under shifting weight. The Roman muttered to himself in his harsh tongue, clearly eager for his duty to end.

Then I heard a voice, weak as morning mist, yet somehow carrying across the barren slope with impossible clarity. Yeshua spoke.

"Father..." The word came as a wheeze, but I caught every syllable. "Forgive them... for they know not... what they do."

The soldier's head snapped up at the words. He moved closer to the center cross, straining to hear more. Something in that voice, even broken by suffering, commanded attention.

My chest tightened. From where I crouched the soldier's face changed, the boredom melting into something like unease, perhaps even recognition. This man who had been tasked with ending criminals now stood before something that fit no understanding of his world.

"My God..." Yeshua gasped, his head lifting with tremendous effort. "My God... why have you forsaken me?"

The words struck me like physical blows. This was not the triumphant messiah of the stories, not the wonder-worker who commanded storms and calmed seas. This was a man drowning in abandonment, crying out to a God who seemed as distant as the stars.

The soldier stepped back, his hand moving unconsciously to his gladius hilt, not in threat, but the instinctive gesture of a man confronted with mysteries beyond his ken. Something had changed in his face. Whatever he was guarding had become, in the space of a few words, something he did not have a category for.

When the soldier finally wandered down the slope to relieve himself against a boulder, I emerged from hiding. Now there would be no witness to what was about to unfold, save for eyes that existed outside of history itself.

I stepped into the open, my sandals scraping against loose stones that scattered and clicked like knucklebones. One thief flinched at the sound, his head snapping toward me with wild, bloodshot eyes. The other moaned, a sound that rose from somewhere deeper than his throat.

Yeshua did not notice. His head sagged forward, hair matted with sweat and blood, breath coming in shallow, desperate pulls that made his ribs stand out like prison bars beneath torn skin.

I tasted bile. Something had driven me to witness this, though I could not say what.

"Do you know why I am here?" My voice cracked like a boy's, betraying me. "I have heard the stories. The miracles. The promises." I faltered, seeing the reality of crucifixion before me, not the clean death painted on temple walls but the brutal truth of a man dying in agony. "My village suffers. Plague takes our children. Roman taxes starve our families. Where is the kingdom you promised? Where is God's mercy?"

The answer was silence, then a groan from deep in Yeshua's chest. He stirred only faintly, his chin lifting and falling again like a man drowning in air. His lips moved, cracked and bleeding: "Water... mother... forgive..." Bare fragments, too fractured to hold meaning, each word costing him precious breath.

I ground my teeth until my jaw ached. I stepped closer, dropping to my knees in the dirt that still held the day's heat. Small stones bit into my flesh through my robes. "Not riddles! I came for truth! Where is the kingdom you promised? Where is God's mercy when children die of fever and Romans bleed us dry with taxes? Why do the righteous suffer while the wicked prosper?"

No clear reply. Only the words of a man unraveling in pain: "They know not..." Then a long, wet wheeze that rattled in his chest like something breaking.

My chest heaved, my heart hammering against my ribs like a caged bird. My voice sharpened to something close to a snarl. "Forgive? Forgive what? My neighbors screaming in their hovels? My own son choking on air that turned to poison in his lungs? Do not speak to me of forgiveness! I want no symbols. No pity. I would know why this must happen!"

The thief beside Yeshua coughed wet laughter that sprayed droplets of blood into the dust. "Talk all you will, stranger. He hears naught but his own phantoms." Then he slumped again, the effort of speaking leaving him gasping.

I ignored him. I spoke less to Yeshua now and more to the void itself, my words coming faster, more desperate. "I believed the stories. The healings. The hope. But all I see is another man dying, abandoned by the God he claimed to serve."

By then I had ceased shouting. The words fell out as confession more than accusation, my voice raw and broken. I knelt in the dust, shoulders heaving, tasting salt on my lips, whether from sweat or tears I could not tell.

Yeshua's head lolled. His eyes flickered open for a moment, glassy with exhaustion and pain, pupils dilated and unfocused, then closed.

I clenched my fists, ready to curse, to pound the ground until my hands split and bled. I had come seeking answers, seeking hope, and found only another broken promise bleeding out on wood.

The eyes opened again. No longer drifting. They fixed on me with sudden, terrifying clarity, pupils contracting to pinpoints of absolute focus. Every muscle in my body went rigid.

The lips moved, pulling sound through ruined lungs, each word clearly costing agony. The voice was shredded, broken, yet it carried something that made the hair on my arms stand up, something that bypassed my ears and spoke directly to my bones.

"You... would know the secrets of all creation... and God?"

The words hit me like a physical blow. My mouth worked soundlessly, lungs collapsed. For the first time, the question I had flung into the silence came roaring back, and it was not accusation but challenge, not comfort but warning.

The wood groaned under the weight of it. The thieves moaned at the edges of the moment. But none of it reached me.

Only that gaze. And the terrible question.

The wind stopped. I felt the stillness before I understood it. A leaf that had been falling hung where it was. The groan of the wood under the weight of the crosses stopped. Everything stopped.

A shadow fell across me. When I looked up, a figure stood at the clearing's edge, tall, draped in robes that drank the light and refuse to give it back. The face beneath the hood was sharp-featured, ageless.

The world was already stopped. I understood this now, looking at the figure standing in the stillness. The wind had stopped before he arrived. The leaf had stopped before he arrived. He was there in it, the way he was there at everything, present, attending, making his note.

Below on the slope the Roman soldier stood midstride, one sandaled foot raised, his mouth open in a shout that would never complete. The blood from Yeshua's wounds had paused, drops suspended between the wound and the ground, motionless.

Yeshua's lips moved one final time, forming words meant only for me: "The truth... will set you free... or make you a willing prisoner."

His head fell forward. The long struggle for breath ceased.

Darkness fell like a curtain, though it was only midday. The sun vanished behind an unnatural eclipse that made the air itself seem to thicken. Thunder rolled across the sky without clouds, a sound like the very foundations of heaven cracking. The earth beneath us heaved and bucked, and I felt it even through my dying body.

But through it all, the dark figure stood unmoved, making a note on his scroll as casually as if recording the weather. The thunder and lightning seemed not to touch him at all.

Time resumed.

The Roman soldier's shout completed itself. The blood flowed again. The wind picked up.

The spear wound had been there since the beginning of it. I had been aware of it the way you are aware of a thing you are managing, the body's report arriving and being stored.

Now it stopped being a thing I was managing. The warmth of it was wrong, warmth moving outward where it should not move. I put my hand to it. My hand came away the color I knew it would be.

I tried to stand. My legs had a different understanding of what was happening than I did. I sat against the stone. The hill was in front of me, the crosses still on it, the soldier moving away down the slope toward his unit. I watched him go. I had been watching everything on this hill all morning and I watched him go the way I had watched everything else, which was with the attention of a man who knows that what he is seeing matters and does not yet know why.

The knowing came in with the blood leaving. Not fear. Something closer to the recognition of a pattern I had not seen clearly until now. The question Yeshua had asked. The thing Grim had written in his scroll. The whole morning assembling into a shape I could almost read.

Then I could not read it. Then I could not hold the shape. The hill was still there. The crosses. The particular light of midday in that place. And then it was not.

* * *

The soldier came back to the body the way you return to unfinished work. He did not look at my face. He worked at the robe until he found the coin pouch, assessed the weight without opening it, and put it in his belt. The sandals next. He checked the soles before setting them aside.

His hands found the ring on my third finger. He pulled at it. The heat swelling had already started. I felt the ring resist, felt the skin bunch ahead of his thumb as he pushed and twisted. He was not careful about it. When it came free something gave in the joint, and the ring bent in his grip. He turned it over, straightened it with his thumb, and looked at where the metal had thinned.

That was when my arm moved.

He stepped back fast. A moment. Then he reached for the pugio and came back.

He came back with the pugio. I saw the blade. He held it wrong for what he tried to do, a throat cut from above requires a different grip than a stab, and the first pass missed the main vessel and opened the skin along the jaw. I felt it. Not pain, not exactly, but the particular sensation of a boundary being crossed, the inside of the body suddenly in contact with the outside world along a line I had no word for.

The blood came fast. I watched it from above and from inside at the same time. I was in the body still, aware of the warmth of it spreading down the front of the robe, and I was also somewhere just above and to the left, watching the soldier work. The two positions. I did not know I could be in two positions.

He adjusted his grip. This time the angle was correct and the cut went through the vessel and the blood that had been fast became immediate, a different order of magnitude, the kind of blood that tells the body the argument is over.

I felt my legs go. Not a decision. The body making its own assessment and acting on it. I was on my knees in the dust of the hill, the robe wet and warm and stuck to the front of me, the soldier already stepping back to avoid the spread of it.

He kicked me. Once, in the side, to check whether resistance was still possible. None remained. I went down on my face. The soil of Golgotha was dry and pale and I could smell it, the mineral smell of this hill on this day in April.

He wiped the blade on the hem of my robe. I watched this from the outside now. I was fully outside the body, suspended perhaps two feet above it, watching the soldier straighten up and look at the ring in his hand and then at me and then at the ring again.

The blood was still moving out of the body. I watched this too. More than I had understood. I had not known, before, how much blood a body held, or how quickly it could decide to be somewhere else.

The soldier walked away toward the next body.

I stayed where I was. Above the body. Looking at it. The body that had held me for forty-one years was on its face in the dust of Golgotha and I was above it and not in it and it was a simpler thing than I had expected. The body. Just a thing, now, in the dust.

And then began the longest awareness I had ever known.

He wiped the blade on my robe. Turned the ring over again in the fading light. It would buy something. Less than it should have.

I felt my heart stutter and stop. Felt my lungs collapse for the final time. But I did not disappear. Instead, I remained, a passenger in my own dying flesh, conscious of every moment that followed.

The soldiers collected the bodies at dusk. Three legionnaires trudged up the slope, their hobnailed caligae crunching on loose stones. The youngest was barely past his first beard, pink-cheeked and soft despite his military bearing.

The sergeant barked orders in clipped Latin, his vine staff marking time against his muscled thigh. They dragged me away from the crosses, my corpse bumping over stones. I felt every jostle, every scrape of skin against rock, though I could not cry out. They threw me into a pit with other criminals (a mass grave hastily dug beyond the city walls). The lime they poured over us burned like liquid fire against my skin, even in death.

I felt the first shovelful of dirt hit my face. Then another. The weight of earth pressing down, sealing me in darkness.

Days passed in the suffocating blackness. I felt my body temperature drop to match the cool earth. My blood pooled and settled, turning my back a deep purple that I somehow knew but could not see. The lime worked its way into my wounds, my mouth, my eyes, eating away at soft tissue with patient hunger.

The first flies found me on the second day, before the soldiers had even finished covering the pit. I felt them landing on my exposed skin, their tiny feet tickling as they walked across my face. They found the spear wound in my chest, crawled into my mouth, explored every opening with methodical precision. I was aware of each egg they laid, hundreds of tiny deposits in my wounds, my nostrils, the corners of my eyes.

The eggs hatched three days later.

I felt them emerge: rice-grain sized larvae, blind and hungry. The first maggot I truly noticed was the one that burrowed into the corner of my left eye, feeding on the tissue there with methodical dedication. Soon there were others (dozens, then hundreds), a writhing mass of larvae that made my flesh their nursery.

Each one was distinct. I felt them moving through my organs, hollowing out my chest cavity, turning my intestines into corridors of decay. They pupated inside my ribcage, and I was aware of their transformation, the way they emerged as flies only to lay more eggs in the feast of my remains.

The first rain came two weeks after my burial. I felt each drop as it penetrated the thin layer of soil above me, turning the earth to mud that seeped through my clothes, my skin, my bones. The water carried away pieces of me in tiny rivulets (dissolved flesh mixing with minerals), flowing deeper into the earth.

Winter brought frost that cracked through the soil and into my bones. I felt each stress fracture as the water in my marrow expanded and split the calcium like breaking kindling. My ribs separated from my spine with small pops that moved through my skeleton. My jaw came unhinged, hanging open in a silent scream I could not voice.

A rat found me in the spring.

I felt its sharp claws digging through the softened earth above my chest. Its teeth, needle-sharp, tore away strips of my preserved flesh. It made a nest in my ribcage, warm and alive against the cold cage of my bones. I felt its heart beating where mine had stopped, felt its young when they were born in the hollow of my chest cavity.

The lime had done its work by then. My skin had become leather, then fragments, then nothing at all. My muscles had liquefied and drained away, leaving only the mineral-white bones and the stubborn tendons that held them together like old rope.

But still, I remained aware. Still, I felt everything.

Years passed. My skull loosened from my spine and rolled away when heavy rains undermined the soil. Animals scattered my bones across the hillside. I felt each rib as it was carried off by scavengers, each finger bone as it was buried deeper by shifting earth. Wild dogs cracked my femur for the marrow, and I experienced the hollow echo as they snapped it like a branch.

One spring morning, I felt small hands close around my left forearm bone where it had come to rest near a clump of wild grass. Children's voices, high and bright with laughter. They had found me while playing on the hillside.

"Look! A stick!"

"Perfect for knocking the ball!"

I felt the bone (my bone) being hefted, tested for weight and balance. Then the sharp crack as it struck a leather ball, the vibration traveling through the calcium that had once been part of me. Again and again they used me in their game, my forearm connecting with the ball with hollow thwacks that I experienced as both sound and sensation.

When their game ended, they tossed me aside carelessly into a thornbush. I lay there for months, bleached white by sun and rain, until another winter's frost finally cracked me down the middle. Even then, each half remained aware, two pieces of the same consciousness watching the seasons change from different angles in the undergrowth.

Decades passed slowly. Part of me rested under a thornbush where my skull had come to rest. Part of me lay buried three feet down where my pelvis had settled. My right hand had been scattered by a badger's digging; I felt my fingerbones in five different locations across the hill.

But the awareness never faded. Never lessened. If anything, it grew more acute as the physical shell that had contained it crumbled away. I became intimately familiar with every inch of soil within a hundred paces, feeling the slow migration of my calcium into the roots of plants, my phosphorus feeding the worms that had once fed on me.

Finally, after what felt like centuries but might have been forty years, the last fragment of my left shoulder blade crumbled into powder, ground down by decades of erosion and the patient work of countless tiny lives. The final trace of what had been Daniel's body merged with the soil of Golgotha.

* * *

The air grew cold again.

"Now," said a familiar voice, "we may begin."

The dark figure stood before me (or before what I had become). I had no eyes to see him with, no form to perceive, yet somehow I was still there, still aware, still myself.

"I am called Grim. The assessment," he said, unfurling his scroll, "can finally commence."

He produced what looked like a wooden wheel from the folds of his robes, its rim divided into countless small sections. With a casual flick of his wrist, he set it spinning.

"Tell me, Daniel," he said as the wheel turned, "have you been a good man?"

The question seemed simple enough. "I... I think so. I tried to be. I helped my neighbors. Cared for my family. I never murdered anyone, never stole..."

"Hmm." Grim made his note. "Well then," he said. "You get to try again."

He was not the only one here. Golgotha on a day like this drew more than one of them, the hill had given up three that morning, and there were others in the streets below. He could see another figure at the edge of the crowd, working, the familiar stillness of a Grim at assessment. He did not cross the distance. Maren would finish when he finished. They did not need to speak.

The Heart

I say the first words. My junior priest Cuāuhtemōc says the response. He has been with me four years, careful with the words, attentive to the order of things, chosen for the quality of his attention. He watches everything without watching anything in particular, which is the correct way to be present in a ceremony.

The man on the stone does not close his eyes. This is what I notice about the ones who have used the three months: they do not close their eyes. The ones who have not, close them.

I do not know what this means. I have thought about it across many years and have not arrived at a conclusion that satisfies me. I record it in the private record I keep alongside the official one, the record of what I notice that the ceremony does not have a category for.

The obsidian blade is in my hand. The stone is curved so the body arches, the chest opens more easily when the back is bent over the stone and the ribs separate slightly from their natural position. I learned this in my fourth year, from the priest who trained me, who learned it from the priest who trained him. I know the blade's weight the way I know my own hands.

Then the man on the stone says something.

He does not ask for mercy. He does not beg. He says it in his own language, which I understand because I have been doing this long enough to have learned the languages of the people we bring from that direction. What he says is: "I am afraid."

Not a plea. A statement. Said the way you might say it to someone beside you in the dark, not asking them to do anything about it, just telling them what is true.

I have heard many things said on the stone. I have a private record of those too. No one has ever said this to me before, not the fear itself, which I have seen ten thousand times, but the saying of it plainly, without demand. The honesty of it.

I say the next words. The correct ones. But he speaks again before I finish.

"Does it go somewhere?" he says. Still in his own language. Still the same flat honest tone. "The heart. Does it go somewhere? Or does it just stop?"

I look at him. This is not a question I have been asked before either.

"It goes to the sun," I say. "The sun receives it. This is what we know."

He is quiet for a moment. Then: "You believe that."

"Yes," I say.

He nods slowly. Not acceptance. Something else, the acknowledgment of a man who has been given an honest answer to a question he asked honestly, even if the answer does not help him.

"My gods say the same thing," he says. "That it goes somewhere. That it matters where it goes." He pauses. "I hope one of us is right."

Nothing in the procedure covers this. The procedure has categories for resistance, for weeping, for the ones who fight at the end. It does not have a category for this.

I say the next words. The correct ones. My voice does not change.

I bring the blade down.

The obsidian finds the space between the ribs the way it always does, the way my hands learned before my mind understood what my hands were learning. The body resists first, it always resists, some refusal that has nothing to do with the man's decision to be here, and then it does not. The opening is there.

He does not scream. The sound is lower than a scream, a long torn thing from deep in the chest, the sound a body makes when it is discovering something it did not know was possible. He does not scream and I do not know why. I have seen men scream. I have seen men go silent. I have never made a record of which takes more.

My hands go in.

The warmth is the first thing. Not the warmth of skin, the inside warmth, the warmth of something that has never been exposed to air, private in a way that nothing outside a body is private. My hands are in another man's chest and I can feel his breath still trying to move, the lungs working around my wrists, the wet heat of him against my forearms.

He makes the sound again. Deeper this time. A long exhalation through something that is no longer unobstructed.

The smell is copper and something beneath copper that has no name because no one who smelled it from the inside thought to write it down.

I find what I am looking for.

It is still working. I know this, I have known this four hundred and eleven times before, the heart does not know yet what has happened to the chest around it. The muscle is doing what muscle does, contracting and releasing, and I can feel each contraction against my palm like something knocking from inside a locked room. Wanting out. Not knowing it is already out.

The severing.

The blood does not spatter. It reaches. The aorta releases everything it has been holding at pressure and it goes outward and upward and it hits my face and my chest and my arms and I do not step back because stepping back would be incorrect. I know this before it happens. I have always known this before it happens. I stand in it.

It is warm on my face the way the inside warmth was warm on my hands.

The heart is in my hands and it is still contracting, still knocking, once, twice, three times, the stupid faithful muscle working the problem it was built to work, and I say the final words and lift it to the sun.

I do not look at Cuāuhtemōc.

But I hear him. A single sharp intake of breath, controlled immediately, swallowed before it became anything. Not from the blood. He has seen blood.

Something else, the man's sound, maybe, the low torn thing, or the smell, or the warmth still on the air, or something that has no name because we do not have a record for what a junior priest feels when he understands for the first time what his hands are going to be doing for the rest of his life.

He does not turn. He holds.

We finish the ceremony. The record is made. The name, the date, the correct form observed. Everything in order.

Afterward, in the preparation room below the temple, I say to him: "You turned."

He says nothing for a moment. Then: "Yes."

"Why."

Another silence. Cuāuhtemōc is not a man who speaks before he has found the right words.

"I don't know," he says. "I have done this a hundred times. I don't know why this time." He pauses. "What did he say to you? Before."

I look at him.

Cuāuhtemōc looked at his hands. There was blood on them, which there always was, but he looked at them the way you look at something unfamiliar.

What passes between a man and the priest who opens his chest is not part of the record. Cuāuhtemōc asked directly. He has four years with me.

"He asked whether it goes somewhere," I say. "The heart. Whether it actually goes somewhere or just stops."

Cuāuhtemōc is quiet.

"What did you tell him?"

"The truth," I say. "What we know."

"And what did he say?"

"He said he hoped one of us was right."

The preparation room is small and the stone walls hold the cool air from the night before. Cuāuhtemōc looks at his hands. I know what he is looking at. I have looked at my own hands the same way, in the early years. You stop, eventually. Or you learn to look at something else.

"The record," I say, "requires nothing about what happens inside us."

He looks up.

"Only what we do," I say. "And what you did was correct."

The quarter turn happened between one moment and the next and was over. The record does not contain it.

He nods. Something in him releases, slightly.

He picks up the cloth from the basin and wipes his hands. He does it carefully, the way you do it when you have done it a hundred times and are only now looking at what you are doing.

"Do you ever..." he starts, and then stops.

"No," I say.

He nods again.

I do not tell him what I felt in my hands. The beating. I have a private record and he is not in it.

I go back to the stone. There are two more this morning. The sun still needs feeding.

The third one is at the end of the day, when the light has gone flat and the heat has dropped to something almost bearable. I have done this four hundred and twelve times. My hands do not shake.

The heart is still working when I reach it. It always is. Muscle does not know what the ceremony is for. It does its work regardless.

I kneel beside the stone and wait for the moment to arrive. The city is very loud below. The market. The canoes. Cuāuhtemōc behind me, saying nothing, which is correct.

The moment arrives. My hands know what to do.

The warmth on my hands is the first thing. Not the warmth of skin, the inside warmth, the warmth that has never been exposed to air. The heart is still moving against my palm. Wanting out. Not knowing it is already out.

I look up at the sky. The last light is the color of maize pollen. I have looked at this sky four hundred and twelve times from this position and it has not changed and it will not change and this is correct.

Then my hands are empty and the warmth is on the air and the stone is done for the day.

I am walking back toward the temple when something arrives that I did not expect. Not pain. Something adjacent. The four hundred and twelve, all at once, the weight of every separate instance, arriving together in a way they have not arrived before. I have kept them separate. I have always kept them separate.

They are not separate now.

I sit down on the temple steps. Cuāuhtemōc does not ask. He sits beside me.

The fever starts that night. By the second morning I know the shape of it. I have seen it take others.

* * *

Eighteen more years. I am meticulous about the records. I train four more junior priests, each of them carefully chosen, each of them good in their own way. Cuāuhtemōc becomes senior enough to conduct ceremonies of his own. He does not turn away again, or if he does, he does not do it where I can see.

The fever comes in the spring of my fifty-first year, two days after the equinox ceremony. I know it for what it is by the second morning. I have seen it take others and I know the shape of it, the way it arrives behind the eyes first, the heat that does not respond to water.

I am in my room in the temple complex. The junior priests take turns sitting with me. On the third day Cuāuhtemōc comes and sits and does not leave. He sits on the floor beside me rather than in the chair, which is what I would have done in his position. He puts his hands flat on the stone between us.

We do not speak for a long time.

Then he says: "The man. The one from Tlaxcala. Do you still think about him."

It is not a question.

"Yes," I say.

"What he asked you."

"Yes."

Another silence. Cuāuhtemōc moves the water bowl a few inches closer to me without asking. He does not say anything about doing this. The fever is doing what fevers do, pulling the room slightly out of true. I am still inside myself but the edges are going.

"Do you know yet?" Cuāuhtemōc says. "Whether one of you was right."

I look at the ceiling. The stone is still. Outside I can hear the city going about its morning.

"No," I say. "I still don't know."

"But you still believe."

"The sun rose this morning," I say. "It rose every morning for twenty-two years of ceremony. I don't know what that proves. It may prove nothing. But I don't know that either."

Cuāuhtemōc is quiet for a moment. He looks at his hands on the stone.

"That's not the same as believing," he says.

"No," I say. "It isn't."

He accepts this. He has always been honest enough to accept the true answer over the comfortable one. It is one of the reasons I chose him. He leans forward slightly, enough that I can see the side of his face, and looks at the light through the doorway.

"I turned that morning," he says, "because of what he said before. I heard him. I didn't know I went to turn until I did." He pauses. "I've done this a hundred times since and I haven't turned again. I don't know what that means either."

"The record is complete," I say. "Whatever it means, the record is complete."

He stays until I cannot speak anymore. He is there when the speaking stops. And then I am not.

* * *

Not the insects that work dry ground. The soil here is too wet for those. What finds me first are the things that live in waterlogged earth, the organisms that have no common name because no one who knew their names thought to write them down.

They are small and numerous and they work in a way that is different from anything I experienced above the surface, not the discrete taking of pieces but a general softening, a dissolution that begins at every surface at once, the boundary between what I was and what the ground is becoming less distinct by the hour.

They find me before the first night is out.

The water finds every space. The lakebed soil is already wet, has always been wet, the water is not arriving from outside but has always been present and is simply now present in me as well, moving through what I am the way it moves through everything else.

It carries pieces of me into the spaces between the roots of the grasses and the reeds, the roots that reach down from the chinampas above, the floating gardens built at the lake's edge, their roots hanging in the water like long pale fingers.

By the second month the roots have found me.

I knew roots from above. The abstract knowledge that they extend downward. I did not know what it felt like to be found by them. They move through me with the patience of things that do not know they are moving, taking what they need without preference or ceremony.

The chinampa above me is growing something. I can feel it growing, the roots drawing upward what they take from me, the material of what I was traveling up through the root system into the stalk and the leaf and whatever grows at the end. Becoming food. Becoming the thing that feeds whoever eats what grows on the chinampa, which is something I have eaten myself at ceremonies, which means I was always already in this exchange and the stone was just one of its moments.

I did not expect to find this thought in the lakebed.
I find it anyway.

The warmth of the soil is constant. This is different
from what I understand of other grounds, the cold that
comes in winter, the freeze, the preservation. This
ground does not preserve. It consumes, steadily,
without pause, at the same rate in every season because
the temperature barely changes this deep, this wet.
There is no winter here. There is only the steady warm
dark work.

The blood of four hundred and twelve is in this soil.
Not just mine, theirs. It soaked into the temple floor
across twenty-two years of ceremony, worked its way
down through the stone and the foundation and into
the ground beneath, dispersed through the lakebed soil
before I arrived in it.

I can feel the soil doing the same thing to me that it
did to them. The same organisms, the same roots, the
same warm dark steady work. The ground that received
the offerings is now receiving me with the same
indifference it brought to everything else.

I thought about this, in the years when I was still
able to think in the way that thinking requires a
continuous location. The ground does not distinguish.
I knew this philosophically. Knowing it philosophically
is different from being inside the knowing.

By the end of the first year little remains that could
be called Itzli. By the end of the second year even that
is gone, dispersed into the lakebed soil, into the roots,
into the organisms with no common name, into the
water that moves through everything, into the

chinampas and what grows on them and what eats what grows on them.

The city built on a lake consumes its dead the way the lake consumed everything before the city, completely, without remainder, without the courtesy of a record.

My records are in the temple. The name of the Tlaxcalan warrior is in them, exact, as required. They will last longer than I did.

I do not know if the heart went somewhere. I do not know if the sun needed it. I was the one who held the knife and I do not know. In the end this is my private record and the lakebed is the only one who receives it.

* * *

Grim came when the last of it had settled into the lakebed and stood on the ground near the temple and opened the scroll.

He read it. Then he read it again. He turned the scroll to see if he had missed something. He had not. The scroll was complete. It was simply not a ledger he had encountered before.

Four hundred and twelve. Each one recorded. Each one with a name and a date and a notation that the correct form had been observed. The scroll had them all.

It also had the twenty-two years of the priest's life before and beside the ceremonies, the training, the junior priests taught, the records kept, the conversation at the end with Cuāuhtemōc. The

Tlaxcalan warrior's question. The honest answer Itzli gave and the honest answer he had carried in his private record for eighteen years after.

The man who had done all of this had not been cruel. He had not done it for pleasure or power or personal advancement. He had done it because he believed, with the sincere certainty of a man who has looked at the universe for a long time, that it was necessary.

The scroll sat in a space his categories did not reach. He had assessed men who had done great harm knowing it was harm. This ledger was different, a man who had done great harm believing it was maintenance. The distinction had no category. He had no wheel designation for it.

The air around the temple was still. The stillness of something trying to determine what it looked at.

He found Itzli waiting with the stillness of a man who had spent his life waiting for ceremonies to begin and knew how to hold himself in the interval.

"You kept the records," Grim said.

"Yes."

"Four hundred and twelve."

"And the maintenance ceremonies. And the training records. And the calendar observations." A pause. "The records are complete."

Grim produced the wheel. He set it turning. It turned for longer than it usually turned, moving through the accounting of a ledger that resisted the wheel's categories, that sat in a space between the designations the wheel had been designed to reach. When it stopped Grim looked at where it had stopped and did not immediately make his note.

"Can I ask you something," Itzli said.

Grim looked at him.

"The stillness. You have that stillness when something has not gone where you were expecting it to go."

He had not been thinking about loss. He had been thinking about the door. He did not correct Itzli.

"The heart," Itzli said. "Does it go somewhere? The ones I sent. Does it actually go somewhere or does it just stop?"

The question sat between them in the warm air above the lakebed. Grim had heard many things from souls at the assessment. He had not heard this question, asked in this way, by this person.

"They go on. What happens after that is not my territory."

Itzli was quiet for a moment. Then: "You don't know either."

"No. I don't know either."

Itzli nodded slowly. The same nod the Tlaxcalan warrior had given him eighteen years ago, not acceptance, but the acknowledgment of a man who has been given an honest answer to a question he asked honestly, even if the answer does not help him.

The priest looked at him. Patient. The look of a man who had done what he had done and would not pretend otherwise and was willing to wait for whatever came next.

Grim made his note. He did not know if the note was correct. He set the uncertainty beside the note, the inadequacy of the wheel for what the wheel had just been asked to do. He would not resolve it. The lakebed did not provide resolution.

He sent the priest on.

He stood in the warm air above the temple for a moment before the birds that had stilled moved again.

The First Breath

I eat the last of the meat. Frozen through, hard as wood. I hold each piece in my mouth until it softens and gives up its taste, the cold salt fat of it. Not enough. Three days of not enough and my body knows the count even when he stops counting.

Sleep comes fast when the cold is this deep. That is one of its tricks.

When he wakes the cold has moved inside me.

I know about this. I have seen it happen in others and knew someday it would happen to me. The shivering that was constant has stopped, which means the body has stopped fighting the cold.

The woman. I think about the woman.

The last good winter. There had been a morning, not a significant morning, no hunt, no ceremony, when she had been working the hide of a deer and had said something to me without looking up from the work, something about the smell of the ground when the freeze broke, and I had answered, and she had laughed at the answer, and they had been in the same moment the same way you are in the same fire, not touching but sharing the same warmth.

I had not known it was a good morning until later. You never do.

The others went one by one. The woman first, three winters back, a sickness that took her in four days and left nothing I could do but sit beside her and then bury her in the soft ground near the water. The two children not long after, same sickness. Then the old male, who simply sat down by the fire one evening and did not get up.

I stayed and the staying got harder and then easier, the way a wound stops hurting once it has gone deep enough.

My hands are in my furs. I cannot feel them. Nothing to be done about this, so nothing to feel about it. The hands are gone, the feet went before them, and the cold is working upward through my legs toward the center of me where the heat still lives.

The sky above the rocks has no moon. The lights are out in their thousands, hard and cold and very far, giving nothing. I have watched those lights all my life. On the worst nights of hunger and cold they were there above me, unchanged. Whatever went wrong below, the lights held.

I think about the ibex on the ridge.

I think about spring, which is real and will come whether I am there for it or not.

I think about the woman's hands working the hide. The particular motion of them. The sound the scraper made.

The lights in the sky do not move. I watch them for a while.

My eyes are open when they stop seeing.

The cold is at my chest now. Not on the outside, from inside. Arriving in the places where warmth was and taking them.

My heart stumbles. I feel each beat asking whether there will be another. I have felt this in animals. I have never felt it in myself.

My hands are the color of the stone behind me. I look at them. Objects.

The lights in the sky do not move. My father showed me these lights.

I leave the body by degrees, the way warmth leaves a stone. I am in the body and then I am above it, looking down at a man against a rock on a ridge in the dark, his breath no longer making a shape in the cold air.

His breath no longer makes a shape.

* * *

The cold keeps me through that first winter. I feel the keeping. Frozen ground holds what it holds with total patience, in stasis, without process, without urgency.

The birds find me in the spring when the ground softens. I feel each one land. The specific weight of each foot. The hop. The beak finding the gaps in the frozen surface. They are doing what birds do. I am what they are doing it to.

Each intrusion is distinct. Not pain. I am past pain, but knowledge. I know where each one works and what it finds. I feel the things that were me being taken up and redistributed.

By summer a pair has found the hollow where the overhang meets the ground, the place I slept for twenty winters. They build. Some of what they use is me. I feel it. I am woven into the nest. I am in the eggs. I am in the blind mouths that open for food and receive it.

Winter returns. The frost finds new pieces to separate. The cold works deeper. Each crack is distinct. I feel each one.

The ibex cross the ridge. I feel their weight on the ground above me. I knew this herd. I read them for forty years. They do not know I am here.

I think about the woman. The sound of the scraper on the hide. The morning when she laughed. I did not ask why. Across the long slow seasons I think about the morning I did not ask.

* * *

Something arrived when the last of it was done.

The birds that had been moving across the ridge stopped. Not all at once, not in alarm, but each one in turn going still where it was. A wren on a branch near where the shelter had been held one foot raised and did not put it down. A hawk that had been quartering the updraft above the gorge hung in place, wings spread, not riding the air but stopped inside it. Below the ridge a deer stood with its ears forward, nose working, finding nothing.

Then something arrived that was not a bird and not a fox and not anything he had a name for.

It settled over him the way cold settles, and it began to read.

He let it. The reading did not feel like harm. It felt like being known. Completely and without remainder, the way he had known the ridge, the way he had known the woman's hands at work. Everything he had been, taken in without judgment. All of it equal in the reading.

The woman was in there. He felt it find her. The shape of the grief, carried through all the dissolution without losing its form. He felt it pause on her the way he had paused on her.

Then it was done with the reading, and it turned him.

Not destroyed. Pointed. In a direction he had not known existed, away from the dissolution and toward something he could not see. The turning was not painful. It was the most decisive thing that had ever happened to him, more decisive than the cold, more decisive than the shivering stopping, a door he had not known was a door opening in one motion and staying open.

He went through it.

* * *

Grim stood on the ridge after the soul had gone and looked at the ground that had been a man.

The birds moved. The hawk tilted a wing and the air took it sideways. The deer dropped its head back to the

51

grass. The wren put its foot down and sang one phrase and stopped.

He opened the scroll and made his notes. Sharp, he wrote. Fully present within its own framework. The woman carried through the dissolution intact. Not lesser, earlier. The difference between an uncut stone and a dressed one was not the stone's quality. It was time, and the right hands, and enough lifetimes of work.

He closed the scroll.

He did not know this was the second time he had stood over this particular soul. He would not know it for longer than he could have calculated.

The Weight of Heaven

I rounded the corner with the lamp and stopped.

I had been in this shaft for six years. I knew every turn of it, every fault in the limestone, every place where you had to angle your body and where you could walk nearly upright. I had been deeper than this, had spent three months on the burial chamber itself, cutting the offering table in the dark with lamps hung on pegs I'd driven myself. I knew this shaft.

I had not been in this corridor before.

A small corridor, branching off the main shaft at an angle the survey plan did not show. Painted. The walls painted top to bottom in the colors the painters used, the blue that meant sky, the red that meant the living, the gold that meant what gold always meant. And at the end of the corridor, on the back wall, a face.

The face of the man whose name I was not permitted to speak.

I stood in the entrance to the corridor and held the lamp and looked at the face.

Thirty-one years of cutting stone for this man. I had cut the granite for my false door. I had cut the alabaster for my canopic jars. I had cut the limestone for my offering table and cut it true, the edges clean, the surface flat enough to hold water without it running. I had been good at this. It was the one thing anyone would have said about me if they had been asked.

I had imagined the face. Everyone who worked the site imagined the face. Some people imagined a king's face, remote and formal. Some imagined a man, ordinary, with ordinary worries. I had imagined a craftsman's face, a man who would look at the stone and understand the work.

The painted face told me nothing about any of these things. It was formal in the way all such faces were formal, the eyes level, the expression that was not an expression but a position. Looking at it was like looking at the sky and trying to find the sky looking back.

From somewhere back down the shaft, around two turns and through the low section: "Kha? Are you coming?"

The voice of the young cutter they had sent to fetch me for the midday break. The boy was seventeen, new, still learning to read the stone.

"Coming," I said.

I looked at the face for one more moment. Then I turned and went back to the work.

My name was Kha. I cut stone for thirty-one years on the tomb of a man whose face I had now seen and whose face told me nothing. I was good at the work.

The dust got into everything. By the third year the cough had started. By the tenth I knew what the cough was. I had seen it take others. I kept working. There was nothing else.

My wife died in the eighteenth year. Fever. It took her in three days and I was at the site when it happened and did not know until I came home and found the neighbors had already wrapped her. I sat outside my house for a long time that night. In the morning I went back to work.

The last year I could not carry the heavy stones anymore. I did finish work instead, the smoothing and the dressing, and I was grateful the foreman allowed it. The morning I could not get up I lay on my mat and listened to the site starting without me, the sounds carrying across the flat ground in the early air, the mallets and the chisels and the overseers calling. I had heard those sounds every morning for thirty-one years.

My neighbor's wife brought water. She sat with me for a while without speaking.

By midday the sounds had become something else. Not absent. Still present but no longer arriving with meaning attached. The market below. The chisels somewhere on the site. A child. Sound continuing, but the part of me that made sense of it was somewhere it could not reach.

The mat beneath me is rough against the back of my neck. I have slept on this mat for thirty-one years. I know every thread of it.

The cough does not come. It has been with me for twenty years and now at the end it is not here. The absence of it is the first sign of something completing.

My hands are on my chest. They have cut alabaster and granite and limestone and they are doing nothing now. I look at them. They are still.

A smell. Lamp oil. Stone dust in my lungs, in the walls, in everything I have touched for thirty-one years.

The afternoon light moves through the doorway. I have read this light my whole life on stone. I watch it move.

My heart slows. I feel each beat as a separate decision. The decisions come further apart.

I leave the body. Not a choice, a release, the way pressure releases from stone when the cut is finally through. I am above the mat. Looking down at the craftsman who cut stone for thirty-one years for a god whose face told him nothing.

The light continues through the doorway.

I do not watch it anymore.

Then he does not watch it.

* * *

The desert receives me without ceremony. Heat from all sides, not the heat I knew working in the sun, but interior heat, the desert drawing the moisture out the way the embalmers do, but without tools and without care.

I feel the moisture leaving. Layer by layer. The body is mostly water and the desert wants it. I feel it going.

My hands go first. The craftsman's hands. I feel the flesh pulling back from the bones, the knuckles emerging from their padding, the sensation of skin tightening over the joints I used for thirty-one years.

56

The sand begins. I know sand. From the inside, sand is thorough. It finds every gap, fills every space the flesh vacates, presses between my bones with the patience of a million grains.

The beetles come. I feel each one. They are methodical. They know what they are looking for and they find it. I feel them working in the spaces the heat has opened.

By the first season I am partly bone. I feel the bones, solid in a landscape that is becoming less solid. The bones are what I was. The rest is in the sand and the air.

Within two seasons I am in more than one place. The wind took some of me east. I feel this. I am distributed.

I feel the false door above me. My chisel marks in it. My work. Standing in the chamber of a man whose name I was never permitted to know. My work holding, above me, while the desert finishes with the rest.

* * *

Grim arrived in the flat heat of midday and stood over the place where the sand had settled and opened his scroll.

The scroll wrote without hesitation. A simple soul in the way that a good tool is simple: made well, used hard, worn honestly. No great sins, no great acts, just the long patient accumulation of a life spent doing what needed doing without complaint and without recognition and without, as far as Grim could see, much bitterness about the absence of either.

He respected this more than he would have said.

He found Kha's consciousness waiting without fidgeting, without performance. Just present. Ready for the next thing.

"Kha."

"Yes."

"Thirty-one years cutting stone for a tomb."

"I did."

"The man in the tomb. Did you ever learn his name?"

Kha was quiet for a moment. "No. We were not supposed to say it. I suppose I could have found it out if I had wanted to badly enough. I did not want to badly enough."

"Why not?"

"What would I have done with it?"

Grim made a note. He turned the assessment wheel and it turned and stopped and he looked at where it stopped and it said what he had already known it would say.

"You worked with care."

"It was good work. The stone was good. I was good at it."

No pride in this. It was just a true thing said plainly.

Grim closed the scroll when Kha spoke again.

"Can I ask you something?"

"You can ask."

"Who cut you?"

"I mean," Kha said, "someone made the tomb and someone made the man who went in it and someone made the men who built it. I was one of those men. I know who made me, more or less, the way you know a thing without being able to explain it. But you." A pause. "You are not like the things that get made. So who cut you? Who dressed you and set you in place and stepped back and said, yes, that is true, the edges are clean?"

Grim looked at where the man had been. The desert stretched flat in every direction. The sounds of the site carried on the hot air, mallets on stone, the same sounds they had made for thirty years, the same sounds they would make for thirty more.

He did not have an answer. The question sat in him differently from other questions, the way a stone sits differently when it has been cut true. He had carried many questions. This one found a place the others had not found.

"I do not know," he said.

"Hm," said Kha, as if this confirmed something he had suspected. "Well. I suppose that's all right."

Grim sent him on.

He stood in the desert for a moment after. The scroll was closed in his hands and the question was in him and this desert did not provide either of them with anything useful. The air around the grave began to move again, the faint dry wind picking up as if it had been waiting.

The Field

He went to the field between collections.

He had been to this field before. He did not remember when. The grass was the same grass as other fields and the sky was the same sky and no reason for this field except that he had come here before and so he came here now.

He stood in it.

The field smelled of something he did not have a name for. Not grass exactly. The warm specific smell of an afternoon that had been doing this since before anyone named it.

He was not here for anyone. No scroll open. The field was empty and the light was the light fields have in the late afternoon, low and sideways, the shadows of the grass longer than the grass.

A while. He stayed.

He thought about saying something. He did not know to whom. He had no evidence that there was anyone to say it to, and some evidence that there was not, and he had been working this job for longer than working had a name and no one had ever said anything back to him that had not come through a scroll.

Nothing said.

He stood in the field and the light moved the way light moves in the late afternoon, slowly, the shadows lengthening, the grass going from green to something that had gold in it, and he watched this happen and did not know what he watched for.

After a while he left.

The next collection waited and he went to it. The grass in the field settled back into the wind's pattern after he had gone, the place where he had stood no different from any other place.

Something waited in the grass behind him, after he had gone.

The Physician's Daughter

"Hold still," I said. "I know it hurts. Hold still anyway."

The man, his name was Yosef, he had told me twice, as if the name might help, had a forearm broken in two places where the stone had come down on it. I had seen this before. My father had shown me how to set it before he showed me most other things, because broken arms were common and needed doing quickly before the swelling made it worse.

"My father was hurt like this," I said, talking because people held still better when there was something to listen to. "He set it himself. Said it was the only time in his life he was glad to know what he knew."

"Is he..." Yosef started, and then his breath went out of him as I worked the bone back to where it needed to be.

"He died three months ago," I said. "His heart. He had known for two years and had not told me." She finished the setting and began wrapping. "He thought I would worry."

"Would you have?"

"Yes," I said. "But I would have worried while he was still alive to argue with, which is better."

Yosef laughed, which was unexpected, and then caught himself — the movement had shifted the arm.

"Don't," I said. "Hold still."

I tied off the wrapping. Outside the courtyard walls the sounds of the siege continued. I had stopped hearing them the way I had stopped hearing my own heartbeat, but they were always there, and occasionally something in them changed and my body registered the change before my mind did.

"Will it heal?" Yosef said.

"If you rest it and keep it clean and do not do anything foolish with it for six weeks. Which in these circumstances," She stopped. No point finishing the sentence. Both of them understood what the circumstances were.

"My name was Miriam," I said. I did not know why I said it that way, with the was. "My father was a physician. He taught me by letting me be in the room when it happened, and when he died I kept working because no one else knew what I knew and the work did not stop."

"You are good at it," Yosef said.

"I know," I said. Not pride. Just true.

I was twenty-seven years old. I had been frightened most of the time since the siege began and exhausted all of the time and there were days I hated the people I was helping for needing so much help. I kept working because stopping felt worse than continuing.

The wall came down.

The sound arrived before the weight did, a low percussion moving through stone, and my body registered it before my mind understood it. I had time to turn my head. Not enough time.

Limestone dust filled the air before the stones arrived. The dust tasted of old walls and mortar and a thousand years of this city. I breathed it in. I was breathing it in when the first stone hit.

The weight arrived in sequence. The first stones took what they took. Then more. My body received them in the order they came. Between the first and the last I was aware of Yosef's arm somewhere near me, the arm I had just set, the six weeks he would need if he rested it.

The circumstances did not allow.

The pain was not what I had trained myself to expect. In four months of working the rooms where pain was I had categorized many of its gradations. What arrived was prior to pain, or perhaps pain had arrived and no capacity remained to receive it as pain.

Still light. Orange, sideways, afternoon light of Jerusalem in July coming through the gap where the wall had been. I had worked in this courtyard for four months and I had not looked at the light once. I looked at it now.

The sentence was still in my mouth. I did not know what it had been going to say.

I rose above the rubble. The courtyard was below me, the stones, the figures underneath them, Yosef's arm at the wrong angle. I saw myself.

I had been frightened for four months. The frightened stopped first.

The light continued through the gap.

The light continued.

* * *

The flies find us within the first hour. Jerusalem in July has those flies, heavy, purposeful, experienced. I spent four months working around them in the rooms where the wounded were. I know exactly what they are doing now.

I feel each one land. The weight of them on my skin, which is still my skin, still has boundaries and temperature and the capacity to receive information. The flies do not know this. They are not interested in what I know.

They find the gaps in the rubble and work downward. Each one is distinct. I feel them moving, the tickle of legs on skin that can still feel, the probing. The eggs they lay I feel as small deposits, each one a decision the fly makes and I cannot unmake.

Yosef is nearby. I know this. Not by sight. I am not in a position to see anything. By the fact of the space he occupies, the way one body knows the proximity of another body in the dark. The wall came down on both of us.

The eggs hatch on the third day. I feel the larvae emerge, small, purposeful, blind. The maggots do not hesitate. They have been doing this work since before Jerusalem had a name.

I feel each one. Where it moves. What it finds. What it takes. They move through the soft tissue first, the places the heat has begun to work on, and then they go deeper. Each one carving a channel through what I was.

The rubble holds the heat. Jerusalem in July, and I am under limestone, and the heat accumulates. The combination of heat and organisms accelerates everything. What would take months in cooler ground takes weeks here.

They build over the rubble in the first generation. I feel the new foundations pressing down through the soil. New weight on old weight. The city continuing above what the city has forgotten.

I do not forget. I am here for all of it. The slow chemistry of bone after flesh is gone. The centuries turning above me. Yosef in the same ground, close enough that our minerals eventually commingle, unable to tell each other so.

I do not forget.

* * *

Grim came when the last of it was done. He had been working in other centuries, other grounds. He came to this one and stood in the dark under the foundations of a building that had been built on the ruins of a building that had been built on the ruins of hers, and he opened the scroll.

He read what it said. He read it again. The temperature in the sealed underground space dropped, but not in the way his arrival usually dropped it.

Deeper. The cold of something holding itself still out of regard for what it looked at.

The assessment was brief. She had worked. She had not stopped working. She had felt the things people feel and kept working anyway, which was not the same as not feeling them.

She had not been kind in the soft sense, she had not had the time or the energy for that, but she had been present, which was harder and mattered more. The scroll had little to say about her failures because her failures were the ordinary failures of a person running on empty in impossible circumstances, and the scroll was not interested in those.

He found her waiting. She was not what he expected, though he could not have said what he expected. She had sat down but not rested. The stillness of someone between tasks, not done.

"Is it done?" she asked.

"Yes," Grim said.

"The man with the broken arm. Yosef. Did anyone finish with him?"

"I do not know," he said.

He had noted Yosef in the scroll, a neighbor, not a husband, though the way she had set the arm had carried the specificity of long familiarity and he had read it wrong. The scroll had corrected him without commenting on the assumption. He did not mention this.

She accepted this. She looked around at whatever she could see of where she was, which was nothing, the same nothing Grim inhabited.

"My father," she said. "Is he here?"

"No. He went on some time ago."

"Good," she said. And then: "Is he all right?"

"He is trying again," Grim said. "As everyone does."

She nodded as if this was the kind of answer she had expected.

He produced the wheel. Set it turning. It turned and stopped and he looked at where it had stopped and the result was the cleanest result the wheel had produced in longer than he could readily account for, and he made his note with something that was not quite satisfaction but was close to it.

"You did well," which he did not normally say.

She looked at him steadily. "I did what was in front of me."

"Most don't."

He sent her on.

Miriam went the way everything went. The same direction, the same nothing at the end of it that he could identify or name. He had been watching this the way you do a thing without deciding to.

Standing in the dark under the foundations of the city for a while longer. The underground quiet held around him.

The Iron

On the second of March 1953 my guards found me on the floor of the dining room at the dacha. I had been there since the night before, since the stroke had come at the table.

They had heard a sound and had not come. You do not come when you hear a sound from my rooms. The ones who came when they were not expected did not come again.

My name was Josef Vissarionovich Dzhugashvili. I had used another name for most of my adult life. I lay on the floor of the dining room at Kuntsevo for several hours before anyone was sufficiently certain I was dying rather than testing them.

The stroke had taken my speech and most of my right side. My mind was still running. This is the thing about a stroke. The mind keeps running. They do not tell you that. It keeps running in the wreckage and it knows where it is. I was aware that I was on the floor. I was aware that no one came.

I ran the calculations that I had been running for forty years: who was safe, who was a threat, what the configuration of power looked like from where I lay on the floor, what any of them would do with this, how to prevent the ones who would use it from using it.

The calculations ran and the conclusions formed. I could not speak the conclusions. I could not act on them. They ran and ran and produced nothing.

I had run the same calculations since I was a young man in the revolutionary underground, sitting across from people who wanted power and calculating how to take it from them before they could use it against me. The calculations had kept me alive. They had kept me in power.

They had shaped the Soviet Union from above the way a hand shapes clay, not gently, not with concern for what the clay prefers, but effectively. The clay was still the shape I had made it.

I lay on the floor from the night before. The floor of the dining room at Kuntsevo was cold against the right side of my face, which was the side the stroke had taken. The left side still received information. I knew which side of the room I was facing. I knew what was on the table above me. I knew who was not coming.

My daughter came at the end. Svetlana, in the room, her face saying clearly what she saw. I tried to send her something across the room, not an apology, I had not built the apparatus for apology and it was too late to build it now, but something that said: I know you are there. I know what it cost to be my daughter. I watched her face. I tried to make my face say this. I do not know what my face said.

The calculations were still running. Who was safe, who was a threat, how to prevent the ones who would use this from using it. They had been running since 1920 on a substrate that was no longer adequate and they ran anyway because they did not know how not to. The conclusions reached their conclusions. No one to deliver them to. I had spent sixty years ensuring I was the only recipient. At the end this meant I kept them.

Then the thing finally stopped.

The floor of the dining room at Kuntsevo is cold. Not the cold of the winter outside, this is interior cold, the stone floor conducting it upward into the right side of my face, which is the only side that is receiving anything now.

I can smell the food from last night. Still on the table above me. The Georgian food. The smell of it reaches me and I note it.

My left eye is open. I cannot remember getting to the floor. I can see the leg of the chair. The pattern in the wood. I cut timber as a boy, before all of this, before I understood what all of this would be. I know what wood grain looks like. This chair is oak. Good oak. I did not choose the chairs in this room.

The stroke took the right side at the table. I read a report. One moment the report was there and then the right side of everything was not available and I was on the floor.

The floor of the dining room at Kuntsevo is cold. The right side of my face receives the cold of it directly, the right side still works, receiving information. The left side of my face is involved in something else.

I can see the leg of the oak chair. The grain of it. I cut timber as a boy before I understood what my life would be. I know what oak grain looks like.

My daughter comes in. Svetlana. Her face says clearly what she sees. I try to tell her with my right eye that I know she is there. I do not know if it arrives.

The calculations continue running. Who is safe, who is a threat, who will move into what is vacating. The calculations have been running since 1920 and the substrate that ran them is no longer adequate but the calculations run anyway on diminishing resources.

The smell of the food on the table above me. The Georgian food I asked for. Still there.

I feel the blood pooling under the right side of my face, the specific warmth of it against the cold floor. The calculations produce conclusions I cannot act on. This is a new condition. I have been in no condition I could not act on since I was nineteen years old.

Then the calculations stop.

I am above the dining room. Looking down at the body on the floor. The body that ran the Soviet Union for twenty-nine years is on the floor of the dacha with its face against the cold oak boards. A small body. I had not thought of it as small.

Then the calculations stop.

* * *

They embalm me and put me in the Mausoleum beside Lenin. I feel the embalming. The fluids entering through the veins, finding the spaces the blood has left, filling them with something that holds the shape of things while preventing the natural process. I feel the holding. The preservation is thorough.

I watch the lines of people from inside the Mausoleum. I cannot see them, the embalming has taken the eyes, but I feel the vibration of them, the distant weight of thousands of footsteps passing above, a continuous procession that I know without seeing.

In 1961 Khrushchev has me removed. I feel the removal. The disruption of the preservation after eight years, the cold air finding the embalmed surfaces, the realization, inside, where the embalming cannot reach, that the location is changing.

The Kremlin wall cemetery. Clay. English and Russian and Mongolian clay are all different but they have the same patience. The clay presses in from all sides with the weight of wet clay, and I feel it pressing, and the embalming I feel working against the pressure.

The embalming delays but does not prevent. The clay knows this. It has received the embalmed before. It waits.

The calculations resume. They have no subject anymore, the Soviet Union has become other things, but the substrate that ran them persists and the calculations run in the abstract, producing conclusions about a configuration that no longer exists.

The clay works slowly through the preservatives. I feel each step. The tissues the embalming had held beginning, slowly, to give way. Decade by decade the clay accomplishes what the embalming had postponed.

The calculations run without subject for decades. Then they too go.

The Kremlin wall cemetery continues above me. The clay continues. I am in the clay that has received the architects of the Soviet Union. I am thorough. I was always thorough.

* * *

Grim came when the clay was done and stood in the Kremlin wall cemetery in the grey Moscow morning and opened the scroll.

The scroll opened. It did not stop writing.

He waited. The scroll kept writing. He stood in the grey morning while it wrote and the city went about its business around the cemetery walls and the scroll continued. An hour. More than an hour. He did not experience time the way the people inside the Kremlin walls experienced it but he was aware of the accumulation of it, the scroll producing and producing without reaching its end.

Names. Decisions. Orders. The machinery of a state that had run without mercy for nearly three decades. The scroll had all of it, the purges and the famines and the camps and the orders and the counter-orders and the precise details of each decision made from above about what happened to people below. Each one. In order. Without omission.

The scroll stopped. Grim read what it had produced. He read it again.

He found Stalin waiting. The mind was still running, he could feel it, even now, the calculations continuing, the assessment of the situation, the evaluation of who this figure was and what it meant for the configuration of power.

"The calculations. They have not stopped."

"No."

"They will not change anything."

"No. They will not." A pause that had the quality of something continuing to run. "But they do not know how to stop."

Grim produced the wheel. He set it turning. It turned for a very long time. The grey morning continued around him while it turned. When it stopped he looked at where it had stopped.

He made his note. The note was clear. The result was what it was.

He sent Stalin on and watched where the sending went. The vast indifferent drawing-in. The direction with nothing at the end of it that he could see or name. The calculations, as far as Grim could tell, were still running as they arrived at the door.

The machinery did not adjust for this. The door did not adjust. The vast drawing-in received what it received without knowing what it was receiving.

Grim stood in the Kremlin wall cemetery for a moment. The grey light held. The city held. Everything held in the ordinary way of things that do not know and are not required to know what is in the ground beneath them.

The Chariot

The king ran at midday.

Ramin saw it first. Ramin had the best eyes in the unit, he could read weather at distances that made other men squint and see nothing, and he said it without inflection, the way I said most things: "The standard is moving wrong."

I looked.

Darius on his horse, turning away from the battle. The bodyguard turning with him. The royal standard moving in the wrong direction, away from Alexander and away from them and away from everything the day was supposed to be.

"That's the king running," Ramin said.

"Yes," I said.

"So the battle is over."

"Yes."

Ramin looked at me. He was twenty-three, the youngest of the forty, and he looked at me the way a man does when he already knows what he's seeing and wants it confirmed. "Then what do we do?"

I thought about it for approximately the length of time it takes to exhale.

Then he shrugged.

Not at Ramin, at the situation. At the king. At the shape of the day, which was not what any of them had anticipated when they woke that morning. The shrug was not despair. It was not the gesture of a man who had stopped caring. It was the gesture of a man who had looked at what was in front of me and decided what I was, regardless of what the day went to be.

Ramin looked at me for a moment. Then I said: "The chariots."

"Yes," I said.

My name was Arshama.

I commanded forty men on a hill on the left flank of the Persian line at Gaugamela, in the year the Greeks call 331 BC. I did not know that it was the last full year in which the world I had served would exist.

I had served Darius since I was nineteen. I had served my father before me. I had stood on the plains of Egypt and on the mountain passes of Bactria and in a dozen engagements whose names he no longer remembered because the names of engagements are for historians and I was not a historian.

I turned to my men.

They had chariots on the hill. Four of them, the big scythed kind, built to break infantry formations, the blades at knee height, the horses trained for the noise and the press of a charge. They had trained with them for two years.

I told them what he intended.

They looked at me. Every one of them understood what I understood, that Darius had run, that the battle was already decided, that the charge would accomplish nothing except their deaths, which would also accomplish nothing. I watched them understand it.

Then they got into the chariots.

They were free men. I had not ordered them. I had told them what I intended. They could have walked off the hill and I could not have stopped them and the day would have ended the same way regardless.

They got into the chariots.

Ramin was on the lead chariot. I drove well.

They charged Alexander's line from the hill at a full gallop, forty men on four chariots making the kind of noise that had broken formations in Egypt and Bactria, and Alexander's infantry had seen them coming and had time to prepare and prepared very well, and that was the end of it.

It was not a long charge. I had time, in it, to feel the horse under me and the sound of thirty-nine other men and the pitch of a noise that had broken formations before. I had time to see Alexander's infantry turning to meet them, the quality of men who have seen the charge coming and have prepared for it and are not afraid.

I had not seen that before. The formations I had broken had not seen me coming.

I had time to understand this. I had time to feel it land, not fear, something more specific, the recognition of a miscalculation made at the moment it becomes uncorrectable. I had made the decision in full knowledge of what I was deciding and I had been right about what I was deciding and here it was, arriving as predicted.

Ramin drove well.

The spear took me at the throat of the horse first and then at my side as the chariot broke. I was in the air for a moment, which was not a sensation I had experienced before. A man on a chariot is never in the air.

The ground of the plain of Gaugamela hit me the way ground hits a man thrown from a moving chariot, which is total and without interest in what the man is.

I was on my back. The sky was October blue, the blue of a Syrian October that is different from any other blue because it has no warmth in it and has no apology for having no warmth. I had seen this sky every October of my life. I had not looked at it from this angle before.

The spear took me above the right hip. I felt it enter. Not pain, not immediately, the body has a latency for that kind of information, a fraction of a second where the knowledge registers before the hurt follows it. In that fraction I understood exactly what had happened and where the spear was and what it had gone through.

Then the pain.

The chariot was still moving and I was no longer on it. I was in the air. A man on a chariot is never in the air. I had this thought clearly, absurdly, while the plain of Gaugamela came up to meet me.

The ground hit me on my right side. The spear was still in me, which complicated the landing. I heard something give in my shoulder. The impact forced the air out of me and the air did not come back easily.

I was on my back. The spear pointed at the October sky. My own spear, from Alexander's infantry, sticking out of me and pointing at the sky I had been looking at all morning.

The blood came quickly, running down into the dirt under me, warm and considerable. I pressed my hand to the entry point. This was reflex. Twenty-two years of soldiering, you press your hand to the wound. The pressure did not accomplish much. The wound was not the kind that pressure helped.

Alexander's infantry moved past me. I watched their feet. Nobody stopped. I was not their problem now. I had been their problem for the length of the charge and I was no longer moving, which made me a different category of thing.

The blood pooled under me. I felt it cooling against my back faster than it left my body. The October ground of the Syrian plain absorbed it the way dry ground absorbs everything.

My father's armor had held until it didn't. The craftsman in Persepolis had done his work well. It had taken twenty-two years and the full weight of Alexander's infantry to prove the limit of it.

The October sky did not move. I watched it. My breathing was wrong, the spear had done something to the cavity of the chest that made the breathing wrong, and I breathed the way you breathe when breathing has become an act of will rather than a reflex.

I felt myself beginning to leave the body. Not a decision. Something the body did on its own, releasing what it held. I was still in it and I was also just above it, watching the plain from an inch and a half above my own face.

The chariot was somewhere behind me. I could not see it. The battle sounds moved away.

I watched my chest stop moving.

The noise of the battle continued on all sides but it moved away from me, which meant the line had shifted, which meant something had been decided without me. I noted it with the part of me that had been registering tactical information for twenty-two years. Then that part quieted.

My armor was good armor. My father's armor. The craftsman in Persepolis had done my work well and it had held in Egypt and in Bactria and in a dozen smaller engagements whose names I could no longer remember. It held until it did not.

The October sky did not move. I watched it for whatever time was left.

The sound the noise made when it stopped being possible was not long in coming.

* * *

The looters came while the dust was still settling. Soldiers from Alexander's line who had watched the charge and now walked the ground collecting what the dead no longer needed. Arshama had done this myself after other battles. It was practical work. The dead had no use for bronze.

They were efficient. My armor first, the good scale armor my father had left me, each scale riveted by a craftsman in Persepolis who had worked my whole life making soldiers harder to kill. Off in minutes. My sword. My sandals, which were good leather and barely worn because I had not marched far enough to wear them down.

The ring my wife had given me when their first son was born, which required some work because my hands had swollen in the heat, and one of the men cursed at the difficulty of it and worked at it without patience.

I had never in my life been unable to do anything, and now I lay on the plain of Gaugamela unable to do anything, and the man with my ring on my finger was already walking away toward the next body, and I felt something I had no name for because I had never felt it before, a fury that had nowhere to go, that had no body to act through, that simply was, complete and useless, the most useless thing I had ever carried.

The birds came after the men. The October sun did the rest. What it did not need the night cold slowed and the morning heat resumed. I was aware of all of it, complete, unwanted, without the consolations I had been told to expect. No afterlife of heroes. No celestial plain.

Just the fury and then the slow understanding that the fury would not change anything, and then just the plain, and what the plain did to what I had been, and the long patience of watching the armies that had killed me march away.

I thought about my men. Each of them by name, in the order they had died, which I knew because I had been present for all of it. I thought about Ramin, who had said the king is running and then the chariots and who had driven well. I thought about what it meant to be a thing that did not change even when changing would have been the sensible choice.

I did not resolve this. The plain of Gaugamela did not provide resolution. It provided time, and I had more of it than I had expected, and I spent it.

* * *

Grim came when the last of the bones had become part of the plain and stood in the dry October air and opened the scroll.

The plain was quiet. It was always quiet now. The armies were long gone, the scavengers were long gone, the historians who would argue about this day for two thousand years had not yet been born. Only the flat ground and the dry air and the silence of a place where something decisive had happened and which now showed no evidence of it.

He read the scroll.

A soldier. Twenty-two years of service. A decision made in the length of an exhale on a hill on the left flank of a battle already lost. Forty men who had gotten into the chariots.

He found Arshama waiting without surprise and without trouble.

"The king ran."

"Yes."

"You saw it."

"From the hill. Clearly."

"And you charged anyway."

Arshama looked at him with the directness of a man who had spent twenty-two years making fast accurate assessments of terrain and enemy positions and his own resources.

"What else would I have done?"

"The youngest one. Ramin. He drove the lead chariot."

A pause. "He drove well."

"Yes. He did."

He produced the wheel. It turned and stopped.

The note was simple. The wheel had not taken long. Just a hill and a shrug and forty men who had gotten into the chariots.

He sent Arshama on.

He stood on the plain of Gaugamela in the dry October air and did not immediately move.

He looked at his hands. This was not something he usually did. He had no idea why he was doing it.

The air around him had gone still. Not the stillness of arrival. The stillness of attention, of something paying close notice to what had just passed through the door. It held for longer than that kind of stillness usually held.

Then it released, and the dry air moved again, and the plain was just a plain, and Grim closed the scroll.

He was not the only one working the plain. A battle this size, ten thousand dead by noon, required more than one. Half a mile to the east another figure moved through the Macedonian casualties with the stillness of a Grim at pace. He recognized the way he held the scroll. Maren. He did not go to speak. This was not the kind of work you interrupted.

The Decision

Ibn al-Alkami had been speaking for ten minutes when I understood that the vizier was right.

The council chamber was cool even in summer, the thick walls of the palace holding the heat at bay. Nine men around the table, the Caliph at the center, the maps of the Mongol advance spread open before them. The news from Persia was three weeks old. Three weeks was not old for news, and yet in three weeks the map had changed in ways that made my chest tighten when I looked at it.

"There is no honor in a city of the dead," Ibn al-Alkami said. He was a small man with precise hands and the habit of speaking quietly, which made people lean forward to hear me, which was, I had always thought, either a technique or a character. I was never sure which. "The Caliph has the power to negotiate terms. That power exists today. When the walls fall, it will not exist."

He was right. I knew it the way you know a structural problem in a building, not from looking at one thing but from the accumulation of small signs that all pointed the same direction. The news from Persia. The news from before Persia. The pattern of what the Mongols had done to every city that had made them lay siege.

He was right and I went to argue against him anyway.

My genuine assessment was that the city needed time, not surrender, and if I had been wrong about the walls I had not yet been proven wrong, and the possibility remained that Baghdad was different, that the libraries and the scholars and the accumulated learning of five hundred years amounted to something the Mongols would not waste, and that this argument could be made and believed and could work.

"The walls of Baghdad have stood for five centuries," I said. I waited for the room to settle on me before I continued. "Men who understood that the city they were protecting built them was not simply a city. It was the center of the world's knowledge. What is assembled within these walls, the House of Wisdom, the libraries, the scholars from every nation, is irreplaceable. Not merely to us. To the world."

"The Mongols have not shown themselves to be students of irreplaceability," Ibn al-Alkami said.

"No. But they have shown themselves to be students of practical advantage. A living city that submits is worth more than a dead city. The tribute alone..."

"They have taken tribute from cities and sacked them afterward."

"From cities that resisted first." I looked at the Caliph. "We have not yet resisted. The walls are intact. The garrison is capable. We are not asking the Mongols to take a city by force. We are saying that taking it by force will cost them something, and that the alternative is worth more to them whole than broken. This is an argument they understand. Trade in silk, in paper, in scholarship: all of this flows through Baghdad. All of it stops if Baghdad burns."

The Caliph looked at the map.

I had known for two years that this moment was coming. I had said nothing about it because there was nothing to say when the person whose character was wrong for the moment was also the person whose position made them the only decision that mattered.

"The walls," the Caliph said. He looked at the map, not at either of us. "You have walked them."

"I have walked them myself," I said. "Three times in the last month. The garrison commanders are capable men. The walls will hold long enough for the Mongols to calculate the cost and find the alternative more valuable."

This was true and it was not the whole truth. The walls would hold. I did not know for how long and I did not know what happened when they stopped holding and I had calculated this probability and found it acceptable and had not said, aloud, what acceptable in this context meant.

The vizier would lose this argument and he knew he would lose it. He looked at me and then, unexpectedly, he looked at his hands on the table. "You have walked the walls," he said. It was not a question and it was not agreement. I did not know what it was. I do not know now.

The Caliph looked at the map. He did not look at Ibn al-Alkami. "My father held these walls," he said. "And his father. The caliphate has held these walls for five hundred years." He paused. "We will hold the walls."

I left the council chamber knowing the argument was lost and the decision made and that what came next was determined.

A guard at the door said something as I passed. I caught the end of it but not the beginning. I did not stop to ask him to repeat it.

The Mongols arrived in the winter month when the river was low. I watched them come from the wall, a hundred and twenty thousand soldiers, the siege engines on the flatboats, the Armenian cavalry on the far bank. I had known this number was possible. I had said the walls could hold against it. I still believed the walls could hold.

The walls held for twelve days.

I was on the eastern wall when the engineers found the weakness in the repair section. I felt the ground tremble when the engines found it. I understood immediately what the trembling meant.

They came through at dawn. I heard it before I saw it, the change in the sound of the siege, the particular quality that meant the thing that had been held was no longer held. I had been listening to sieges for thirty years and I knew the sound.

I did not run. Nowhere to run and I was not a man who ran. I stood in the street near the House of Wisdom and watched them come through.

I had been wrong about the scholars. Wrong about what irreplaceability meant to them. I thought they would calculate the value and find it exceeded the cost. They were not calculating.

The sword took me across the back. It came from behind and to the right and I did not see it and I did not feel it arrive, only the sudden failure of my legs to receive signals from my spine. I went down.

The cold stones of the Baghdad street received me. January, the river wet in the air, the cold of this city's winter coming up through the limestone into my face.

I looked at the street. At the level of the street. The Mongols were moving past me at the level of my eyes, their boots on the stones, methodical, unhurried. I had watched armies all my life. I knew how armies that had won moved. They moved like this.

The blood was pooling around my left cheek. It was warm. The stones were cold and the blood was warm and the contrast was the most vivid sensation available to me.

Someone kicked me in the leg. Not with intent. I was in the way and they stepped over me and their boot caught my calf on the way through. I felt it. I noted it with the part of me that was still noting things.

The sword had gone through something in my back that controlled the lower body. I felt my hands but not my legs. My hands were flat on the stones. The stones were very detailed at this distance. I had never looked at the street of Baghdad at this distance before.

The blood reached the edge of my vision and moved past it. There was a great deal of it. I had known, intellectually, how much blood a body held. Now I was on the outside of the knowledge.

I felt myself separating. Still in the body, still aware of the stones and the cold and the blood and the sound of the army moving through the city, and also rising slightly, viewing the scene from just above my own back, watching the Mongols move through the street of Baghdad over the body of the man who had said the walls would hold.

The walls had held for twelve days.

The river ran black somewhere above me. I knew the direction without seeing it.

I thought about the vizier's face across the table. The way a man looks when he is watching someone make a mistake that cannot be corrected later.

The river ran black above me. I could not see the river but I knew the direction and I knew what was in it and the cold of the stones held the knowledge without needing to be told.

* * *

Then the engineers found the weak point in the eastern section, where a repair twenty years ago had used different stone, and the battering began there and continued until it did not need to continue anymore.

From the walls I watched what followed. The Mongols were methodical. They had done this before and they knew how it was done and they did it efficiently, block by block, street by street.

I had believed they would spare the scholars. I had believed the House of Wisdom was different. I had looked at the history of what they had done in other cities and found exceptions, places where the libraries had been preserved, where the scholars had been taken as prizes rather than killed, where practical value had outweighed the momentum of destruction, and I had believed Baghdad would be one of those.

I watched the books of the House of Wisdom carried to the Tigris and thrown in.

The river ran black. I had never seen a river run black before. I knew what was in the river. I had watched them carry the books from the House of Wisdom, had stood at the edge of the Tigris and watched them go in, the centuries of accumulated knowledge of the world entering the water and the water turning black with it.

I had not believed, watching them carry the books, that this was actually going to happen. I could not have explained, standing at the river with the water black around my knees, what I had thought went to happen instead.

The mounds of the slain took three days to build. I saw it from where I was. On my knees by then, not from choice but because my legs had failed me somewhere in the second day and had not resumed their function, and the men building it were methodical, the same methodical efficiency they brought to everything, and the Mongols arranged the skulls with the same mathematical precision they arranged their formations.

When it was finished it was taller than the minarets.

I thought about the argument I had made. The irreplaceability. The practical value. The tribute that would flow from a living city. I thought about the governor of a northern province who had refused terms and whose city was now a similar arrangement, thought about the pattern I had seen and had argued away from and about the vizier's face across the table and what had been on it.

I died with the city. My death was one death among two hundred thousand.

* * *

The ground of the Tigris floodplain is old and saturated and has held many things across a very long time. It held Dawud with the patience of ground that has been receiving the dead of this valley for four thousand years, ground that has no category for what it receives, no distinction between the man who built something and the man who failed to protect it.

The Tigris was still running black when the ground took him. The books he had believed were irreplaceable were in the river, the ink dissolving, the paper softening, the five hundred years of accumulated learning moving in the water toward the sea.

He was in the ground beside the river and the ground and the river were doing the same work, returning what they had received, and neither of them knew or cared that what the river was receiving was different from what the ground was receiving, that one was a man and the other was the reason two hundred thousand people were in the mounds.

The water came into the ground when the river rose in spring. He felt it moving through what he had been, carrying pieces of him the way it carried pieces of everything else, the soil of the floodplain, the residue of the city above, whatever had dissolved into the water from the river and settled into the ground beside it.

He was in the water and in the ground and in the things that grew in both and he could not tell anymore what was him and what was the dissolved books and this was the thing he had not been able to calculate, sitting at the council table looking at the map, and could not calculate now.

By the second season little remains that could be called Dawud. By the third season even that was gone, carried into the floodplain and the river and the sea. What had been a scholar-soldier who had argued, sincerely and incorrectly, for the irreplaceability of the city of knowledge returned to the ground that had received the knowledge itself.

The ground did not distinguish.

* * *

Grim came when the last of it had settled and stood on the bank of the Tigris and opened the scroll.

He read it. Then he read it again.

What was in the scroll was not simple. He had expected this, a man present at the decision that had ended two hundred thousand lives would not produce a simple scroll. What he had not expected was the character of the complexity.

No cruelty here. No pleasure in the destruction. No self-interest that he could identify. A man who had looked at a situation, made an honest calculation, reached a conclusion he had believed was correct, and argued for it in the belief that he was protecting the thing he loved.

He had been wrong in a way that killed two hundred thousand people.

The scroll had them all. The names of the soldiers. The scholars who had died with their books. The children. The particular count of the dead. All of it in the ledger beside the sincere argument, the walked walls, the honest assessment of the garrison's capability, the calculation that had found the probability acceptable.

He held the scroll. The Tigris moved beside him.

He found Dawud waiting. The years in the ground and the seasons in the river had done their work. He had arrived at the full shape of what he had done.

"The vizier was right." Not a question.

"Yes."

"I knew it when he spoke. I argued against him anyway."

"Yes."

"I believed the argument. Both things were true at the same time."

Grim looked at him. The distinction Dawud made was a real one. He had been present at assessments of men who had done great harm knowing it was harm. The ledger in his hands was something different and the wheel would reflect that difference and would still have to account for two hundred thousand.

"The books. The House of Wisdom. Is any of it..."

"Some survived. Carried to other cities before the siege. The scholars who had copies elsewhere. Not most of it." A pause. "Not most of it."

Dawud received this.

Grim produced the wheel. He set it turning. It turned for a very long time, longer than Itzli's, longer than most, moving through a ledger that resisted every category the wheel had been built to use. A man of sincere conviction whose sincere conviction had produced catastrophe. A man who had looked at history and reasoned carefully and been wrong in the specific way that careful reasoning is most dangerous, when it reaches a conclusion and stops looking.

When the wheel stopped Grim looked at where it had stopped and understood that the wheel was correct and that correct was not the same as adequate.

He made his note. He set the uncertainty beside it.

"Does it matter that I knew? In the end. That I understood what I had done."

"It matters that you did not require the dark to understand it. You saw it in the moment it was too late to change."

"Is that enough?"

Grim looked at the river. The Tigris was clear now. It had been clear for centuries. The books were gone.

"No," he said. "It is not enough. But it is what there is."

He sent Dawud on.

He stood on the bank of the Tigris for a long time after the sending, the scroll closed in his hands, looking at the water and thinking about the calculation that had found an acceptable probability and about what acceptable meant and about the difference between believing something is true and believing it should be true and about how many times across his long work he had found those two beliefs occupying the same space without having noticed.

The God King

I was a god.

This is not a claim. It is not pride speaking from beyond the grave. It was the actual administrative and theological fact of my existence from the moment I was born until the moment I stopped breathing, and it was understood by everyone in every corner of the world that mattered.

The priests confirmed it at my coronation with rituals performed for two thousand years before me. The people built their lives around it. The army fought in my name because my name was the name of heaven on earth. When I spoke, it was not a man speaking. When I ordered a thing done, the gods themselves had ordered it.

I believed this.

I believed it the way you believe the ground. That was what the divinity was. When I walked into a room the room changed. I had felt this since childhood, had known it as certainly as I knew the smell of the river in flood. It was not something I claimed. It was something I was.

I ordered men killed. I ordered cities razed. I ordered names removed from monuments, because a man whose name is gone is a man who never existed, and the order of things requires that certain men never have existed. This is Ma'at. The proper functioning of what is. A god does not act from anger or preference. A god acts from the necessity of order. That is what I did.

In the thirty-eighth year of my reign I received a report from the governor of the northern territories. He delivered it kneeling, which was correct, and he read it without looking at me, which was also correct, and what the report said was that the northern territories were failing, the irrigation channels silting, the grain yields falling, the population declining, and that resources beyond what the territories could produce would be required to maintain them.

I listened to the report. When he finished I asked him a question.

"Is this a report," I said, "or are you telling me something else?"

He kept his eyes on the floor. "It is a report, divine one."

"Then make the notation that the resources will be allocated," I said. "And make the notation that the governor of the northern territories has served faithfully."

He made the notation. He left.

The resources were not available. He had known this when he delivered the report. I had known it when I received it. Neither of us had said it, which meant it had not been said. Not in the official record. It would not require a response I could not provide.

This was also Ma'at.

I had been doing this for forty-eight years.

My tomb took twenty years to cut. I never saw it. It was not permitted for the living king to look upon his own house of eternity. I was told it was magnificent. I believed this also, because the people who told me would not have told me anything else.

When the priests came to tell me I was dying I sent them out. I was not dying. Gods did not die. Gods transformed. I would do it in my own time without priests standing over me cataloguing my decline.

I died alone in the inner chamber with the lamps burning low, in the fifty-third year of my life and the thirty-first year of my reign.

The last thing I was certain of was the smell of the lamp oil.

The pain had been in my chest for three days. I had told no one. Gods do not tell people about their pain.

It arrived now fully, a fist closing inside the chest, squeezing the function out of what the function was supposed to do. I was aware of my own heartbeat in a way I had never been aware of it in fifty-three years of life, each beat effortful, each beat asking a question about whether there would be another.

The lamp oil smell was the last thing that arrived with information attached. After that the information stopped arriving.

Then I was above the inner chamber. Looking down at the body of the king on the floor, the lamps burning low, the smell of the oil still in the air. The body of the person who had been a god for thirty-one years. A small body, from above. All bodies are small from above.

I waited for the transformation to continue.

Nothing came.

I waited.

* * *

They come for the body within hours. The embalmers. I commissioned them myself, the finest in the two kingdoms. I feel every decision they make.

The brain comes first, and it comes out through the nose. A long hooked instrument inserted while I watch from wherever I have gone. I feel the hook moving. I feel what it finds and what it removes. The brain that calculated the flood levels and the tribute and the political marriages of thirty-one years, pulled out through the nose in pieces while the embalmers work efficiently and without ceremony.

Then the cuts. Left side, the flank. The blade going in. I feel it, not as pain but as wrongness, the violation of a boundary that the body spent thirty-one years maintaining. The hands reach inside. I feel the hands inside my body, practiced and efficient, finding and removing what they need. The lungs. The stomach. The intestines. Each one lifted out and placed in its canopic jar while I watch from above.

They leave the heart. The heart stays. I feel the heart remaining when everything else has been removed. The heart alone in the empty chest cavity, which is a strange sensation, the cavity that held everything now holding only this one muscle.

The natron begins. Forty days of it. I feel every day. The slow desiccation as the natron draws the moisture out, the skin tightening over the bones, the features sharpening as the padding beneath the skin is drawn away. My face becoming more itself and less itself at once.

The oils come after. Cedar oil. Myrrh. Substances rubbed into every surface, worked into every fold. I feel each application. The hands working the oils into the preserved skin with the thoroughness of long practice.

The linen goes on in layers. Each strip wrapped and overlapped. Amulets placed at intervals on the body as the wrapping proceeds. I feel each weight. The linen tightening over the preserved form until I am a specific shape, the shape the living king had, held by cloth and oil and prayer.

The mummy board goes on last. My own face, gilded, looking up at the ceiling. Then the first coffin. Then the second. Then the third. Each one heavier than the last.

The sarcophagus lid comes down.

The sound it makes settling into place is the sound of a door closing that has no handle on the inside.

I am in the tomb they told me was magnificent. In the darkness I cannot see it. I wait for the transformation that was supposed to follow. Nothing follows.

I wait.

* * *

They came in the second year or the twentieth, I had no way to know which. Two men, moving quickly, not priests. They had a lamp. The light of it reached me through my sealed eyelids, the first light since the tomb was closed, and I felt it the way you feel sun on your face, as warmth as much as brightness. They spoke to each other in low voices, working quickly. They were not praying.

They took the gold from the outer coffin first. Then the amulets they could find. Then they were gone and the darkness came back and I was still there.

More time passed.

Others came, across what must have been centuries, in ones and twos and once a group of four who spent a long time and took a great deal and argued with each other in a language I did not know. Each time the lamp came, the light through my eyelids, the brief warmth of it, and then the dark again.

I stopped waiting for the transformation to continue.

I had been wrong about some things.

This thought came to me slowly, the way water works into stone, over years without number. I had been wrong about the divinity. Not about its reality. I had felt it too thoroughly for too long to doubt that entirely, but about its nature.

It had not protected me from this. It had not transformed me into anything. It had left me here in the dark with the knowledge that I had ordered men killed and cities razed and names erased, and now I had all the time that existed to think about that.

Thinking about it in the dark for a very long time was different from thinking about it in the throne room with the priests confirming that heaven had sanctioned everything.

In the throne room the sanctioning had felt real. Here, in the dark, under the stone, the sanctioning felt like a story I had told myself, a story everyone around me had agreed to tell. The men who had died because of it had not agreed to any story at all. They had simply died.

The governor of the northern territories had not said it. I had not said it. The notation had been made. The resources had not been allocated. The territories had declined. The people in them had declined with the territories.

I had a great deal of time to think about this.

* * *

The last robbery happened in a blaze of light that was nothing like lamplight, white and flat and coming from everywhere, and the voices speaking over me were in a language I had never heard in any form. They were careful. They wore gloves. They took notes.

They did not take the gold but they took almost everything else, the wrappings, the amulets, me, the coffin boards, all of it lifted out and carried into a brightness so total it was almost dark in its own way.

They put me in a room. A dry room, carefully controlled, the air the same temperature every day. Other things were in the room with me, boxes and cases and objects from other tombs, other kings, other centuries. I lay in my case and the dry air moved over me at its constant temperature and the light came on in the morning and went off at night and people came sometimes and looked and left.

Decades of this.

The last thing to go was a fragment of linen from the innermost wrapping, caught in a crack in the case, too small to have been noticed.

The dry air took it grain by grain over twenty years until one morning in what I would later understand was the year 1922 of a calendar I had never heard of, the last of it released its final connection to the material world and became dust and the dust went into the ventilation system of a museum in a city built on the ruins of a civilization built on the ruins of mine, and I was done.

* * *

The cold came into the room.

Grim materialized between the specimen cases and the electric lights dimmed. Not flickered. Dimmed, as if something in the room drew on the same source. They held at half strength for a moment and returned. In the glass cases nearest where he stood, frost spread from a single point outward in branching lines across the inside of the glass.

He opened the scroll. He read what it said. Then he looked across the room at where Amenhotep's consciousness still sat, aware and impossibly old, as old as the dark he had spent three thousand years inside.

The assessment took a long time.

Not because the sins were complicated. They were not complicated. They were the sins of a man who had been handed absolute power at birth and had used it as men with absolute power generally do, without restraint, without much thought for the people on the receiving end of it. The scroll covered them methodically. Each ordered execution. Each razed settlement. Each name chiseled off a monument. The governor's report. The notation that had been made. The territories that had declined.

The list was long and Grim worked through it without rushing and Amenhotep offered no defense because no defense remained that had not already failed him in the dark over the past three thousand years.

What made it long was that Amenhotep kept stopping to ask questions.

"Am I being judged?" he asked, early in the assessment.

"Yes."

"By what authority?"

Grim looked at him.

"I was a god." The words came out differently than they would have in the throne room. Smaller. "The gods judged men. Men did not judge gods. That was the order of things."

"That was one order of things. There are others."

Amenhotep was quiet for a while. Then: "The darkness. The tomb. Was that part of the judgment?"

"No. "That is what happens to everyone. The body must fully return before the assessment can begin. You happened to be embalmed, which took longer."

"Three thousand years."

"Give or take."

Another silence.

"I had time to think."

"I know."

"I thought about the men I ordered killed."

"I know that too."

"The territories." "The governor's report. I did not say it and he did not say it and the notation was made and the people declined anyway."

"Yes."

"Does it matter? That I thought about it?"

Grim looked at the scroll. He looked at the long list. He looked at the consciousness across from him, which was nothing like the consciousness that had gone into the tomb, stripped of everything except what was actually there underneath the theology and the gold and the thirty-one years of absolute certainty.

What was underneath was not nothing. It was not much. But it was not nothing.

"It matters," Grim said, "that you stopped believing the story. Most don't."

"I had three thousand years."

"Most still don't."

He closed the scroll. He produced the wheel and set it turning and it turned for longer than usual before it stopped, as if it too was uncertain what to do with this case.

When it stopped Grim looked at where it had landed and made his note.

"What happens now?"

"You try again. Without the gold. Without the priests. Without anyone telling you that you are something other than a man."

"Will I remember any of it?"

"No."

Amenhotep was quiet for a moment. Then: "The others. The ones whose wheel lands differently than mine. Where do they go?"

Grim looked at him.

"On. They go on to what they have earned."

"Which is what, precisely?"

"That is not my territory. My work ends at the handoff."

Amenhotep considered this with the look of a man who had spent thirty years receiving incomplete reports from officials who thought incomplete reports were safer than complete ones. "You send them somewhere and you do not know what is there."

"I know they are received." The words came out the way they always came out. He had said them before. He had not examined whether they were true.

"Received by whom?"

The question was a reasonable one. Grim had not thought about it as a reasonable question before this moment.

"That," Grim said, "is above my station."

Amenhotep made the sound of a man who had heard that answer before, from officials who did not know the answer and had learned to dress the not-knowing in the language of hierarchy. He did not press further. He had spent enough time in the dark to know when pressing would not help.

Grim sent him on.

He stood in the museum storage room in the flat electric light, the specimen cases around him, the careful dry air, the ventilation system moving it all at the same constant temperature.

He thought about the stone cutter. Thirty-one years cutting a tomb for a man whose name he was not permitted to say. The false door standing in the dark for three thousand years. No one knowing who had made it. The air in the storage room warmed slightly,

briefly, an anomaly the building's climate system
would record and not be able to explain.

The Taiga

The morning the horse broke through, I heard it first.

Yura was ahead of me by thirty feet, leading the mare across the crossing we used every late winter, the bend where the current slowed and the ice built thick. He had made this crossing forty times. The mare had made it more. And then the sound changed and she felt it before it gave way and she tried to stop and couldn't, and they both went through.

My husband Pavlo was behind me with the sled. I did not look back at him. Nothing could be done that I could not do first.

The rope was coiled on the sled. I had it in my hands without thinking about having it. The mare was thrashing and Yura tried to hold her head up and that was wrong, you cannot hold a horse's head up in open water, the horse will pull you under, and I said his name once and when he looked at me I threw the rope.

"Let her go," I said. "Hold the rope and let her go."

He did not want to. The mare was his. I watched him understand that she was already gone and I watched him hold the rope and I pulled.

The water was the temperature that kills. He was in it for less than a minute and he could not speak when he came out, could not work his hands. I got him onto the sled and Pavlo drove and I held Yura against me the whole way back to camp and talked to him the entire time, not about anything, just talk, because the voice is a tether and when someone's body is trying to leave them you keep talking.

He lived. His hands were wrong for two seasons afterward. He never blamed me for the mare.

My name was Nara. I was born on the Lena River in the year the ice broke early and we lost two boats, which my mother said was a bad sign and which turned out to be neither a good sign nor a bad one, just an early ice-break, which happens.

I learned early that my mother had a talent for seeing signs in things and a poor record of reading them correctly. I watched what she did and learned to watch the things themselves instead.

A place on the Lena, maybe half a day's travel east of our summer ground, where the water ran a different color for a hundred meters. Not brown like silt. Something else, greenish, metallic-looking. I passed it twenty times over thirty years and never stopped to look at what was below.

I made most of the decisions in our camp by the time I was thirty. Not because my husband was weak, he was not, but because I was better at them and he knew it and was not bothered by knowing it, which was one of the reasons I had married him. He was good with the dogs and with the large decisions, the ones that required a man's standing in the community. I was good with everything else.

I was not always kind. This is true. When the fish were short I made choices about who ate first that I stand by now and do not feel good about. When a girl in our camp kept making errors that cost us fish I was harder on her than she deserved because I was frightened of the winter and she was there.

When my eldest son made a marriage I thought was wrong I said so in the hearing of his wife and this was a permanent harm to a relationship that never fully healed.

These things sit in me the same as the things I did right. I do not weigh them against each other. They are all what I did.

Pavlo died in the thirty-second year. Not dramatically, he sat down after the evening meal and did not get up. Fast, which is a mercy. I sat with him through the night the way I had sat with Yura on the sled, talking about nothing, because you keep talking.

The fever came in the late winter of my fifty-second year. I recognized it from inside the way I recognized the sound of ice about to change, a weight settling in the chest with the quality of something that intends to stay. I read it clearly. I had been reading signals my whole life.

I told my family what needed doing about the spring stores and the agreement with the Bykov camp. I told them in the efficient way I told them necessary things. They heard me. We did not name what we all knew.

The fever moved through me. Hot in the interior way of high fever, not from outside but from the center outward, the body burning what it could reach. I had been cold in many ways: wet cold, dry cold, the cold of the Lena in November. This was the opposite of all of it and it was mine.

The dogs came in without being called. Three of them, the old bitch and her sons. They lay against my legs without ceremony. I had been reading animals my whole life. I knew what it meant when they came in unbidden and lay down. They could smell the change. I could smell it too, in myself, which was a new thing.

Katya sat with me. She had her father's quietness and my hands. I was glad she was there and I did not tell her I was glad because she knew and because I was tired.

The warmth of the dogs against my legs. The fever burning inward from the center, the body consuming what it can reach to maintain a temperature it cannot maintain.

Katya is there. I do not tell her I am glad. She knows. I am too tired to say what she already knows.

The light through the hide covering. I read it the way I have always read light. What hour. What direction. What the weather is doing. By midmorning it tells me the weather will be clear. By afternoon I can no longer read it.

The dogs lie against me without ceremony. They came in without being called. I have been reading animals my whole life. I know what it means when they do this.

My breathing changes. I feel it change the way I have felt it change in others, the quality of it shifting from something automatic to something labored, the body deciding each breath is worth the effort and then deciding the question is harder than it was.

The heat burns through me from inside. The dogs are warm against my legs. The warmth from outside and the heat from inside meeting at the surface of the skin, and in that meeting I feel myself becoming less distinct from the air in the room.

I leave the body during a breath. Between an exhale and the inhale that does not follow. I am above the sleeping platform. The dogs below, still pressed against the body. Katya's hand on the body's hand. The body that trapped and skinned and navigated the Lena basin for fifty-two years.

The dogs look up. They know something has changed. They do not move.

* * *

They bury me in the permafrost. I feel the fires they build to soften the ground, the heat of them coming down through the soil, and then the work of the shovels, and then the cold when the fires are gone and the ground closes over me.

Permafrost holds completely. This is what I learn from inside: other grounds work through what they receive, taking it apart in stages, giving it back to the roots and the water. Permafrost keeps. The cold presses in from all sides and does not release what it holds.

I feel myself freezing. Layer by layer, from the outside in, the cold finding each tissue and holding it in place. The water in each cell becoming crystal. The specific sensation of becoming still in a way that stillness has never meant before.

The seasons pass above me. I feel them by the way the ground above the permafrost changes, the seasonal thaw reaching down, finding the top layer, softening it, then retreating. Each cycle I feel the warmth approach and stop short of where I am.

The Lena runs its cycle. I can feel the ice-break in spring, the vibration of it traveling through the frozen ground, the shudder of a river releasing from its winter. I count the ice-breaks. A way of keeping time.

Pavlo is somewhere in this ground. Not near, his people buried him on the other side of the river. But in the same permafrost. I feel the general fact of him the way you feel weather coming. Not specific. Present.

A warming cycle reaches me in what I estimate is my three hundredth year. I feel it differently from the seasonal thaws, this one goes deeper, finds places the seasonal warmth has never reached before. The crystal structures shift. Something that has been held is becoming held differently.

The organisms come when the permafrost thaws enough to allow them. Slow organisms, adapted to cold, working at cold temperatures with cold patience. I feel each one. They are unhurried. They have been waiting three hundred years.

The Lena is the same river. The ice still breaks in spring. I have been reading it from inside the ground for what I estimate is three hundred years and it has not changed. I have changed. I am in the river now, worked into it by the thaw water, carried downstream, distributed into the watershed.

I think about the dogs. Whether the old bitch's sons' descendants still work this territory. Whether they still come in without being called at the end.

* * *

Grim came in the brief summer when the ground above me smelled of the short grass that grew in the warm weeks, and he stood on the bank of the river and opened the scroll.

He read it. A life lived in difficult conditions, the decisions of a person responsible for other people's survival. Some harm done and known about. A horse lost to the river and a boy pulled out. The general weight of a woman who had managed what she was given to manage and had known her own errors without requiring ceremony around the knowing.

He found her waiting with the patience of someone who has waited through many difficult winters and knows that the waiting is not the hardest part.

"The fish."

"Every year. Except the year of the early ice-break. That year we were short."

"The boy in the water. Yura."

"He lived." A pause. "His hands were wrong for two seasons. He never blamed me for the mare."

"You couldn't have saved the mare."

"No. I know that. He knew it too."

119

He produced the wheel. Set it turning. Watched it land where it landed, solidly in the middle of the range, the result of a life that had done more right than wrong and had not pretended otherwise. He made his note without hesitation.

He sent Nara on. The river ran. The summer grass moved in the wind above the bank.

He was already in the next territory before the grass had stopped moving.

The Silk Road

"The gradient changes past the second marker," Bao said. "When the road tips and you think it's getting easier, it isn't. There's a false flat for half a day and then the real climb starts."

Liu was seventeen. He had made the short runs before but never the full eastern passage. He nodded at the road.

"How do you know when it's the false flat?"

"Because the rocks on the left side change color. Grey to brown. When you see the brown rocks you're still in the false flat." Bao looked at him. "You'll see it and think: my father was wrong, it is getting easier. Then you'll see the brown rocks and you'll know."

Liu looked at the road. "What if I forget?"

"You won't. The thing you're told to watch for, you watch for. That's how the road teaches."

Luo brought tea without being asked and they sat in the courtyard in the evening and Bao told Liu about the waystation masters east of the pass, which ones were honest and which would short your grain if you weren't counting. Liu listened the way his mother listened, not talking, but nothing missed. Bao had always thought this was what he'd inherited from her, not him.

I should have told her that. I thought about it now and then. I never quite managed it.

At the last waystation before the final pass, there was a woman sitting outside the door in the late afternoon who looked at me in a way I could not read. Not threatening. Something more like recognition. I had never seen her before. She did not speak. Three days from home on the return run, I knew it was fever and not the ordinary kind. The ordinary kind you sweat through. This kind had the weight behind the eyes, the heat that did not respond to water.

Liu was ahead somewhere on the road, they had separated at the waystation three days back, Liu returning early with the lighter cart, the plan always having been that Bao would follow. The plan had not accounted for this.

I hobbled the horses at the flat ground between two low hills and built a small fire and lay down beside it. The fire was low. I did not have the energy to build it higher.

Nineteen years on this road. Twenty if you count the first time with my father. I knew every waystation master by name, knew which bends held water in which season, knew the sound the road made at night in different weathers.

I thought about my wife. The particular smell of the courtyard when I came through the gate after a long run, the way she always had something warm ready without making a point of it. I had never told her I noticed.

I thought about Liu, who would be home by now. Who would learn, eventually, that the brown rocks meant the false flat was still going.

The stars came out. The same stars whether you were three days from home or thirty. My father had shown me these stars on this road and he had looked at them every clear night since and they had not changed.

The fever came before dawn and moved through me differently than the fevers that had passed. Those had been argument, the body pressing back, negotiating, finding its way through. This one did not negotiate.

I felt it arrive in the way I felt a mountain pass arrive, a change in the quality of the air, a different kind of cold, a sense of elevation that could not be reduced to anything simpler than itself.

I hobbled the horses. The fire had burned down. The flat ground between the two hills held the darkness the way flat ground holds darkness, without obstruction, completely.

I felt my heart working harder to do less. The fever makes the heart work harder and delivers less oxygen. I knew this. I have watched it happen. From the inside the knowledge does not help.

I thought about my wife. The courtyard smell when I came through the gate. I had never told her I noticed it. This was an important thing to not have said.

I thought about Liu. The brown rocks. Whether he would remember.

The stars my father showed me on this road were above me. They were not moving. I watched them for the time available.

I left the body lying beside the fire on the flat ground between the two hills. I was above it. Looking down at a merchant three days from home with the horses hobbled and the fire burned low, who had been on this road for nineteen years and would not complete the return run.

The horses were still.

I thought about my wife. The courtyard smell. I had never told her I noticed it. I thought about this, not with regret, just the specific inventory of a thing not said that could no longer be said. The stars were the same stars my father had shown me on this road. I watched them until the watching stopped being something he did and became something that was happening without him, and then it was not happening either.

* * *

The ground between the two hills is alkaline and dry. It receives me with the patience of desert ground, without urgency, without preference, working at the pace the heat and the dryness determine.

The horses leave after two days. I feel them go, the pressure of their hooves on the ground, moving away, the rhythm of horses that have been patient for as long as patience allowed and are now following the need that hunger creates.

The alkaline soil works at the surfaces first. My hands, the hands that held the traces, worked the routes, checked the brown rocks for their color for nineteen years. I feel the skin tightening over the bones, the alkaline drawing the moisture out, the tissues pulling back from the joints.

The heat cycles. Hot days dry what the cold nights have softened. The cycling cracks things that would hold in less extreme ground. I feel each crack. The bones separating at the joints, the connective tissue giving up its hold. This is the process. I am in the process.

By the first winter my bones have begun to separate. The cold that drove the caravans off the road works on the connective tissue that holds thin bones together. I feel each separation as a distinct event.

Liu comes in the spring. I feel his footsteps. The specific weight of a seventeen-year-old boy who has learned to walk the road carefully. He walks the flat ground between the hills. I feel every step.

He stands for a long time. I feel him standing. Then he turns and goes back the way he came. He knows what the brown rocks mean. The brown rocks told him.

By summer I am in the road itself. Worked into the dust by the wind and the traffic. Pressed into the surface by the feet of traders going east and west. I am in the road I traveled for nineteen years.

I think about my wife. The courtyard smell. I still have not told her. I will not tell her. This is the shape of the thing I did not say.

* * *

Grim came when the road had finished and stood on the flat ground between the two low hills and opened his scroll. A decent man. A working man. No great sins, no great acts, the long ordinary accumulation of a life spent doing honest work in the world.

He found Bao's consciousness settled and quiet, a man who had been waiting without impatience.

"You came a long way on this road," Grim said.

"Nineteen years. Twenty if you count the first time with my father."

"Your son came looking for you."

A pause. "I know. I felt him on the road."

"He found the cart."

"Yes."

Grim made his notes. He produced the wheel. It stopped where he expected. He recorded the result.

"Your wife," Grim said. "She had something warm ready."

Bao was quiet for a moment. "She always did. I never told her I noticed."

"No," Grim said.

"I should have told her."

"Yes," Grim said. Not unkindly. Just true.

He watched where Bao went. A direction. Nothing at the end of it that he could see or name.

He was still watching when he heard footsteps behind him on the road. He turned. Another figure stood twenty paces off, robes the same lightless dark as his own, a scroll under one arm. Tall. Older, in the way that Grims were old, which had nothing to do with appearance and everything to do with the quality of stillness they carried.

"Maren."

"You are in my territory," he said, but pleasantly. Not a complaint. An observation.

"The soul originated west of here. I followed the road."

"Close enough." Maren came and stood beside him and looked at the flat ground between the hills. "Merchant?"

"Nineteen years on this road. Fever."

"I had three of those last month. The fever is moving east." Maren glanced at Grim's scroll. "Clean assessment?"

"Clean enough."

They stood without needing to fill the silence.

"I have been watching where they go." Casually, already decided. "After the handoff. Have you ever watched?"

Grim looked at him.

"It is probably nothing. I am probably just not looking in the right direction."

"Probably."

Maren nodded and turned back toward the east. "Safe travels," which was the thing Grims said to each other, the old joke between them that never got old because it was never entirely a joke.

Grim watched him go.

He stood on the road a moment longer and watched Maren go. Something different in the way Maren moved. Had been there before, maybe, but was now visible. He did not know what he was looking at.

He counted the cart tracks. Eleven. He did not know why.

The cart tracks were still visible in the dust.

The Conquistador

I saw a child once, I will say this much, a child who was perhaps four years old, standing in the street of a city that was not yet burning but would be burning by the end of the day. The child looked at me with a look I recognized because I had seen it on the faces of dogs that had been beaten, not fear of the beating that was happening but fear of the next beating, the permanent crouching anticipation of something that was always coming.

I was the thing that was always coming. I was the reason for that look. I knew this and I did not stop what I did because stopping was not a choice that was available to me, or so I told myself, and I told myself that for the next fifteen years.

My name was Diego. I was a carpenter's son from Extremadura. I came to this country at nineteen and believed everything I had been told.

I did well, by the terms that counted. They gave me land. People to work it — which is a way of saying they gave me people.

I had a house and a wife, a Spanish wife brought over in the third year, and children, four of them, and I went to mass and I did not talk about what I had done and neither did anyone else because we had all done it and the not-talking was a shared agreement that held as long as no one broke it.

I broke it once. Late in my life, with a priest who was not the usual kind of priest, a young one who had come over on one of the later ships and had not been here for the beginning and asked questions the older priests had stopped asking. I told him some of it. Not all. Some.

He absolved me. That is what priests do. I did not feel absolved. I felt like a man who had been told his debt was cancelled by someone who did not hold the debt.

I was sixty-one years old when I died, which was old for this country, old for any country at that time. My heart stopped one afternoon while I was sitting in the shade of my house looking at the land I had been given, the land that had belonged to people I had helped remove from it.

I had sat in that shade many afternoons. I had looked at that land many times. I do not know what I thought about on those afternoons. I think I tried not to think.

The last afternoon I did not try. I let myself think about the child in the street of the city that was not yet burning. I let myself think about the child's face. I let it be there without looking away from it.

The last afternoon I did not try to keep the mechanism running. I let myself think about the child in the street of the city that had not yet been burning. What the child's face had looked like. I had been not thinking about it for a long time.

I thought about Diego the carpenter's son from Extremadura. Nineteen years old, going somewhere, believing everything he had been told. He had been real. That had been real. I thought about what I had done to the real thing.

The fever had been working for three days. I felt it reach the place fevers reach when they are finishing. Not the worst of it. I had felt the worst of it, the heat and the confusion, but the quieter place that comes after the worst, when the body is doing what it is going to do and the arguing is over.

I was aware of the jungle sounds outside. I was aware of the light through the wall. I was aware of a thought I had been not-thinking for twenty years arriving with the quiet of something that had been patient.

The child's face. What I had done. The knowledge arriving now with its full weight, which is what it has always weighed, which I have been managing and not feeling for twenty years, which the fever has removed what manages it.

The fever has taken the mechanism I built to not feel this. The mechanism is gone. The feeling has been waiting behind it for twenty years.

My heart is working hard in the heat. The jungle outside, the sounds of it, still arriving as separate things after twenty years. The light through the wall. The smell of the place I am lying in.

I feel my heart change its rhythm. The fever and the knowledge together doing what either one alone might not do.

I am outside the body before it stops. Looking down at the man in the room, the fever on his face, the knowledge on his face, the two things that came for him at the same time.

My heart stopped. The knowledge was still there when it stopped.

I took it with me.

My heart stopped. The knowledge was still there when it stopped. I took it with me.

* * *

The jungle does not wait. This is the first thing. The heat and the wet together, the combination of tropical ground in the wet season, do not allow waiting. The process begins immediately, before the body has finished its final cooling.

I feel the heat of the ground, not the ambient heat but the heat of biological activity, the vast metabolism of the jungle floor doing its work on everything that comes to it. The ground is warm and alive and it begins immediately.

The fungi come first. Hair-thin threads extending through the leaf litter, finding the surfaces, beginning the work of chemical dissolution that precedes everything else. I feel each thread. Each one extending into what I was.

Then the insects. The jungle floor has more insects per square foot than any other ground in the world, and they are organized in their way, each species knowing its place in the sequence. I feel each one. Where it works. What it finds.

The soft tissue goes in weeks. Not months, weeks. The jungle is efficient in a way that the cold grounds are not. What would take a year in colder soil takes less than two months here.

My bones remain longer. The jungle wants them too but bones require more patience. I feel the fungi working at the surfaces of the bones, the slow dissolution of calcium, the steady patient claiming of what is solid.

The people who work this land after I am gone know what is under it. They pass this knowledge down in the way that knowledge which cannot be written is passed down, in the body, in the work, in the telling. I feel them walking above me. Their footsteps are different from the Spanish footsteps. They know the ground differently.

I think about the child's face. I have thought about nothing else for twenty years. From inside the ground of the country I helped take from the child's people I think about the face. I find no resolution. The ground finds none either. The ground takes everyone the same way.

* * *

Grim came when the last of the bones had gone back to the earth and stood on the land in the morning light and opened the scroll.

He read it. He read it again. He stood with it for longer than he usually stood.

The scroll was long. He worked through it without rushing and without looking away.

He found Diego waiting. He had made his peace with the waiting. That was different from having made his peace with what he waited for.

"I know what you have," Diego said before Grim spoke. "I have known for forty years. I have been sitting with it for forty years. You do not need to show me."

"I show everyone."

"I know. Show me then."

He showed him. Diego watched without flinching, which was not the same as watching without feeling. When it was done he was quiet for a long time.

"The child. In the street."

"Yes."

"I have thought about that child every day for forty years."

"I know."

"Does that matter? The thinking about it?"

Grim looked at the scroll. He thought about Amenhotep in the tomb for three thousand years and what the darkness had and had not done to him. He thought about the difference between a man who arrived at an accounting and a man who had been running from one.

"It matters that you did not look away at the end."

"I looked away for forty years."

"And then you did not."

Diego absorbed this. It did not comfort him.

Grim produced the wheel. It turned for a long time before it stopped. The result was not clean. It was not the worst he had seen.

It was the result of a man who had done genuine evil in the service of a story he had believed, and had then spent the rest of his life knowing the story was wrong and not knowing what to do with that knowledge, and had at the very end looked at what he had done without the story in the way.

It was something. It was not enough. It was what there was.

He looked at the scroll. He looked at Diego.

"You go back. Without the ships. Without the priests telling you God is watching and approving. Without anyone putting a sword in your hand and telling you it is necessary."

"Will I be better? The next time."

Grim thought about the soul he had been carrying since Jerusalem, the one that had asked hard questions at Golgotha and gambled away bread money and pushed a friend near a well. The soul that kept coming back unremarkably, without great evil and without great understanding, trying again.

"I do not know."

He sent Diego on and watched where the sending went. The direction. The nothing at the end of it.

The Viking Shore

Twelve children sick in two weeks and the medicine I had was for three, maybe four. Ragna sat in the corner with her hands in her lap and did not offer an opinion. Ragna had buried two husbands and four children of her own and had been in this room more times than I had and knew that opinions did not help.

I set out what I had on the table. Not enough. I already knew it wasn't enough. I counted it anyway because counting was the thing you could do and I had learned, in eight years of doing this, to do the thing you could do and not think about the rest until the rest arrived.

"The Eriksson children," Ragna said. Not an opinion. An observation.

"I know."

"The youngest is a week ahead of the others. If she turns..."

"I know," I said.

Ragna was quiet. I looked at my hands.

The Eriksson children were three. The youngest was already worse than the others. There was medicine for one of the three, maybe. I looked at the table and made the calculation that I would carry for the next forty years, and I made it without flinching because flinching did not help either.

"You know what you're going to do," Ragna said.

"Yes."

"Then do it."

I did it. Two of the Eriksson children survived. The youngest did not.

Nine others in the camp survived because of what was on that table, and the youngest Eriksson would not have survived regardless. I had understood this by the second morning and had confirmed it by the third, and none of that made any difference to the weight of it, which I would carry without complaint because complaining served nothing and the people around my needed to believe I held.

So I held.

My name was Astrid. I had been running this settlement since the morning my husband Leif sailed south and west with forty-two other men toward the monasteries the traders described, and not one of them came back. I had known what that meant. You do not need the details when you know the shape.

That first winter I had made the wrong decision about the grain and it cost them half of what they had and I had spent three nights running the arithmetic with the numbers that did not work and then I went to Ragna and asked what I knew about stretching stores and did what Ragna told me and the numbers still did not work but they worked well enough.

Three people died that winter. Old Einar from the cold, which he would have died of regardless. The widow Kari's infant. A boy of nine who went through the ice on a dare and did not come back up. That last one had nothing to do with the grain or the stores or any decision I made. It happened the way things happen. I told myself this for forty years.

We built new boats in the twelfth year. By the twenty-fifth the settlement was larger than it had been when the men sailed.

My eldest daughter. I want to say I was harder on her than the others because I was training her. That was part of it.

The other part was that she looked like Leif in the jaw and the way I set my shoulders when I had made up my mind, and some mornings I looked at her across the fire and something in me closed that should have been open. I knew I did it. I did not stop.

I ran it better than I had. This is true. I told her so.

What I did not tell her that the holding had cost more than the years showed. You give what the settlement needs and you keep the rest for the work and there comes a point where what you keep is not enough. I had reached that point ten years before I handed it over and had kept going because stopping was not available to me.

Watching her be easy in it, easy in a way I had never been, I did not know what to do with that. I was glad for her. I sat by the fire and let her carry it and that was enough for the last five years.

Seven grandchildren. The youngest had never known it any other way.

I died on a morning in early spring when the ice was breaking up on the fjord. I heard it from inside, the deep cracking and groaning carrying across the water, the sound of the world releasing winter, the sound I have been hearing every spring for seventy-one years.

My daughter held my hand. I let her. This was not always easy for me and now it was easy.

The breathing changed. I have watched breathing change in others for forty years, the quality of it shifting, each breath becoming deliberate, the body asking whether the next one is worth the effort. Now I was on the inside of the question.

I felt my heart slow. Not dramatically, slowly, the way the last ice on the fjord thins before it breaks. Beat by beat by beat with longer between each one.

My daughter's hand. I have known the weight of this hand since it was small. I feel it.

The ice broke. The sound of it coming through the walls of the house, the sound of the fjord releasing. I have heard this sound every spring. This spring I am in the sound differently. I am releasing with it, the thing that was in me going out with the tide on a morning that smelled of brine and pine smoke.

I was above the bed. Looking down at the woman who had run this settlement through nine winters, my daughter still holding the hand of the body. The hand still warm.

The ice broke and the water ran.

The ice broke and the water ran and I went with it, more or less, out with the tide on a morning that smelled of brine and pine smoke and the particular cold clarity of a world just beginning to thaw.

* * *

They bury me with the things I valued and the words said over me by the woman who knows the words. The ground of this country is cold and does not give up what it holds easily.

The first frost of the following winter reaches me, working down through the soil in fingers of cold that find the gaps. I feel each finger of frost finding me. It is not the frost I knew from above, the frost I wore against and built fires against and stuffed walls against. This frost is in me, working through the spaces between tissues, expanding in the water of the cells, cracking things open that have held since I was buried.

Spring returns and some of what the frost has cracked moves with the meltwater, pieces of me carrying downhill toward the fjord. I feel this. I am in more than one place.

The roots of the pines find me. The grass finds me. Each root is an intrusion I feel distinctly, thin and purposeful, pressing into what I was, taking what the root needs. I feel what it takes. I feel where it goes.

Decades.

My daughter dies and is buried near me. I feel her arrive in the ground, not her presence exactly, not her voice, but the fact of her, the density of a person I have known for forty-seven years settling into the same earth. I want to tell her something. I cannot tell her anything. We are in the same ground and I cannot tell her.

The settlement continues above us. I feel the footsteps of people going about the work of staying alive, generation after generation. Sometimes a foot stops over where I am. Sometimes it does not.

Eventually even the knowing of my daughter fades. The ground has finished with her too, taken her into the roots and the water. We are both in the fjord. We are both in the pines. We are in the same things.

* * *

Grim came to the settlement in the grey light before dawn and stood on the shore and the tide stopped.

Not slowed. Not paused between waves. The water that had been moving toward the shore simply held where it was, a low wall of grey-green sea hanging in place, the white at its edge frozen mid-curl, and the fjord behind it flat and still as iron.

A gull that had been working the tideline hung in the air six feet above the water, wings spread, going nowhere. The settlement above the shore was silent. No wind. The smoke from the long house fire stood straight up into the still air and did not move.

Grim opened the scroll.

What he found in the ground was long and complicated. Not the clean result he had found in Miriam, not the single terrible ledger he had found in Diego. Something harder to hold, a consciousness that

141

had made the right decisions and the wrong ones and the necessary ones that were both at once, and had known the difference and had made them anyway, and had paid for them in the currency of a person who keeps paying long after the debt should be settled.

The scroll noted the youngest Eriksson child. The widow Kari's infant. Twelve children in the ninth year and what she had decided about the sick and the well. The favoritism toward the eldest that she had known was happening and had not stopped.

The hardness she had put on like a coat and never fully taken off. The five years at the end when she had finally let the rope out and how much easier it had been than she expected, which was its own kind of grief.

It also noted forty years. Forty years of getting up.

He found her waiting with the quality of the shore itself, not peaceful, not at rest, but done. The stillness of someone who has finished a long piece of work and is not yet sure what they feel about it.

"Your daughter. She ran it well after you."

"She was easier in it than I was. I do not know if that is because I made it easier for her or because she is easier than me."

"Does it matter?"

She thought about this. "No. I suppose not."

He ran the assessment. The wheel turned. He watched it work through what it had been given, which took longer than most. When it stopped he looked at where it had stopped and made his note. Not clean. Not uncomplicated. Solid, in the way that a thing is solid that has been tested from many directions and has not broken under any of them.

He sent her on and watched where the sending went. The same direction. The same nothing at the end of it that he could see or name.

Then he reached for Maren's collection schedule, the habit of a long association, the casual checking-in of two colleagues who shared borders and occasionally shared work.

The machinery had reassigned Maren's territory.

Not to Grim. To someone else, a designation he did not recognize, which happened sometimes when territories were reorganized. No note. No forwarding. Nothing that said Maren had been consulted or had any warning.

Maren always said goodbye. In all their long association, across centuries of shared borders and occasional shared work, Maren always said something first before moving on.

Grim stood on the shore and looked at the water.

The Grass

I had been sitting with her for three days.

Not every death took three days. Some took an afternoon. Some took a week. The old woman, Walks-Before-Dawn, had been at the edge for three days and had not gone yet, and I sat beside her the way he always sat, close enough that she could feel the warmth of me, not so close that I was in the way of whatever she worked through.

Her daughter was on the other side. A young woman, still learning this, still looking at me sometimes as if I could tell her what to do. I never told them what to do. You could not tell someone how to be present at the thing that had no instructions.

On the third afternoon Walks-Before-Dawn opened her eyes.

She looked at me directly. Not through me, the way the dying often looked, but at me.

"Is it good?" she said. Her voice was almost gone. "Where it goes. Is it good?"

The daughter reached for her mother's hand. I let her.

I thought about what I knew and what I believed and where those two things were not the same thing.

"Yes," I said. "It is good."

She accepted this. She did not ask how I knew, which was the thing I had feared she would ask. She closed her eyes.

An hour later she was gone.

I stayed until the daughter had what she needed and then I walked back to my family's fire and sat and looked at the sky, which was the blue of late autumn, the blue that has no warmth in it but is very clear.

My name meant something like the one who reads what the sky is saying, which was also what I did, though not only that. I read weather and animals and the patterns of game and the mood of the grass when the wind moved it.

I had been reading these things since I was seven and had mostly been right and once been wrong in a way that cost people food for a week. I carried that the way you carry a scar, you do not get to put it down.

I sat with the dying because the dying asked for me. I did not refuse. I never found a word for what made me stay.

I had two wives and seven children and one of the children had died young. I had sat with other parents when their children died. When my own child died I understood for the first time that sitting with the grief of another is a different thing from sitting with your own grief. I had known this was true. I had not known what it felt like.

The raid came at dawn from people who needed the territory my people were using. They needed it. My people were using it. This is how it has always gone and how it will always go. I understood this in the moment it was happening.

The raid came from the direction I had not been watching. I had been watching the sky. The autumn sky, the specific blue I named for myself as a boy and never found a word for. I turned at the sound.

The arrow was already past the point where turning would change what it did.

It went through my side. Not a spear, an arrow. The force of it was a surprise. You watch arrows land in animals and you understand the force theoretically. The theory is not the thing.

I was down on one knee. The body made this decision. The body understood the arrow before I did.

I put my hand to it. Reflex. The hand came away dark, darker than blood from the skin, darker than I expected. The liver, probably. I know wounds. I have sat with enough people through enough wounds to know what the color means.

I went down to both knees. Then to my hands. The grass was at the level of my face. The autumn grass. The grass I have been reading for thirty-five years for what it tells about weather and animals and the movement of people.

A boot caught me in the side. The raider coming back through, checking whether I was still capable of trouble. I was not.

I was on my face in the grass. The blood moved through the stems, the grass absorbed it the way grass absorbs everything, without preference, without record.

The autumn blue was still above me, visible through the grass at the angle I was at. The color I named for myself as a boy.

I left the body. Not all at once, the way dawn arrives, in stages. I was in the body and the grass was in my face, and then I was just above it, and the autumn sky was both above and below.

The blue did not change.

* * *

The great grass receives me on a morning that smells of cold and old grass and blood. The ground is still warm from the last of the summer. The grass roots close over what the grass floor has received.

The frost comes in the first weeks and finds me. I have known frost my whole life, read it in the grass, predicted it from the quality of the evening light. I have not known what frost feels like from inside the ground. It is not cold the way air is cold, it is cold the way something that has been cold for a very long time is cold, without urgency, without temperature as a concept separate from the thing itself.

It works into the joints first. I feel each one, the specific expansion of water becoming ice in spaces that water occupied as water. The cracking. Each crack distinct. The body I lived in for thirty-five years separating at the joints with the patience of a very slow chisel.

147

Spring comes. The thaw working from the surface down, approaching from above. I feel it approaching, the gradual softening of the ground above me, a warmth that has never reached this deep before. When it arrives it is not gentle. It arrives and the things it has been holding release quickly.

They find me. I know this came. I have explained this to children, the ground gives what it receives back to the grass and the grass gives it to the animals and the animals give it back to the ground. I have said this. I am in the saying now.

The roots. Each one a distinct intrusion. I feel where each root goes after it leaves what I was, up into the stem of a grass plant, into the leaf, into the seed. I am in the seed.

The buffalo come in their season. I feel them moving above me, the weight of a herd, the pressure of ten thousand hooves, the rhythm of a movement that has been crossing this grass since before my people were here. I am in the grass they eat. I am in the buffalo.

Walks-Before-Dawn is in the same ground. I feel the general fact of her the way you feel a known presence in a dark room. We are in the same grass. The grass does not distinguish.

The sky above is the blue I read my whole life. I cannot see it anymore. It is still there.

* * *

Something arrived when the last of it had gone into the grass.

It was not the thing his people expected. He had sat with enough dying people to have heard them describe what they saw at the edge and the descriptions were consistent and he had taken that as evidence. He expected the consistent thing.

What arrived was a figure that belonged to no category he had, carrying something rolled and held in a way that suggested it was important, radiating a cold that had nothing to do with the weather, paying attention to him specifically in the way of something reading a situation before deciding what it means.

He sat with it the way he sat with dying people. Present. Not demanding it be something other than what it was.

Grim opened the scroll. He read what it said. He found the hunter waiting with the quality of someone who has arrived at a situation without a category for it and has decided that sitting with it is the correct response.

The scroll offered no translation for the name. It produced instead: the one who reads what the sky is saying.

He ran the assessment. The wheel turned and stopped where it stopped, solidly, without difficulty. The wrong direction and three days without food. Seven children and one dead. The old woman at the edge of the thing and the question she had asked him.

Grim looked at where the sending had gone. "What you told her. That it was good."

The hunter was quiet for a moment. "I don't know if it's true."

"I know."

"I told her what she needed."

The hunter was quiet for a moment. He paused in the way of a man deciding whether to say the thing he was actually thinking about. "I sat with people my whole life," he said finally. "When they were going. Nobody asked me to. I just, ended up there."

"Was it true? What you told her."

The hunter looked at him. "You ask that a lot?"

"No," Grim said. He didn't, usually. He didn't know why he had.

Grim looked at where the sending went, which was a direction he had always seen and had not, until recently, thought to look past. He did not answer immediately.

"I don't know. That is also not a lie."

He sent the hunter on and watched longer than usual. The grass moved in a wind that existed for it and not for Grim. The sky above was the blue of late autumn.

The hunter had spent a life sitting with people at the edge of the thing they did not understand, present for the gap between what they expected and what actually came. Had made a skill of inhabiting the not-knowing on behalf of others. And then, at the end, had applied the same practice to his own ending.

Grim had been making the handoff for longer than he could count. He had always assumed someone was receiving. He had not looked.

The Plague Cart

My name was Thomas and I drove the cart.

This is what I did. I got up before light and I hitched the horse and I drove the cart through the streets and I stopped where I was told to stop and I loaded what was there to be loaded and I drove it to the pit outside the town walls and I unloaded it and I drove back and I did it again.

Some days six. Some days twenty. The worst day thirty-one and I know the exact number because I counted, the way you count things when the counting is the only thing between you and the size of what you are doing.

I had done other work before this. I had worked my father's land and then the land of the man who bought my father's land and then I had come to the town when nothing remained on the land and I had done the work that was available which was this work, the cart, because most men would not do it and I needed to eat.

I knew what the sickness was. I knew it before the physicians knew it, or before they would say it, which is a different thing.

I knew it because I saw what it did and I saw how it moved, house to house, street to street. The ones who touched the sick got sick. The ones who did not sometimes did not. I drew the conclusion that a man with more learning would have drawn and I acted on it.

I wrapped my face. I did not touch the bodies with my bare hands. I washed after every run with the strongest vinegar I could find.

I did not get sick.

I do not say this with pride. I say it because it is true and because it is also the thing that broke me at the end, not the bodies, not the smell, not the sounds from the houses when I came to collect. What broke me was that I did not get sick.

Every person I loaded into that cart had touched someone they loved or eaten food someone else had prepared or simply breathed the air of a room where someone sick was breathing, and they were dead, and I was not, and I could see no reason why that should be the case. No reason that had anything to do with who they were or who I was.

I drove the cart for eleven months. The sickness slowed in the spring. By summer the worst was past, which did not mean it was over, which did not mean the people were back who were gone. Half the town was gone. You could walk streets at midday and hear nothing. You could go a week without seeing a face you knew.

I drove the cart until not enough work remained for a cart anymore, which happened in the autumn of the second year, and then I found other work, and I did not talk about what I had done, and most people did not ask.

The cough started that winter. Not the plague cough, something else, something that settled in my chest and did not leave. The physicians said it was nothing and then they said it was something and then they said nothing could be done about it, and by the third winter I knew they were right because I felt what it did and I recognized the shape of it from the cart.

I was thirty-four years old.

The room above the tanner's smelled of hides and the damp of a building that has absorbed thirty years of the work below it. I had lived in this smell for two years and had stopped noticing it and now I noticed it again, which was the first sign that the night was a different kind of night.

The cough had changed. I had been tracking what it did the way I had tracked what the sickness did on the cart, noting, logging, the professional habit of a man who learned to pay attention to the details that precede the event. The cough had changed in a way the physicians had told me to expect and that I had not believed I would experience. I believed it now.

I was alone. This was not different from any other night. I had been alone in this room since coming to the town and the alone of it had become ordinary, a condition rather than a feeling.

What I noticed, in the changed cough and the changed dark, was not the loneliness. I had managed that, but the absence of anyone who knew my name before the cart. No one in the town who had known me as anything other than the cart man. I thought about this. I thought about whether it mattered. I decided it did not matter.

The breathing changed next. I have watched breathing change in three hundred and forty-one people. I know every stage of it. I am in the stage I watched most.

I noted this with the professional attention I gave everything.

The room above the tanner's smelled of hides and damp and thirty years of the work below. I have lived in this smell for two years. It is the last smell.

I was alone. This was not different from any other night.

The breath came. Then the next one took longer. Then the next one longer still. I counted the intervals the way I counted everything, noting, logging.

I felt my heart slow inside the slowing breath.

I was above the room. Looking down at the cart driver on the bed, alone, the man who knew what was in the lime pits.

The noting stopped.

* * *

They put me in the same pit I filled. I feel the recognition of it, the uneven sides where the tired men dug the second half narrower than the first. I know this pit. I stood at the edge of it every morning for eleven months.

I am the three hundred and forty-second.

The lime comes before the soil. I have poured it myself many times. From below it is something I have no word for, not the neutralizing agent I understood it to be from above, but a presence, a chemical heat that is not pain but is adjacent to pain, working at the surfaces of what I am with the patient efficiency of a substance that does not know what it is touching.

I feel it finding the gaps. Working into the spaces between. The lime is thorough in a way that the cold grounds are not. It is designed to be thorough.

Then the soil. And then I become aware of the others.

Not voices. Not presence with qualities I have words for. But three hundred and forty-one people in the ground around me, in various states of what the lime is doing to all of us. I feel the distribution of them.

I know some of them. The widow from the street behind the tanner's, a large woman, difficult to lift. I know the weight of her. I know the lightness of the carpenter's son, who was twelve and weighed almost nothing. I carried each one. Now we are in the same ground.

I feel the widow nearby. I feel the carpenter's son further away, they put him in a different layer. I feel the priest who said words over us. I feel the words did not change what we are.

The lime works through us. The months pass. The ground above settles as we give up what we hold. I feel the settling, the weight of the soil adjusting to the new density below.

We are in the same ground. We were strangers. We are in the same ground now, the three hundred and forty-two, the lime working through all of us without distinction.

*　*　*

Grim was not alone when he came.

This was not unusual in itself. Mass death required multiple Grims and the plague had produced mass death on a scale that made even Grim's long experience feel inadequate. What was unusual was the chaos of it, the way the souls were stacked and overlapping, some recent, some months old, some so intermingled with others in the pit that the scroll had difficulty separating them. He had requested help. The help had come.

Maren worked the far end of the pit. Two others Grim knew less well were working the middle sections. The sound of multiple scrolls opening and closing, the murmur of assessments running at once, creating a quality in the air that Grim had felt before but rarely, the machinery under strain.

He found Thomas near the surface, one of the later arrivals, and opened his scroll.

Clean. Cleaner than most. A man who had done difficult work with more intelligence and care than the work required and had asked nothing for it. The wheel would not take long.

He was halfway through the assessment when Maren appeared at his shoulder.

"Can I ask you something." Not quietly this time. The tone of a man who had been sitting with something for a while.

"What kind," not stopping.

"Where do they go?"

Grim's hand paused over the scroll. "What?"

"When we send them on. Where do they go. I have been trying to remember if anyone ever told me and I cannot remember if anyone ever told me."

Grim looked at him. Maren watched the pit, not Grim, his face the careful neutral of a man who had already decided he was going to say the thing and was saying it.

"On. They go on."

"On where?"

Grim did not answer immediately. He started to, once, three souls later, formed something that was almost the beginning of a sentence, and stopped. He didn't know what he had been about to say. He finished the section. The question sat between them, taking up more room than it should.

"That was what I assumed. That the assessment determined it. That the wheel result sent them to the appropriate destination."

"You assumed."

"Yes."

"So did I." "But I tried to follow one. After the handoff. Last month, a woman outside Lyon, clean assessment, good result. I sent her on and I watched where the sending went."

Grim waited.

"I could not tell. It goes somewhere. But I could not see where. I could not tell if it was different from where a worse assessment would have sent her. I could not tell if the wheel result changed anything at all about the destination."

On the other side of the pit one of the other Grims called out for help with a soul that was resisting assessment, tangled up with two others in a way that required careful separation. Maren looked over at the sound but did not move immediately.

"We have been doing this a very long time. And neither of us knows where they go."

Grim had no answer to this. He had not asked the question. He was not sure when the not-asking had stopped being ignorance and started being choice.

Maren went to help with the tangled souls.

Grim turned back to his work. The scroll kept writing. The pit kept giving up its dead. He assessed, noted, sent on. He watched where the sending went and saw what Maren had seen, which was nothing. A direction without a destination. A handoff with no one visibly receiving.

He had always assumed someone was receiving. Above the pit the air had gone wrong in a way that had nothing to do with smell or temperature. A pressure to it, a weight. Birds that should have been circling had moved off to a treeline two hundred yards away and stayed there, facing in.

"You counted," Grim said. "Every one."

"Thirty-one on the worst day," Thomas said. "I know the exact number."

"Why did you count?"

Thomas thought about this. "Because someone should know the number. Because they were people and someone should know how many there were."

Grim looked at him for a moment. Then he produced the wheel and set it turning.

At the end of the day, when the pit was done and the other Grims had moved on, Grim and Maren stood together at the edge of it. Maren had a flask. He offered it without speaking.

They stood at the edge of the pit in the last light. Below them, three hundred and forty-two people were in the process of becoming part of the ground of this town.

Maren put the flask away. He crouched at the edge of the pit and picked up a small piece of lime from the soil there. He turned it over once, looking at it, then set it back at the edge. He stood. He looked at the town, at the smoke from the tanner's chimney, at the lit window of the house on the corner.

"I do not know where they go," Grim said.

Maren looked at where he had set the piece of lime. He did not pick it up again.

Somewhere in the town a dog was barking at something it could smell but not see.

“Same time next century?” Maren said.

“Same time,” Grim said.

The Hold

I will not dress it up. I ran slaves. Fourteen voyages from Liverpool to the coast of West Africa and across the Atlantic and home, between 1697 and 1731, and the sum of those voyages is six thousand and twelve people. I know the exact number because I kept exact records, the way any merchant keeps records, because the records are the money and the money is the point.

My name was Edmund Holt. I was born in Liverpool in 1668, the son of a ship's chandler, and I went to sea at sixteen and worked my way up through the trades and found slaving when I was twenty-three and found that it paid better than anything else I had tried and that the men who financed it were the men who ran the city and the men who ran the city were the men I wanted to be, and so I became one of them.

I did not think about it the way people who were not doing it thought about it. The ones in the hold were cargo. This sounds like I am making an excuse.

I am not making an excuse, I am telling you the mechanism. I do not fully understand the mechanism myself. You keep the records. You maintain the ratios. The ratios are numbers and numbers are not people. That is what I told myself. I am not certain I was telling myself. I am not certain who I was telling.

The losses were significant. On my best crossing I lost eleven percent. On my worst I lost thirty-one percent, a fever that moved through the hold in the second week and could not be stopped. I went over the side of the ship on the worst night of that crossing and did not look into the water where we had put them. I did this deliberately. I knew the mechanism.

I had a wife and four children in Liverpool. I was at home perhaps a third of each year. My wife was a capable woman who managed the household well and asked me nothing about the voyages. My children grew up in a house full of the money the voyages produced and did not ask about it.

I retired in 1731 when I had enough money that I could stop and still live as I had been living. I lived another twenty-two years in a large house in Liverpool with a view of the harbor. I watched the ships. I watched them for twenty-two years.

The gout in January of 1753 moved somewhere new. Not my feet, where it had argued for a decade, but deeper, a systemic fact, the body indicating that the negotiation I had been winning for eighty-five years was near its end.

The physician came. The priest came. They sat on either side of the bed and the harbor was visible through the window and I watched the ships. I had watched them for twenty-two years. I watched them now.

The mechanism held. This is what I want to say about my death: the mechanism I built to keep the cargo and the ledger correct, it kept running. I can feel it running now, from the bed, the machinery of a system maintained for forty-one years still maintaining itself in the rooms of my mind where I keep it.

The harbor was in the window. The physician on one side. The priest on the other. I watched the ships.

The gout had moved from my feet to something systemic, the body indicating in the efficient way bodies indicate that the negotiation I had been winning for eighty-five years was over.

My breathing slowed. The harbor continued outside. A ship I did not recognize moved into the dock, new ownership, probably, or a new master. Twenty-two years of watching this harbor and I knew every regular vessel. This one I did not know.

The mechanism ran. The number sat in it, six thousand and twelve, at its full weight, with nowhere to go.

I felt my heart complete its argument with itself. The harbor continued. The unfamiliar ship reached the dock.

I was above the bed. Looking down at the merchant-slaveholder in his last bed, the harbor in the window, the number in him that had no place to go.

I did not look away from the harbor. The mechanism ran to its conclusion with the number sitting in it at its full weight and nowhere to go. This is what I took with me.

* * *

The clay of the sailors' church cemetery in Liverpool presses in from all sides the way the hold pressed in, from every direction, complete. I had not expected the comparison. I had not thought about the clay having that quality. It does.

I feel the weight of it. Cold November clay, wet, holding its shape around the shape I occupied. The clay is patient. It has been receiving the sailors and the merchants and the slaveholders and the sailors' wives since before Liverpool had a dock, and it knows what to do.

My hands go first. The hands that wrote the ledger. I feel the cold working into the joints, the clay pressing the flesh back toward the bone, the water in the cells doing what water does when it has nowhere to go but further into the clay.

I hear the harbor. Not with ears, the ears are gone, but feel it. The vibration of ships moving in and out. The rhythm of the dock work. The loading and the unloading. I know this rhythm. I listened to it for twenty-two years from the window. From inside the clay I feel it in a different register.

The stone above me is well-cut. I feel the inscription on it through the ground, not read it, feel the depth of the chisel marks. The letters of my name and dates and the passage from scripture that the priest suggested and I accepted without thinking about it.

Others are in the ground around me. Sailors who did sea work of different kinds. Some of them were in ships I know. I feel them in the ground, the general fact of other people in clay, at various distances.

The six thousand and twelve are not here. They are in other grounds, in the places the ships took them. I am in the clay of Liverpool. The six thousand and twelve are in the grounds of other continents. The ground does not connect us. The clay does not connect us. The number connects us.

The number sits in me for as long as I sit in the clay. The clay works through everything eventually. The number is the last thing the clay reaches.

* * *

Grim came when the clay had finished and stood in the churchyard in the grey November light and opened the scroll.

The scroll wrote. It did not stop writing. Grim waited while it wrote, standing in the cold churchyard while the scroll produced its accounting, which took longer than most, because the ledger was extensive and the scroll was thorough.

Six thousand and twelve. Each one recorded, because the records were the money. The scroll had them all. It also had the mechanism, the deliberate construction of a way of seeing that had allowed a man to do what he had done without knowing he did it in the fullest sense of knowing. The scroll noted this not as mitigation. As information.

He found Edmund Holt waiting.

The mechanism had not survived the assessment. Whatever had kept the cargo was not available to him now. He sat with what the scroll contained in a way he had not sat with anything in his life, and the sitting was not comfortable, and he did not try to make it comfortable.

Grim produced the wheel. It turned for a very long time. When it stopped, Grim looked at where it had landed and made his note, which was clear and unambiguous and which he made without hesitation.

"You go back."

The word came out small. "I know."

He sent him on. The grey light continued. The harbor below the churchyard did its ordinary business. Ships moved in and out of it the way they always had and would.

The wind from the harbor brought the smell of it up the hill, tar and salt and something underneath, a sourness that was not the sea.

Grim closed the scroll.

The Gardener

I brought back the huia.

This is the thing I want to say first because it is the thing that matters most and because there is satisfaction in saying it plainly without qualification. The huia had been extinct since 1907.

Three hundred and eighty years of gone, three hundred and eighty years of existing only in museum drawers and old photographs and the descriptions of people who had seen them and written down what they saw, and then they were not gone anymore, because we brought them back, and the first time I heard one call in the bush above the Whanganui I sat down on the ground and stayed there for a long time.

My name was Ezra. I was born in Wellington in 2231 and I died in the field station near Rotorua in 2287. I was fifty-six years old.

I was a conservation geneticist, which in 2287 meant something different from what it had meant in the previous two centuries, which were the centuries of loss, the long terrible inventory of what the world had given up. My century was different. My century was the one that had decided, with the determination of people who have watched something precious destroyed and have finally reached the limit of watching, that the direction could be changed.

Not everywhere. Not all of it. But some of it. Enough of it to matter.

I worked on birds. Specifically the birds of the Pacific that had been lost to introduced predators and habitat destruction and the long cascade of consequences that followed from both. The huia was the most famous, the most symbolically significant, the one that people who knew nothing else about extinct New Zealand birds knew the name of.

But others too, the piopio, the laughing owl, the native thrush, and I worked on all of them across thirty years of work that required patience with very slow progress and very occasional moments of something that was not quite triumph but was close to it.

The huia call was one of those moments. There were others. The morning we confirmed the first successful laughing owl breeding pair in the wild. The day the piopio population crossed the threshold into self-sustaining. Small moments, unspectacular to anyone who had not spent thirty years working toward them.

The stroke came on a Tuesday morning in October when I looked at the population graph. The wrongness arrived not in my vision, the graph was still there, numbers still there, but in my understanding of it. I looked at the upward trend and I knew what an upward trend was and I could not find what it meant. The knowledge of what it meant was not where I had left it.

I reached for my pen. My arm went somewhere other than where I directed it. The pen did not arrive in my hand. I was on the floor.

The floor of the field station. I knew exactly where I was. I saw the corner where we kept the field equipment, the shadow pattern in October light. I tried to get up. My body did not receive this. I tried again.

My body did not receive it the second time. I noted the failure without alarm because alarm did not seem useful.

The huia were calling in the bush above the station. Not for me, they did not know I was there, they called because huia call. The specific cascading note I had worked thirty years to hear in the wild.

I heard it from the floor. The meaning of it did not arrive differently than it ever had. Something I had worked toward for thirty years, present in the air above me while I lay unable to get up. I heard it until I did not.

* * *

The New Zealand bush knows what to do with what it receives. The restoration work of two centuries had not just returned the birds, it had returned the soil community, the fungi and the invertebrates and the organisms of a mature bush ecosystem that had been absent from most of this ground for a hundred years.

The mycelium came first. Hair-thin threads extending through the leaf litter and the upper soil layers with the patient efficiency of organisms that had been building networks in this ground for millions of years. They found me before the bacteria found me. I felt them finding me, the threads extending through what I had been, taking what mycorrhizal fungi take, incorporating it into the network. I was in the network.

The worms came after. New Zealand worms, the native species returned along with the native ground cover. They moved through what the fungi had already worked on. Each one distinct.

The huia called in the bush above me on the morning of the third day. Not for me, they had no knowledge of me. They called because huia call, the cascading note that had been absent from this hillside for three hundred and eighty years and that I had spent thirty years working toward hearing in the wild. I had heard it four years ago, sitting on the ground for a long time.

I heard it now from under the ground.

The laughing owl called in the evenings. I had heard recordings but the recordings had not prepared me for the real thing, which I had also heard in the last years of the program. Both continued above me in the restored soundscape of this hill.

My colleagues continued the work. I could feel them on the monitoring paths, their footsteps on the soil above me, distinguishable from the heavier animals by their rhythm and spacing. They moved in pairs. They were doing what I had done. The work did not stop because I had stopped.

By the second year my phosphorus had entered the root systems of the trees I had spent thirty years planting. I was in the trees. I was in the soil they were making.

The huia ate what the trees produced. I was in what the huia ate. I had worked toward this without knowing I worked toward it. That seemed correct.

* * *

Grim came in the morning, when the mist was still in the valleys and the bush was loud with things that had no knowledge of what had just been lost from it.

He stood over the place where Ezra had been returned to the hill and opened the scroll.

The light around him bent and held and then bent further and kept bending, the prismatic quality building past anything he had produced before, the air in his vicinity scattering light into colors that had no business being there, visible for thirty meters in every direction, the mist catching it and holding it so that where Grim stood was a quiet center of refracted color in the grey morning.

A huia landed on a branch eight meters away. It looked at the light with the alert curiosity of a bird that has no evolved fear of this because nothing in its evolutionary history had prepared it for it. It stayed for a long time.

He read the scroll for a long time.

Thirty years. The laughing owl. The piopio. The population graph trending upward. A man who had decided that the direction could change and had spent his life providing evidence for that decision. Not everywhere. Not all of it. But some of it.

He found Ezra waiting with the quality of someone who has just completed a very long project and is not yet sure what comes next.

"The huia."

Ezra looked at him with the attention of someone who has spent thirty years learning to notice things.

"You can hear them?"

"I can hear everything."

A pause. The huia on the branch called once, the cascading note moving through the misty air, and both of them were quiet while it did.

"The population graph. When I died. Was it,"

"Trending upward. Fragile. But upward."

Something in Ezra's face released.

Grim started the wheel and then stopped it before it had properly turned and just looked at the scroll for a moment. He didn't know what he was looking for. He started it again. The wheel turned and stopped. He made his note.

He made the note.

He sent Ezra on.

The huia on the branch called again. Then it flew, disappearing into the mist with the flight pattern of a bird that does not know it should not exist.

Grim stood in the misty morning for a long time after.

"I am sorry," Ezra said. He had not yet gone. "For whatever it is."

Grim looked at him.

He had been closing scrolls for longer than closing had a name. He had sent more souls through the door than there were words for numbers. He had watched what went through the door, Miriam and Kha and Arshama and Jean and Nell and Giulia and Astrid and Soon-yi and David and Amara and Marcus and Yenna and all the others, the millions and billions of others across the eternity of his work.

He had known what the door led to, had been inside it, had felt the vast indifferent consuming, had found the line between present and ceased and had not crossed it.

He had kept closing scrolls.

The huia called from somewhere deeper in the bush, distance making the sound smaller but not less itself.

He closed the scroll.

Then he stood with the closed scroll in his hands and did not move, and the mist moved around him, and the bush was loud with things that did not know he was there, and something that had been building in him since before Maren asked the first question on the Silk Road reached, in the misty morning above Rotorua, the place where it stopped being weight and started being decision.

He put the scroll away.

He looked at the door.

The huia called from deeper in the bush, very faint now, the specific cascading note getting smaller with distance. He could still hear it. He could always hear everything.

Not yet.

He had looked at it before. He had looked at it thousands of times, it was part of the work, the door was always present, the sending went through and the assessment was complete and the door was part of the furniture of the machinery. He had looked at it the way you look at a wall — a fact with no surface for questions.

This was different.

What had gone through just now, the huia population trending upward, the laughing owl, thirty years of a man deciding what the direction of things should be, had gone through the door in the usual way, in the direction of the usual vast consuming, and something in the watching of that sending had caught.

Maren had asked the question on the Silk Road. He had been thinking about it since then without knowing he thought about it, the way a sound persists after the sound has stopped. Where do they go. And now: what is the vast indifferent consuming that receives them. And: is the thing that consumes them aware of what it is consuming.

He had been through the door. He had seen the souls arrive and be processed and the processing had no cognition in it, no awareness, only the machinery of consumption. He had come back from that seeing with one clear fact: the being that consumed the souls did not know the souls existed. Did not know anything existed. Was simply a process, vast and indifferent and ancient, doing what a process does.

But Maren had asked. And Maren had gone further than he had gone. And Maren had not come back.

He looked at the door.

The Astronomer

The boy would not stop asking questions.

This was, in theory, why I had taken him on as an apprentice. My father had done the same for me. The questions were the point. And yet at three in the morning, with the large planet in the correct position and the fourth moon at the precise point in its arc that I needed to record, the questions arrived like stones in still water.

"How do you know it's a moon and not a star?" Marco said.

"Stars do not move against the background. Watch."

I waited. He watched. A minute passed. The fourth moon moved.

"Oh," he said.

"Make the notation."

He made it. His hand was careful and his numbers were clean; I had chosen him partly for that. He was fifteen and thought slowly but thought correctly.

"Does it always move this fast?"

"No. The speed changes. The pattern repeats. That is what I am mapping. The pattern."

"And then what do you do with the pattern?"

I looked at him over the lens.

"You write it down," I said. "So it exists. So someone knows it exists. So when someone else looks later they do not have to start from the beginning."

He thought about this. "What if no one looks?"

"Then the pattern still exists," I said. "The moon moves whether we write it down or not. The writing is for us, not the moon."

He accepted this and wrote it down also, which I had not asked for but which was correct.

My name was Giulia. My father ground lenses and I had grown up in a house full of glass and light and the patience of a man who worked toward a precision most people would never see. He had taught me mathematics because he needed help with the calculations and I was better at them than he was by twelve and he was not bothered by this, which I understood even then was unusual in a father.

The work I did appeared in the records under my father's name. I had understood this arrangement clearly enough that I had never expected anything different. What I had was the work. The moons moved whether or not my name appeared beside the mathematics that described their moving.

Four years of nightly observation. The notebooks filling with the patterns, the patterns resolving into mathematics, the mathematics describing something no one had described before.

Marco lasted two of those four years, until he was placed with a mapmaker's workshop where he could learn a paying trade. When he left he asked if he could have a copy of his notations. I gave him the full two years.

"Are these worth anything?" he said.

"Not to anyone who doesn't know what they're looking at."

Marco picked up one of the notebooks and looked at the cover. Then he put it back.

He said something about the stitching on the corner coming undone.

She was already at the lens.

He looked at the roll of paper. "My uncle said I should have gone into the trade six months ago."

I looked at him for a moment. "They are for the person who knows what they're looking at. Whoever that turns out to be."

He left. I kept working.

The fever came in my thirty-fourth year. I noted it as data. On the fourteenth night I noticed it had moved from the surface of my body to somewhere interior, not hotter but deeper, as though it had established itself inside where the body's ordinary warmth lived.

I was alone at the lens when the numbers stopped. This happened in order: first I could see them, then I could see what they were, then I could no longer hold what they meant. The pattern I had spent four years accumulating was in front of my and I could see it and I could not hold it. Like trying to hold water with the hands open.

I was not afraid. I noticed this with the same attention I gave everything. The fourth moon was in the correct position. I had watched it for a thousand nights and it was where it should be.

I put my hand on the cold brass of the lens. The brass is cold from the night air. I have put my hand on this brass every night for four years.

The numbers have stopped arriving. This happened in order: first I could see them, then I could see what they were, then I could no longer hold what they meant. The pattern I was tracking, the pattern that no one else knew existed, moved away from me in the way the moons move: measurably, predictably, following a law I had worked out and cannot now reach.

I am not afraid. I notice this.

The fever has moved from the surface of my body to somewhere interior, not hotter but deeper, as though the fever has stopped fighting with the skin and has moved inward to work on something more essential.

My hand is on the lens. I can feel the cold of the brass through the fever. The cold is real. The fever is real. The fourth moon is in the correct position. I watched it for a thousand nights and it is where it should be.

I feel my heart change. The specific quality of a heart that is working harder to do less. I have felt this in patients, pressed my fingers against the pulse and felt this quality, and now I feel it from inside.

I leave the body at the lens. I rise above the observatory. Looking down at the woman with her hand on the cold brass in the lamplight, the notebooks on the shelf behind her, the fourth moon in the correct position outside the window.

The pattern continues. I worked it out correctly. The moon does not care that I worked it out.

* * *

The Italian winter clay receives me slowly. This is its nature in that season, methodical, unhurried, working through what it receives at the pace the cold determines.

The clay presses in from all sides. Not like water, clay does not give the way water gives. It holds the shape of what it receives while working at the surfaces. I feel the working. The cold chemistry of the clay finding the outer layers and beginning.

I had spent four years recording a pattern no one else knew. The clay records a different pattern now, the chemistry of what it receives at what temperature, the sequence of what the clay claims and in what order. This pattern is also mine, also no one else's.

My hands go into the clay with the methodical patience of clay. The hands that held the compass and the measuring instrument and the pen. I feel them lightening as the flesh gives what the clay wants. The bones of my hands becoming distinct. I can feel each bone separately in a way I could not feel them when they had their padding.

The notebooks went into the cellar when the house was sold. I feel the cellar flood the following spring, the water moving through the ground above me, the pressure of it, carrying things. The notebooks were in water. The calculations existed in me and in those notebooks. The water does not distinguish between the two.

Forty years after my death, a man in another country works out the mathematics I worked out. He does not know he is working it out again. He receives the credit. I am in the clay of the Veneto by then, distributed into the root systems of vines.

The fourth moon continues in its arc. Faithfully, correctly, following the law I derived from a thousand nights of observation. The law holds whether I am here to confirm it or not.

I had always been right about the moons. The clay does not care about this. The moons do not care. The law holds.

* * *

Grim came in the spring, when the last of it had returned to the earth, and stood in the field that had been the cellar that had been the house and opened the scroll.

He read what it said and then he stopped and read one section again.

182

A name sat in the margin of the calculations, written in a different hand. He did not know whose it was. The scroll did not explain.

The scroll recorded everything. It had recorded Giulia's calculations with the same precision she had brought to making them. They were there in the scroll, the four years of nightly observation, the mathematics of the moons, in her handwriting in the record where history had written nothing.

Grim held the scroll open for a long time.

He found her waiting with the alertness of a person whose attention has always been primarily on the thing in front of them rather than on themselves.

He ran the assessment. The wheel turned and stopped where he expected it to stop, high, clean, the result of a person who had done serious work seriously and asked little of the world in return.

"The notebooks," she said while he was making his notes. Not a question. A statement that wanted verification.

"Gone," he said. "Within a generation. A flood."

She received this without surprise. She had known the notebooks were vulnerable.

"And the calculations themselves?"

"In the record," he said. "Here. Only here."

She looked at him. The look of someone who has spent a life doing work for an audience of none and has just confirmed the audience was precisely none.

"But accurate," she said.

"Yes," he said. "Completely accurate."

Something in her settled.

"Then one more question."

"Yes."

"The patterns I mapped. Is there more of that out there? More mathematics. More lights."

Grim thought about what he had seen across a very long time, the lights in their arrangements, the patterns that existed at scales she had no instruments to see.

"Yes," he said. "More than I have ever tried to count."

She absorbed this with the look of someone who had suspected as much and was glad to have it confirmed. Not excited. Satisfied. The way you are satisfied when the data supports the hypothesis you had formed.

"Good," she said.

He sent her on.

He watched where the sending went. The same direction. The same nothing at the end of it. He watched longer than usual, as if watching longer might eventually show him something different. It did not.

He stood in the field for a long time after, the scroll closed in his hands, thinking about the calculations and then not thinking about them, his attention drawn without reason to a beetle working across the clay near his foot, and then to the light on the far hills.

Thinking about Marco, who had asked what the pattern was for, and what she had said. So someone knows it exists. So when someone else looks later they do not have to start from the beginning.

He left the field and did not look back.

The Revolutionary

They were setting type at two in the morning when the boy asked me if I was afraid.

The boy. Bertrand, seventeen, the printer's assistant I had taken on six months ago, had not spoken for three hours. He was fast and quiet and he did not make errors, which were the three things I required. I had not asked Bertrand to be here tonight. Bertrand had simply arrived when I had, and had started working, and I had not sent him away.

"I am not afraid," I said. It was mostly true.

"They killed Dupont," Bertrand said. I was setting type without looking at Jean, my hands moving through the letters with the mechanical speed of the practiced. "Dupont printed less than this."

"Dupont printed a personal attack on a member of the Committee. This is an argument. There is a difference."

"Is there?"

I looked at the type I was setting. The argument was good. It was the best thing I had written, clear, without rhetoric, in language that a printer's assistant could understand because I had written it as a printer's assistant and not as a philosopher.

It argued that the machinery the Revolution had built to destroy tyranny had become a tyranny of its own and that this was not what they had meant and that it was not too late to mean something different.

I believed every word of it. This was either brave or stupid.

"There is a difference," I said, "in principle. Whether there is a difference in practice is what we are finding out."

Bertrand's hands kept moving. "What do you want me to do? If they come."

"Go out the back. You were never here."

"And you?"

"I was always here. It is my press."

Bertrand said nothing for a while. The type clicked into the composing stick, letter by letter, the argument taking its physical form in lead.

"I believe what it says," Bertrand said, finally. "What you wrote."

"Good."

"Do you think it will matter?"

I thought about it. The honest answer was that I did not know. The hopeful answer was that it had to matter, that words on a page could change the direction of a thing that had gone wrong. I had believed this since I was Bertrand's age and I believed it now and the belief had not yet been proven wrong and had not yet been proven right.

"I think it will be read," I said. "By someone. And that someone will think something they did not think before. Whether that changes anything is not something I can calculate."

"That's not a good answer."

"No," I said. "It isn't."

They finished the setting in silence. I ran the first sheet at four in the morning. I pulled it from the press and looked at the words in the lamplight and they were correct and the argument was intact and the ink was even and the work was good.

I gave Bertrand a copy at dawn.

"Don't carry it in the street," I said.

"I know," Bertrand said.

I watched the boy go. I folded my copy and put it in my coat.

My name was Jean. I had been a printer's assistant and then a printer and then a man who printed pamphlets for the Revolution because it was the work that was available and I could do it. Not famous. Not important. One of thousands of men who believed the same things and did the available work and hoped it would add up to something.

It had added up to something. I had watched it add up. The old order had fallen the way structures fall when the foundation is gone, quickly at the end after a long slow undermining, and the world on the other side of the falling was supposed to be different and for a while it was different, in the way that a room is different just after you have cleared it of furniture, full of possibility and light.

Then the furniture came back. Different furniture, darker, heavier, arranged to serve different people than before but arranged to serve some at the expense of others exactly as before. The machinery of the Revolution that had been built to destroy tyranny discovered it was good machinery and found new things to do with itself. The Committee. The tribunal. The list of names.

I watched this happen and I did not leave and I did not stop believing, which was either admirable or stupid.

I watched men I had worked alongside become men I did not recognize, men who used the language of liberty to mean something that had nothing to do with liberty. I watched the blade fall on people who had believed what I believed, who had done what I had done, whose names ended up on lists for reasons I could not always follow.

My name ended up on a list.

The tribunal was brief. I said what I believed and it did not matter and they said what they had already decided and it was settled.

The morning of my execution I thought about the pamphlet. The one from the second year. I thought it was a good pamphlet. I still thought it was a good pamphlet.

The cart came at nine in the morning. The smell of the streets was the smell Paris had carried all summer, the stench of a city in fear, unwashed and sharp, with something sweet and wrong underneath that you could not separate from the heat and the rot of the gutters.

They had been running the machine since spring and the city smelled of it.

I knew that smell. I had walked past the square many times. I had told myself each time that what was happening was necessary, the cost of what they were building. I did not know if I had believed that. I had believed it sometimes.

Others were in the cart. I did not know them. They did not speak. The streets were full of people. Some watched with nothing on their faces. Some watched with satisfaction. Some turned away. None of it mattered in any way I could affect.

The square smelled of old blood. The machine itself was taller than I had expected, and simpler, a wooden frame and a groove and a heavy blade held up by a rope and a mechanism, and below it a basket. The mathematics of it were simple. I understood machines. I had worked with type and press all my life, the logic of moving parts, the precision of an action that produces the same result every time.

A board they strapped you to. It tipped forward. The wood smelled of the men who had been strapped to it before me, their sweat still in the grain of it, and I thought: that smell was the last thing they knew in this position, and now it is the last thing I will know in this position, and in that there was a strange fellowship, a line of men connected by a piece of wood and the smell of their fear.

The blade came down.

Here is what they do not tell you about that kind of death: it is faster than you understand while it is happening, and slower than you expected when it is done.

The blade separated my head from my body in less time than it takes to register what is happening. The mechanism was designed for this. Thirty years of printing had taught me to respect a well-designed mechanism. I respected this one.

What I was not prepared for: I was still thinking. The head was in the basket and I was still thinking. The eyes still received light. The ears still received sound, the crowd, the cart moving away, a dog somewhere. The brain, which had not yet received the information that the machinery it had been running through was no longer there, continued processing with the thoroughness it had always brought to the world.

I could see the base of the machine from inside the basket. The straw. Someone else's blood on the wicker. My blood joining it quickly, more than I had imagined, warm through the straw.

I looked up at whatever the basket allowed me to see of the sky. Blue. A Paris summer sky, the same sky I had looked at for fifty-three years, from a new angle.

The brain noted the absence of the body. The reliable familiar weight and warmth of it, the hands I had set type with for thirty years. Gone. The brain kept trying. It was still trying when the darkness came.

The darkness came.

And then I was above the square. Above the machine and the basket and the cart and the crowd. Looking down at the mechanism that had just separated me from the thing I had lived in. It was very clean, from above. The square smelled of summer and blood and the specific Paris smell of a city that had been afraid all year.

I was in the air above the Place de la Révolution and the morning continued below me and I watched it and thought about the pamphlet I had written in the second year, whether it had been any good, and thought that it probably had been.

* * *

Here is what they do not tell you about that kind of death.

There is a moment after the blade and before the darkness in which everything still works. My eyes still saw. My ears still heard. The machinery of the brain, which had not yet understood what had happened to it, continued processing with the thoroughness it had always brought to the world.

The incoming information was the square from a new angle. The cobblestones. The legs of the crowd. The base of the machine's frame, close and very large. The basket approaching fast, and then the jolt of arrival, and then the sky above the square tilted at the angle of something that had come to rest on its side, and the sound of the crowd, and the smell of blood which was copper and iron and very close now.

The brain noted the absence of the body, which should have been there, the reliable familiar weight and warmth of it, and found the absence wrong in a way it could not resolve. It kept trying. It was still trying when the darkness came.

The machinery received what it received, as it had for every soul before me and would for every soul after, the darkness did not hold.

I was still there.

Not whole. Not the I that had been in the cart or stood before the tribunal or set type by lamplight for thirty years. Something smaller and stranger, something that had been in all of those things without being any of them, the part that had always been watching from slightly behind the eyes, noticing what it noticed, thinking what it thought.

And this part was still present in the square in Paris on a summer morning with the smell of blood and the sound of the crowd and the light that comes off cobblestones when the sun is high.

The rest of the morning happened without me. I felt it happen. The cart moving on. The crowd dispersing. The men who came with the buckets. The city going on with the long work of going on with itself, indifferent, having seen so many.

What was left of me stayed in the square until what was left of me was gone from the square, taken with the men and their buckets to the place outside the city where they put what the machine produced. I felt the journey. I felt the arrival. I felt the lime, which was efficient and thorough and not quick.

Then the long wait in the ground outside the city that had been building on top of itself for a thousand years and would keep building, turning its dead into the foundations of what came next.

I was in the pit with everyone else the machine had produced. I recognized none of them. They had believed different things or believed the same things or believed nothing at all. The lime and the dark and the ground did not make any of those distinctions. They were all in the ground together and the ground did not ask.

Decades.

* * *

Grim came to the grave and stood over it and opened the scroll.

A decent man. A sincere man. A man who had held to his convictions past the point where holding to them was safe, and had paid the price of that period, which was extravagant even by the standards of periods that extracted payment.

He found Jean waiting. His conclusions had just been overturned.

"I did not expect this."

"No one does."

"I mean, after. I expected nothing. I had considered the question of what comes after and concluded nothing was the most defensible answer. Being here was not among my conclusions."

"Most people find that."

The assessment continued. The wheel turned and stopped and Grim made his notes. Jean watched the process with the attentiveness of a man who finds mechanisms interesting and has just encountered a very unusual one.

"Where do I go? After."

"Back. You try again."

"Try what again."

"Living. Choosing. The whole arrangement."

Jean thought about this with the careful deliberateness of a man who had spent his life thinking carefully about arrangements.

"Without remembering any of this."

"Without remembering."

"Then what is the point of the trying?"

It was not a question Grim had a good answer to. He gave the answer the machinery provided, that something carries, something accumulates across lives even without conscious memory, the trying is the point. He believed this answer. He had believed it for longer than he could count and had not examined it. He was examining it now, which was probably too late.

"You accumulate," Grim said, after a moment. "Across lives. Something carries."

"Even without memory."

"Even without."

Jean did not look satisfied. He looked like a man who had spent his life insisting on clear answers to important questions and was being told the important question did not have one. Which was accurate.

Grim sent him on.

He followed.

Not through, he did not go through. He watched the trajectory the sending took and kept watching past the point where he normally looked away and returned to work. He watched past the edge of his own territory, into the part of the machinery between the handoff and whatever came next.

He saw the direction. He had always seen the direction.

He watched longer.

The direction went somewhere. He could feel the somewhere the way you feel a room through a wall, the sense of mass and space on the other side, not visible but present. He pushed his attention toward it the way you push against a door that is not quite latched.

The door did not open.

But it moved. A fraction. Enough to tell him something was there. Enough to tell him it was not the open differentiated space he had always assumed, not the vast sorted landscape of souls arriving at their various earned destinations.

The somewhere on the other side felt singular. Dense. The same somewhere, regardless of what the wheel had said. And whatever was there was not receiving the souls. It drew them in the way a void draws air, without awareness, without intention, simply by being what it was.

He pulled back.

He stood in the street above the grave in the Paris morning, the city moving around him, the horses and the carts and the people who had survived what Paris had just done to itself getting on with the business of getting on. The smell of the city was the smell it always had after the machine had been busy, a city trying to smell like itself again and not quite managing.

The Factory Child

I had been there longest.

I was eight, which meant I had been at the mill for two years, and I had a way of moving through the machines that looked almost casual, one hand trailing along a frame to feel the vibration, body angling at the hips to pass through a gap that looked too narrow but wasn't. I had the machines the way some people have weather, not knowledge exactly, more like a fluency, the ability to read a system that could not be explained, only practiced.

"Watch the third one on the left," I said, the first morning. "The rhythm's off. It catches."

Nell watched. It caught.

"You felt that?" I said.

"In the floor," Nell said. "Before it happened."

I looked at myself with the serious assessment of someone deciding whether a thing is true. Then I moved on to the next frame and Nell followed me and that was the beginning of the only friendship I had at the mill.

Neither of them talked much. The mill was too loud for talking and they were both tired, always, in the way that children who work twelve hours a day are tired, which is a tiredness that lives in the bones and does not fully leave even in sleep.

What they had was the moving through the machines together, and the occasional word when they were close enough, and the knowledge of where the other one was on the floor at any given moment, which was the same knowledge you had of any dangerous thing that could hurt you if you stopped paying attention.

Three months in, the overseer moved me to a different section. He said nothing about why. I was simply there one morning and then not there the next. Nell watched the door I had come through for a week before I understood that I was not going to come back through it.

I kept working. Nothing else to do.

Her name was Nell. She did not know her family name. She did not know if she had one. A woman I did not remember clearly, large, in a grey dress, brought her to the mill and left her there, and that was the beginning of my life as I remembered it.

I was six years old.

The mill was loud. This is the first thing. The machines made a sound that was not like any other sound, not like weather or animals or people, a sound that was the same every day all day.

I stopped hearing it after a while the way you stop hearing your own heartbeat. But it was always there.

I remembered first the sound and then the heat and then the smell of the oil they used on the machines, a thick smell that got into everything.

I was a scavenger first. This meant crawling under the machines while they were running to pick up the cotton waste that fell, because the machines did not stop and the cotton had to be collected and a small child could move through the spaces that an adult could not. I learned quickly where the moving parts were. Most children learned this without losing fingers and some did not.

I did not lose fingers. I was quick and she paid attention and I had a talent for reading the rhythms of the machines, knowing when a part was about to move, feeling it in the vibration of the floor before the movement happened. The overseer noticed this and after two years he moved me to piecing, joining broken threads on the spinning machines. It required the same quickness and the same attention and was considered better work because you did not have to crawl.

I was good at it. I was known for being good at it.

The cough started when I was nine. It was a common cough at first, the kind that came with the winter damp, and then it was not common anymore, it was the mill cough, the one that the older workers had, the one that did not go away when the winter did. By the time I was ten it was in my chest permanently, a wet heaviness that was there when she woke up and there when I went to sleep and there in the spaces between.

I kept working. The cough was what it was.

I died in the spring of my tenth year in the room above the mill where the children slept. In a narrow bed with two other children in it. Neither of them woke up when I went.

The cough had changed three weeks before. Agnes had told me what it meant when the cough changed. Agnes knew. Agnes had watched others.

The room smelled of oil and bodies and the damp of a building that has absorbed years of the machinery below. I have breathed this smell for four years.

The mill ran below me even at night. The machinery ran without stopping. I had learned to sleep with the sound and now, at the end, I heard it. The wheel. The looms. The sound it makes all day every day.

I thought about grass. I did not know why. I had a memory of grass from before the mill, just the feeling of it, the smell of it, the color of it. Not a specific place. Just grass.

I felt my breathing slow. I have felt this in others. I knew what it meant.

I was above the room. Looking down at the narrow bed with three children in it, two sleeping, one not. The mill running below. The oil smell. The spring night outside the window.

I stopped.

Then I stopped.

* * *

They bury me in the section of the churchyard set aside for mill children. A section the parish had not anticipated needing when they set aside the rest. I feel the cold English spring ground close over me.

The ground of the churchyard is old ground. It has been receiving the dead of this parish for four hundred years. It knows what it is doing. The organisms in it are the organisms of old English churchyard ground, patient, thorough, experienced with what comes to them.

The spring warmth reaches the ground and the organisms resume. I feel them find me the way they find everything, without recognition, without distinction. I am what they find. They begin.

Each one is distinct. I feel where each one works and what it takes. The organisms of the churchyard work methodically through what they have, each species in its sequence, each claiming what it claims.

I had thought about grass near the end. The grass that grows over the churchyard in summer grows over me now. The roots go down through the turf into the ground and I feel them, thin, purposeful, finding what is available. I am in the grass. I am in the grass of the churchyard.

The mill runs below me. I can feel it. I thought about grass when I was dying. I don't know why. The mill ran before I arrived and it runs after.

The other children are in the same section. Agnes is nearby. I feel the fact of her in the ground, the presence of the girl who showed me the third machine on the left. We are in the same churchyard. We are becoming the same ground.

The mill runs for forty years after I die and then it stops. The machinery is sold and the building sits empty and the vibration changes, less, then quieter, then nothing. The ground absorbs the silence the way it absorbed the sound.

No one comes looking. The grass grows over it all. The children I was buried beside are in the same grass. What made us distinct is in the roots. The roots do not distinguish.

* * *

Grim came in the summer, when the churchyard was green over everything, and he stood by the fallen stone and he opened the scroll.

He read it quickly. Little to read. A life of ten years, most of it in a mill, the moral ledger nearly empty because there had been almost no opportunity to fill it in either direction. She had not been cruel. She had not been kind in any sustained way, there had not been the circumstances for it. She had worked and she had been good at the work.

And she had thought about grass at the end.

He found her still and drawn in on herself, a child who had learned that stillness is safer than movement, and he crouched down to be at her level. It seemed correct. The temperature in the churchyard dropped sharply. The numbered stones of the other mill children shifted slightly in the earth, a collective settling, as if the ground had been told what was above it.

"Nell," he said.

She looked at him.

"It is finished," he said. "The mill. The cough. All of it. It is finished now."

She kept looking at him. She assessed him the way she had assessed the machines, reading the rhythms, determining what was safe.

"Is there grass?" she asked.

Grim thought about it.

"Yes," he said. "There is grass."

She accepted this. She did not ask anything else. She waited for whatever came next with the patience of a child who had learned that waiting was what you did.

No wheel for this assessment. Nothing to assess. He sent her on, as gently as the sending could be done, and then he followed the sending the way he had followed Jean's, pushing his attention past the edge of his territory, toward the door he had felt move.

He got closer this time.

The door was the same. The singular somewhere on the other side was the same, dense and undifferentiated, the same place it had sent Jean, the same place it sent everything. He pushed harder than he had pushed with Jean.

The door did not open. But through the fraction of the movement he could feel something on the other side. Not souls arriving at their destinations. Not the vast sorted landscape of earned outcomes.

Something on the other side not receiving them but drawing them in. Vast. Indifferent. Unaware of what they had been.

He pulled back.

He stood in the green churchyard in the summer light for a long time, the fallen stone at his feet.

Then he reached into the old records, further back than he usually reached, looking for something he had not known he looked for until Jean's door had moved. He looked for Maren. Not the territory reassignment. The record before that. The reason for it.

He found the entry after a long search, buried in administrative language so old it was almost unreadable, the kind of language that had been designed to say something without being understood to say it.

The machinery had not reassigned Maren.

The record used no other word. No designation. No explanation. Just the absence of a forwarding, the absence of a note, the absence of anything that would tell Grim where Maren had gone or what had become of him. Gone. The territory reassigned to someone else. The records closed.

Grim stood in the churchyard and did not move for a long time.

This should not be possible.

Grims did not cease. They were not born. They did not die. They existed outside the cycle that governed everything else, outside the decay and the assessment and the reincarnation, permanent in the way that the machinery was permanent, present before the first soul and after the last. Not a belief. Not a theology. The foundational fact of what Grim was, the one thing that had never required examination.

And yet Maren was gone. Not somewhere. Not reassigned. Gone in a way that left no record, no trace. The territory reassigned as if nothing unusual had occurred. As if a Grim simply ending was a thing that could occur.

It sat in him the way a blade sits in a wound, not painful yet, the shock still working, the full shape of it not yet arrived.

Maren had gone looking. Past the door, into the singular dense somewhere on the other side. He had gone and he had not come back and the official record called it a reassignment and Grim was now alone with what that meant.

He tried to account for where Maren had gone in the language of the machinery and could not. The machinery had no category for where Maren had gone. It had reassigned the territory and closed the records as if the not-going-back were a routine administrative outcome rather than the thing it was, which Grim was now standing in the churchyard trying to name.

He was not permanent.

Nell had asked if there was grass. He had said yes. He did not know if that was true.

The Mud

"If we get through the wire," Brandt said, quietly, "then the shell craters."

"I know."

"The craters on the left held last week."

"I know."

Brandt was quiet for a moment. "What did you do before?"

He had been a clockmaker in Düsseldorf. I had not been anything that helped here either.

"Taught mathematics. Secondary school."

Brandt almost laughed. "Mathematics."

"Geometry. Calculus. The relationship between the angle and its sine."

"Does that help? Here?"

I thought about this. The mud was up to my knees at the edge of the trench. I knew this mud. I had been standing in it for eight months. I knew which parts would hold and which would take you to the knee and which would take you to the waist and not let go.

"No," I said. "Not at all."

Brandt laughed then, one brief quiet sound into the dark.

Heinrich. Twenty-two when I arrived, twenty-three when he didn't leave. Before the war I taught mathematics to thirty students in a village school in Bavaria. I knew each of them by name. I knew the quality of each one's confusion, where the concept stopped arriving cleanly, what angle of approach would make it land. This is teaching. You find the angle. You try again. You watch their faces for the moment it lands.

I thought about them sometimes in the mud. Not abstractly. Specifically. Karl who could not hold the relationship between the angle and its sine without a drawing. Margarethe who understood calculus before she understood arithmetic and had to be taught backward. The youngest, Friedrich, who was nine and already thinking about things I could only keep up with if I ran.

I wondered which of them had come here too. The mud did not make introductions.

The war had stopped requiring conviction by the second year. By the third year the question of belief had become irrelevant the way the question of whether you believe in weather becomes irrelevant when it is raining.

The push was at dawn. I moved through it beside Brandt, toward the wire, the mud doing what it always did, taking each step as a separate negotiation. I knew which sections to avoid and he avoided them. I moved well. Brandt was to my left, close enough to hear my breathing, and they were almost at the wire when I put my foot wrong, not in a bad section, just wrong, the weight distributed incorrectly, and I went down.

Not into a crater. Not into the deep mud. I went down to one knee and came back up, but the moment was enough. The sound came from the left, the direction I was not looking, and it was not like any other sound, and then there was not.

Somewhere behind me on the ridge, twenty meters back, a sound came that I had not heard in three years of this ground. Not shelling. Not rifles. Something animal. I noted it and did not turn. The round hit me in the left shoulder. I knew what it was. I had known rifle fire for three years, I had learned to identify caliber by sound, and I knew from the way my left arm stopped receiving signals that the round had gone through something structural.

I was down. The mud received me the way it received everyone. Face first, the particular cold wet of Western Front mud, the iron smell, the rot smell, the chemical smell of ground that has been shelled for three years and holds everything that shelling produces.

I got my right arm under me and pushed. I got up as far as my knees. The left arm was not cooperating. The sleeve of my uniform was wrong, the shape of it wrong, something missing from the shoulder joint that the shoulder joint required.

The blood moved fast. I pressed my right hand to the wound and the hand came away immediately red. The round had opened something significant.

I went back down to my face in the mud. The mud was cold. The blood was warm. The contrast.

Someone's boot came past my head. Close. Not a kick, they had not seen me or were not interested. The push continued above me, men moving toward the wire, the sounds of it moving away.

I noted the things I could still note. The mud against my face. The specific weight of my equipment. The sound of Brandt. I thought I heard Brandt's breathing somewhere to my left but I was not certain and I was not going to raise my head to check.

The cold arrived in stages. It had been below freezing all morning. The cold that had been outside my uniform was now inside it, moving through the wet wool, finding the places where the blood had cooled and continuing past them.

I thought about the students. Karl and his angles. The window that stuck.

I felt myself separating from the mud. Not rising. I was not going anywhere, the body was not moving. But some part of me that was not the mud-covered body shifted slightly above it, looking at the back of my own head from two feet away.

The grey sky was the same grey it had been since I arrived in this sector in October.

I did not know if Brandt made it to the wire.

I was on my back in the mud. I did not know how I got there. One moment I moved and then I was here and the sky was the grey that the sky always was on the Western Front, the grey that had no graduation in it, no difference between dawn and midday and dusk, just grey from one end to the other.

The mud was cold through the back of my uniform. I had been cold for three years. This was the cold of being in the mud, which was a different cold from the cold of standing in the trench. I noted the difference.

The wire was ahead of me. I could not tell if Brandt was at the wire or past it or somewhere in the mud between here and there. The grey sky gave nothing.

I thought about Karl, who could not hold the angle and the sine together. Who had gotten there eventually, slowly, by working the problem from both ends until they met. I had been patient with Karl because patience was what that kind of mind required and I had seen what patience produced.

I thought about the village school. The window that stuck in the winter and the way the light came through it in the afternoon, sideways, hitting the chalk dust on the air in a way that made it visible. I had taught in that light for three years and never once stopped for it.

The mud held me. It had been holding men on this ground for three years. It did not distinguish.

I did not know if Brandt made it to the wire.

* * *

The mud here did not decay things. This was what I learned from the inside that I could not have known from the outside: the mud at the Western Front preserved. The same qualities that made it a horror to fight in, the density, the lack of oxygen below the surface, the chemistry of what three years of shelling and three years of bodies had made of it, those qualities held what it received.

Other grounds took their dead and returned them. This ground kept them.

Months passed and I was still there.

Still complete, or nearly complete. The mud pressed in from all sides with the weight of a hand pressing on the chest, not painful but constant, the pressure of it never releasing, the mud above and the mud below and the mud on every side, and no way to push back against it because pushing back requires a body and the body was what the mud was keeping but not releasing.

A year. Two years. I thought about my students. I thought about Karl and my difficulty with angles and Margarethe who understood calculus backward and Friedrich who was nine and already past where Heinrich could follow me. I thought about whether any of them had come here. Some of them had been the right age. The mud held many men the right age and the mud did not tell me their names.

I felt the others in it the way you feel weather coming, not specific, not named, but present. The general weight of them. German and French and British and Belgian and all the nationalities the war had brought to this strip of ground. The mud had no opinion about nationality. It held them all with the same indifferent thoroughness, the same refusal to release.

I thought about Brandt. The clockmaker. I could not tell if Brandt was in this mud or somewhere else. The mud did not make introductions.

Years became decades. The war was over, I knew this not because anyone told me but because the quality of what pressed down from above changed. No more shelling. The ground settled. What had been no man's land became farmland again, slowly, the farmers working around what the ground held and not asking too many questions.

I felt the plows. I felt them stop at the places where the ground resisted and redirect. The farmers knew what was under their fields. They worked around them the way you work around stones.

Then one morning, I calculated sometime in the 1990s, based on the weight and vibration of the machines above me, they came not to farm but to dig. Deliberately. With care. Brushes, not shovels, near the surface.

The pressure released in stages as they uncovered me layer by layer, and for the first time in more than seventy years I was not pressed on all sides, and the air reached me, and the air had oxygen in it, and the things that needed oxygen to work began their work.

Two weeks. That was all it took once the air reached me. Seventy years of preservation undone in two weeks.

I felt it all, the rapid progression of what the mud had held at bay for seven decades, doing now in days what it would have done in weeks when I was fresh. The researchers who had uncovered me were careful with what they found. I finished in a laboratory, in controlled conditions, attended. It was nothing like what I deserved and nothing like what I had expected and I was grateful for neither.

I thought about Brandt. Whether the clockmaker had made it to the wire. Whether I was in this mud or in some other section. Whether there was a place in Düsseldorf where the clocks Brandt had made were still running, still keeping the time Brandt would never know again.

The mud does not make introductions. I had never found out.

* * *

* * *

He arrived with five others.

He was not alone in the way that he had not been alone at the plague pit, multiple Grims working a single site because the volume required it. But the plague pit had been chaotic, the assessments overlapping and urgent, the machinery straining against the scale of what it was being asked to do.

This was different. This was the machinery running at a sustained capacity it had been running at for three years, and the Grims who worked this ground had the efficiency of people doing an impossible task long enough that the impossibility had become ordinary.

Six of them. Moving through the mud in the grey dawn light, each one working their section, the assessments running in parallel, the scrolls opening and closing in the rhythm of industrial death. Grim had worked this sector before. He knew the ground. He knew which parts of it held the most, where the pushes had been most concentrated, where the wire had been.

He moved through it with the same learned knowledge that Heinrich had moved through it with.

Maren worked the section to the north.

Grim saw him across the grey ground, the familiar stillness, the way Maren held the scroll when he read a difficult assessment, slightly angled, as if the light were better at that angle even though there was no light that would make a difference to what he read. They had worked together long enough that Grim could read Maren across a distance the way you read weather, in the posture, in the set of the shoulders, in whether the scroll was open or closed.

The scroll was open. Had been open a long time.

Grim finished his current assessment and moved north.

"Difficult one?" he said.

Maren looked up. Something in his face that Grim could not immediately read. A young man, he said. A schoolteacher. He died thinking about a baker's fire from his childhood.

"That happens."

"Yes." Maren closed the scroll. "Grim. How long have we been doing this?"

Grim looked at the ground. The mud. The wire in the distance. The grey sky that had been grey for as long as anyone here could remember.

"Long enough," he said.

He had thought to say something more precise, a count, a marker, the name of a battle that would serve as a reference point, and had not. He was not entirely certain the count was right. The beginning of a very long thing had that quality: most present as shape, least present as fact.

"Long enough to know where they go?"

The question arrived differently than it had on the Silk Road. Then it had been casual. Now it was not.

"You have been watching," Grim said.

"For some time," Maren said. "You?"

"Yes."

"And?"

Grim was quiet for a moment. Around them the other Grims worked their sections, the assessments running, the machinery doing what it did. The sound of it, if it had a sound, would have been the sound of an enormous, indifferent engine.

"The same place," Grim said. "Every time. Regardless of the assessment."

Maren nodded.

"I am going to look further," Maren said. "Past where I have been looking."

Grim felt something cold move through him that had nothing to do with the temperature of the morning.

"Maren," Grim said.

"I know," Maren said.

"You do not know what is past the door."

"No," Maren said. "But someone should find out." He looked at Grim with the directness of someone saying a thing they have thought about carefully. "If it is not one of us, who?"

They stood in the mud of the Western Front in the grey dawn while the assessments ran around them and the machinery processed its three years of accumulated dead. The mud in a ring around where they both stood had gone completely still. The other four Grims had drifted further away without knowing they had done so.

"Safe travels," Maren said.

Not a joke this time.

Grim watched him go back to his section.

He turned back to his own work. The scrolls. The assessments. The wheel turning and stopping. The sending. The watching of the direction and the nothing at the end of it.

The Number

I taught literature to secondary school students in Warsaw. I was good at it. The good of a teacher who likes the subject and likes the students and can hold both things at once without one diminishing the other. My students read Polish poets and German novelists and French playwrights and I made arguments to fourteen-year-olds about why this mattered.

Some of them believed me and some of them did not, and the ones who believed me I sometimes still saw years later in the street, adults by then, and they would stop me and say something about a particular poem or a particular morning in the classroom and I was always glad when this happened.

My name was Rivka Stern. I was thirty-seven years old in September 1942 when the Germans came to our building. I had been a teacher for eleven years. I was not married. I lived with my mother, who was sixty-nine and who had a bad hip and who I was afraid would not survive the journey, wherever the journey went.

The journey went to Treblinka. My mother did not survive the selection. I understood what the selection did within minutes of arriving, from the direction people were sent and the speed with which the guards moved away the old and the very young. I had been reading German for twenty years. I understood the instructions.

I did not say this to anyone around me because understanding it and saying it were different things and I was not sure saying it would help anyone.

They gave me a number. I will not write the number here because the number was the point of giving it, to make the name irrelevant, and I do not intend to help it with that. I was a literature teacher from Warsaw. That is what I was.

I worked in the camp for eight months. I will not describe what I saw in those eight months because the description would require more than I can give it and because the scholars have described it and the survivors have described it and the records exist and anyone who wishes to know what those eight months were like in that place can find out. I will say only that I did the thing I had always done.

I paid attention. To the people around me. I paid attention to who needed what. I paid attention to the way a person's face changed when they stopped being able to hold on and I tried to be near them when I saw the change coming, because a teacher who sits with people is a useful thing to be even when there is no classroom.

In April of 1943 I woke one morning and my body would not get up. This is different from not wanting to get up. The body that had gotten up every day for eight months in that place lay on the bunk and when I told it to rise it did not.

I was not afraid. This surprised me. I had been afraid for eight months in the sustained way that living under that kind of authority produces. Now I was not. What I felt instead was something closer to having reached the end of a very long sentence and finding the period.

I listened to the sounds of the morning the way I had listened to everything in that place, noting, cataloguing. The light changed. I thought about my mother's hum while she was cooking. I thought about how I had heard it my whole life and never told her.

My breathing slowed. I noted this with the professional attention I had given everything.

Miroslava, from Łódź, came and took my hand at some point in the afternoon. She had said her name looking me in the eyes on our second day, in the way that meant: I am telling you this so that one of us will know.

I felt her hand. Then I felt it less.

I was above the bunk. Looking down at the literature teacher from Warsaw. Miroslava still holding the hand. The grey light continuing. The sounds of the camp continuing. The machinery of the place continuing without me.

A woman whose name I had learned. Miroslava, from Łódź, she had said it looking me in the eyes on our second day in the way that meant: I am telling you this so that one of us will know, took my hand at some point in the afternoon and held it. I felt her hand. I could not locate mine in the same way I usually could. I noted this. The grey light continued. Then it did not.

* * *

They burn the body.

I want to say this plainly because it is different from every other thing in this account. The ground did not receive me. Fire did.

Fire is different from every other process. Fire does not take weeks or months or years. Fire is hours. I feel every stage of it, the temperature arriving at the surface, the sensation of combustion working through what I was, faster and more total than any ground could manage.

The heat is not pain. Pain has architecture, it requires a nervous system to process it, and by the time the fire reaches the temperatures it reaches, the nervous system is no longer available. What I feel is not pain. It is the sensation of transformation, fast and total.

The smoke rises. I am in the smoke. Some of me goes into the air above the camp, carried on the updraft, dispersed into the sky of a country that continues above what is happening in this camp. Some of me goes into the river. Some into the ground.

I am in several places at once within hours. Not the slow distribution of years that the ground produces, immediate, total, scattered across a landscape that goes on living as if this were a normal thing for a landscape to contain.

Miroslava is in the smoke a few weeks later. I do not know this until it happens. Then I know it. I cannot tell her that I know.

We are in the same air. We are in the same river. The river runs to the sea and the sea receives everything and the sea does not distinguish between the literature teacher from Warsaw and the woman from Łódź who held her hand.

The smoke dispersed into the air of Europe in 1943. Some of it is still dispersing. I do not know where Miroslava went. I know where we both went.

* * *

Grim came when the last of the ash had settled and stood at the edge of the river and opened the scroll.

The scroll was brief. A life of thirty-seven years, eleven of them teaching. The months in the camp. The quality of attention paid across all of it, to students and to neighbors and to strangers and to a woman whose name she had learned so that the woman would not be unknown to someone. Clean enough. Cleaner than most.

The cold that came with him was colder than it usually came. The river did not slow. It kept moving the way rivers move, without pause, without interest in what was happening on its bank. The cold held and held and did not release until the assessment was done.

He found her waiting.

She did not ask him what he was or what this was. She had spent eight months paying attention to things that were terrible and continuing anyway. She did that now.

"Rivka Stern. Literature teacher. Warsaw."

"Yes."

"Your students."

"Some of them will be all right."

He did not know if this was true. He made a note that she had said it.

The wheel turned and stopped quickly — not much to weigh here. The result was clear. He made his note.

He sent her on. He watched where the sending went. The same direction. The same vast indifferent drawing-in on the other side of the door, pulling her toward it the way it pulled everything, without knowing she was there, without knowing what she had done in eight months in a place designed specifically to make people into nothing, without knowing that she had done it and had remained something anyway.

He stood at the river for a long time after.

He opened the administrative section of the scroll, the part where location and date and cause of death were recorded, and he looked at the category for cause of death and the category did not have a designation for what he looked at. He created one. It took him a while to find language for it. When he found it he wrote it carefully and closed that section.

He did not close the scroll immediately. He held it.

Then he closed it and walked.

The Cartographer

I learned cartography from a man who had learned it from a Moroccan who had learned it from a tradition going back to Ibn Battuta, the great traveler, who had walked more of the world than any man before him and had the courtesy to write it down.

I learned that a map was a form of argument, that every choice of what to include and what to leave out was a position, that the borders you drew and the ones you did not draw were equally statements about how you understood the world to be organized.

I spent forty years making those arguments in ink on paper, traveling the rivers and the dry country and the forest edge and the desert approaches, measuring and recording, talking to the people who lived in each place about how they understood its boundaries, its resources, its relationship to everything around it.

I spoke eight languages well and four more badly. I drew the land as the people of the land understood it, which was not how the Europeans understood it.

The Europeans arrived in force when I was in my fifties. They arrived with their own maps, cruder than mine in their rendering and more powerful in their application, because they arrived with the armies to make their maps real.

I watched territories I had spent years documenting become lines on paper in rooms I was not invited into, watched the careful distinctions I had recorded between this people's land and that people's land dissolved into administrative units that served no one who lived there.

A man from one of the French expeditions found me in my sixty-third year and offered to buy my maps. I told him what I thought of this in four of the languages I spoke well and one I spoke badly. He left. The maps stayed with my family.

I do not know what happened to the maps after I died. I hope they burned. I hope some grandchild found them and understood what they were and burned them before anyone else could make use of them. I spent forty years making an argument about how the land was organized. They used it to do the opposite of what I intended.

The only comfort available to me is that this is what arguments do, they escape the intentions of the people who make them and find their own uses in the world, which is terrible and also how knowledge works.

I died of a fever in the dry season, in my own house, in my own bed, with my wife beside me and two of my sons in the doorway. The fever took three days and was not gentle about it.

On the third day the sounds of the house came to me from a great distance and the light through the window was very bright and then not bright enough. The fever had moved to somewhere interior, not hotter but more total, the body burning from the center out.

My heart worked hard in the heat. Each beat effortful. Each beat the body asking the question.

I thought about the river I had first mapped at twenty-two. The way it smelled in the morning, a river smell, specific and unrepeatable. I have mapped forty rivers. I know the smell of each one. This one I knew first.

I felt myself leaving the body. Not dramatically, the way a current leaves a riverbank, smoothly, without announcement. I was in the body and then I was above it, looking down at the cartographer in his bed, my wife's hand on the body's hand, my sons in the doorway.

I thought about the river.

On the third day I could not see clearly and the sounds of the house came to me from a great distance and I thought about the river I had first mapped at twenty-two, the way it smelled in the morning before the heat came, green and cold and absolutely real, and then I did not think about anything.

* * *

The dry season keeps me first. The soil of this country is hard and reluctant in the dry months, it holds what it holds, resisting the process that other soils welcome. I feel the holding. I am held.

I note where I am. This is the reflex of forty years. I note the depth. The soil composition. The root that has found my left hand, an acacia root, I think, from the texture of it. My left hand, which I have mapped with for forty years, is now being mapped by a root.

Then the rains come.

I have mapped the rains of this country for forty years. I know which wadis flood. I know how far the water travels from each source. I know what the water does to the soil. From inside the soil I know differently, not the water as an event but the water as a presence, moving through, carrying pieces of me downstream.

Not all at once. Over one rainy season, what the dry heat reduced and the rains loosened traveled. I felt it happening, parts of me separating, moving with the water, reaching new locations. I was in more than one place.

By the second rainy season I was in perhaps a dozen locations. I knew this the way I knew the shape of a territory from inside it, not by seeing but by the accumulated knowledge of presence.

I was in the road. Worked into the dust of it by the same rains that carried me there, pressed into the surface by the feet of traders. The road I had mapped. I am in the road.

My wife came to where I was buried and stayed. I felt her footsteps. I have known her footsteps for forty years. She sat in the dry season, visited in the wet. I felt each visit. I could not tell her anything.

She died four years after me and was buried beside me. I felt her arrive. Without surprise, without drama, the way a known person arrives in a familiar room. We are in the same ground. We are becoming the same ground.

I tried to map this. It was the reflex of forty years. I had no instrument. I was the territory and the cartographer at once and the cartographer cannot have the distance that mapping requires.

* * *

Grim came in the morning, in the dry season, when the air smelled of dust and the dry sweetness of the acacia that flowered even in the worst heat. He stood over the grave and opened the scroll.

Outside the city walls, where the camel caravans came in from the north, a man was leading three animals along the trade road. He stopped. The camels stopped with him, their heads turning in the same direction, all four of them oriented toward something in the cemetery that gave no signal any of them could have named. They stood for a moment that stretched past what stillness usually permitted.

Then the man touched the lead camel's neck and they moved on, and the animals moved with them, and they did not look back.

The scroll wrote steadily. Grim read what it produced and read it again.

The maps were in there. All of them, complete, every line Yusuf had drawn across forty years of walking. The territories as the people of the territories understood them. The careful notations in eight languages and four more badly. Everything that had been lost or used wrong or burned or sold was present in the scroll, faithful and exact, in the handwriting of the man who had made it.

He read what the scroll had and read it again.

He found Yusuf still working through something.

"The maps are in the record."

"I know. I made them."

"All of them. Complete."

"Yes." A pause. "Are they of any use to you?"

"They tell me where things were. How people understood their own ground."

"Then they are doing what I made them to do. That is more than most of them managed."

The assessment ran. The wheel turned and stopped and Grim made his notes. Yusuf watched the mechanism with the professional attention of a man who had spent his life making instruments of measurement and was now encountering one he had not previously catalogued.

"You are troubled," Yusuf said.

Grim looked at him.

"You ask the questions you are supposed to ask but you are asking something else underneath them. I have interviewed enough people in enough languages to know the shape of a man whose attention is not entirely where he has placed it."

Grim was quiet for a moment.

"There is something I am trying to understand."

"About where we go."

Grim was still.

"You are watching after the handoff," Yusuf said. "I felt it when you sent my wife on. Four years ago. Something following the sending and then pulling back." He waited. "I was curious whether you would do it again."

"I will," Grim said.

"Good. You should know where your maps lead."

He sent Yusuf on and followed the sending the way he had followed Jean's, pushing his attention past the edge of his territory, toward the door.

The door was there. The same singular dense somewhere on the other side. He pushed and it moved its fraction and he felt what he had felt before, not souls arriving at their destinations, not the sorted landscape of earned outcomes. Something vast pulling them in without knowing they were there. The way a drain pulls water. Without intention. Without awareness. Simply the nature of what it was.

He pulled back.

He stood in the morning heat of Timbuktu, the dust smell and the acacia sweetness and the sound of the camel caravan already distant on the trade road, and he thought about a cartographer who had spent forty years mapping territories that were then used to erase the people who lived in them.

The door had moved further this time. He did not know if that was progress. He did not know if further was a direction that meant anything in what was behind the door. He put the scroll away.

The camel caravan was gone from the road.

The Between

He watched a woman argue with a vendor about a price. He watched two men loading a cart. He watched a boy run across the square for no reason visible to anyone, just running, the way children sometimes ran, because the square was open and the morning was there.

He was not here for anyone. No scroll open. An hour between collections, perhaps two. He had come to stand in it.

He tried to watch.

His attention found the old man on the bench near the gate. Assessed the color. The stillness of someone who had stopped compensating. He had six months, perhaps. Less if the winter was hard. The man held something in his hands, a small object, turned over once, then held still. Grim could not see what it was. He looked away before he worked out what he looked at.

He looked away.

His attention found the woman at the upper window, standing too still, looking at nothing in the street below. He knew that look. He had seen it on every continent in every century and it always meant the same thing and he was already moving before he had decided to move.

She stepped back from the window.

He stopped.

Not today. She had stepped back. Whatever she had been deciding, she had decided the other way, and she was still inside and the window was empty and the square continued and the boy was still running.

He stood in the market square and the light continued on the stones and the morning continued around him and the machinery was quiet and he could not tell the difference between that and rest.

The next collection arrived. He felt it arrive the way you feel a change in pressure, something resolved itself, somewhere, and a scroll waited, and the hour was gone or had never fully been.

The old man on the bench did not look up.

The Cauldron

One room I remember clearly. October, I think. I had stopped counting by then. A machine hall I had worked in for six years before the war. I knew every corner of it. Two of them, backs to me. I had the angle.

There had been a woman on the third floor of this building before the battle. I had seen her twice from the street. She had been carrying something red both times. I do not know what it was.

The first shot was clean. The rifle jammed on the second.

My name was Vasily. I had been a factory worker before the war and a soldier in it and something else in the last months that I do not have a word for. By the end I was none of those.

I did not have time to clear it. I finished with the stock of it, which is not what a rifle is made for but which it can be made to do if you are determined about it. This took longer than it should have. I did not hear myself do it. The shot in an enclosed space had taken most of the sound.

My hands were wrong afterward. Not injured. The hands of a man who has just done something with his hands that his hands were not designed to do.

The ringing stayed. I carried it out of the hall and across the rubble and I was still carrying it when the round came. The last thing I heard clearly was the shot in the machine hall. Everything after that was sound moving through the ringing.

Afterward the weight of the rifle felt different in my hands. Not heavier. Just different. I carried it for three more months and the difference never went away. I have not thought about why since then. I am thinking about it now.

The Germans were not monsters. This is the thing I had to understand and did understand. They were men who were cold and frightened and doing what they had been told was necessary, the same as us. They died the same way we died.

Their faces at the end were the same faces. A dying man's face is a dying man's face regardless of which side of a ruin he is dying on, and I saw enough of them to know this and knowing it did not help and nothing helped and the city burned and we fought in it.

I died in January when the temperature was thirty below and I had not been warm for three months. I died from a wound that would have been treatable in any other circumstance and was not treatable in this one because there was nothing to treat it with and nowhere to treat it and no one available to do the treating.

I lay in the rubble of what had been an apartment building. I knew this building. I had lived two streets from it for eleven years. I knew which floor this room was on from the angle of the gap in what had been the ceiling.

The grey sky through the gap was the same grey it had been since October. The particular grey of a Stalingrad winter that had nothing in it, no differentiation, no weather, just the grey that was the sky here in this season.

I was cold in a way that I had stopped registering as cold because I had not been warm since the first week of November. This was different. This was the cold arriving in specific places, which meant the wound did what wounds of this kind did in conditions of this kind.

I had a rifle. The stock of it was against my cheek. The metal of it was cold the way all metal was cold here. I had been holding this rifle for three months and it had become the thing you hold when you have nothing else to hold.

The rubble smelled of old plaster and something burnt and underneath both of those, the smell of the city itself, the smell of a city in winter that is being systematically destroyed, brick dust and frozen ground and something I had no name for that was the smell of a place ending.

I thought about the tractor factory. Before the war, the smell of machine oil and heated metal. The sound of the floor when the production lines were running at full capacity, a sound you felt in your chest more than you heard it with your ears.

The gap in the ceiling showed me a rectangle of grey sky. I watched it for whatever time was left. The grey did not change. It did not need to change.

The wound was on my left side. I had put down the rifle for a moment, there had been a reason, I no longer remembered the reason, and they came through the wall then. A blade. From below and to the left, entering between the ribs.

I felt it enter. Not pain, not at the moment of entry, from the outside you expect pain but from the inside it is pressure first, the sensation of something being pushed through space that cannot quite accommodate the pushing. The pain came after, when the body had a moment to understand.

I hit the German with the stock of the rifle. Reflex. He went back through the gap in the wall. I do not know what happened to him.

I was on the floor of what had been an apartment building on Pavlov's Square. I had lived two streets from here for eleven years. I knew this building.

The blood moved fast through the space between the ribs. I pressed my hand to it. The hand accomplished less than hands are supposed to accomplish in this situation.

The cold arrived through the wound. January, thirty below, and the wound opened a channel between the outside and the inside that my body had not had before. The cold moved in through this channel with the same indifference the cold had brought to everything in Stalingrad since October.

I was on my back now. I watched the grey rectangle of sky through the gap in what had been the ceiling. I had been looking at this sky since October.

I felt myself separating. I was in the body, aware of the floor, the cold, the blood slowing, and I was also above it, looking down at a soldier in a ruined apartment building.

The grey did not change.

I watched my body from above until it stopped.

The tractor factory had made good tanks. I had seen them come off the floor and go directly into the battle and I had thought: this is what we are now, a city that makes the machines that are destroying the city. I had thought this without feeling much about it because there was not much capacity left for feeling things about the large shapes of what was happening. There was only the next thing in front of you.

The gap in the ceiling showed me the grey rectangle I had been watching.

The grey did not change. It did not need to change. It had been that grey since October and it was still that grey and it would be that grey after.

I watched it for whatever time was left.

Then I did not watch it.

* * *

Stalingrad in January does not give its dead up easily. The cold that kept me was the cold of a city that had been systematically unmade, not winter cold but the cold of burst pipes and blown-out walls and the absence of warmth that tens of thousands of people had put into these buildings across decades of living in them. That warmth was gone. What the cold found in its place it froze solid and held.

I was in the rubble of an apartment building on Pavlov's Square. I knew this building. I had lived two streets away for eleven years. I knew what it had been, four families on each floor, a woman on the second floor who grew herbs in her window, a man on the ground floor who repaired clocks.

The battle had taken the building apart floor by floor and the rubble had come down on me and I was in it, in the cold, in the close dark of concrete and brick that did not decay and did not release and held what it held.

Around me in the rubble were others. Not in the ground, in the building. Soldiers from both sides who had died in the same rooms, in the same stairwells, sometimes within feet of each other. The cold had kept them as it had kept me. I could feel them the way I could feel the walls and the beams, as facts of the space I was in. Many of them.

This was the thing about Stalingrad that people who were not there did not understand: it was not a battle, it was a city, and the city was full of buildings, and each building had its dead, and I was one of the dead in this building.

I was aware of the others the way you are aware of people in a room in the dark, by their position, their weight, their presence. Many rooms and many buildings, and the scale of it was something I could not hold as a thought.

The thaw came in spring. The freeze had suspended everything; the thaw resumed everything at once, and the resumption was rapid and total and I was present for every stage of it.

What the cold had held the warmth released. The smell of it carried across the rubble fields in the first warm days. I was part of that smell. I was part of what the thaw released into the air of a city that had, by then, no civilians left to breathe it, only soldiers and the dead, and then mostly the dead.

The city was rebuilt over me. Not around me, over me. They graded and compacted the rubble and built on it, and the weight of the new city pressed down through the decades the way the cold had pressed in. Different weight. Heavier.

The clock repairman's building became something else and I was in the foundation of it, in the material of what it was built on, and I felt the people who lived in it above me going about their ordinary lives in a city that had been built on top of what had happened here, which is what cities do, which is the only thing cities can do.

Decades.

* * *

Grim came to Stalingrad on a day in summer when the city was warm and full of people going about the ordinary business of living, and he stood in the street above where the apartment building had been and opened the scroll.

He was not alone.

Five of them working the city that day. Stalingrad had given its dead up slowly across the decades of reconstruction, and the assessments had accumulated in the same way the rubble had accumulated, in layers, the most recent on top, the oldest deepest, and what the city had been doing for thirty years, returning its dead to the world, had been generating work that Grim and his colleagues had been managing in sections, returning when the city gave up another layer.

He knew all five of the Grims working with him that day. Had worked with most of them before, at other sites, in other years. The one he did not know well was the one working the section of the old factory district, a Grim whose name Grim did not know because they had only worked together twice before and there had been no occasion for names.

The factory Grim had been working quietly all morning. His scroll open, his assessments running. Normal.

Then he stopped.

Not paused between assessments. Stopped the way a machine stops when something has gone wrong inside it, a cessation that was different in quality from a pause. He stood in the middle of the factory district with his scroll open and did not move.

He finished his current assessment and crossed to the factory district.

The factory Grim was still standing in the same position. Scroll open. Not reading it. His eyes, if you could call them eyes, focused on something that was not the street in front of him.

"Are you all right?" Grim said.

The factory Grim turned. His face was wrong. Grim had seen that look in souls, the ones who arrived already broken. He had not seen it in a Grim.

"I cannot," the factory Grim said. His voice was wrong. Thin. "I cannot do this assessment."

"Which one?"

"Any of them." He looked at the scroll. Then at the street. Then at Grim. "Do you know what is in this ground? Do you understand what they did to each other here? Both sides. In this factory. In this street. Do you know what they did?"

"Yes," Grim said.

"And you can still," He stopped. Looked at the scroll again. "I have been doing this for, I do not know how long I have been doing this. Long enough that I have stopped counting. And I can no longer, I look at this ground and I look at what is in it and I cannot..."

The scroll hung open in his hands, unused.

He had not seen it reach this point before.

"Go," Grim said. "I will finish this section."

"You cannot finish your section and mine both."

"I will manage."

The factory Grim looked at him. Something in the look that Grim could not read clearly, something between gratitude and shame and a third thing that had no name.

"Do not report this," he said.

Grim looked at him.

"Please."

The word sat between them in the summer air of Stalingrad, in the rebuilt street, in the warm day that had no relationship to the winter that had happened here.

"Go," Grim said again.

The factory Grim went. Grim watched him go and then turned back to the work and finished the factory district's assessments on top of his own section, working faster than he usually worked, the scroll open continuously, the wheel spinning, the assessments running and running.

He made his report at the end of the day. His section. His assessments. His results. Complete and accurate.

The factory district Grim went unmentioned. That section, unmentioned. The conversation in the street, unmentioned.

Why he had done it, unexamined.

Three weeks later he checked on the factory district Grim through the collegial channels that Grims used to communicate across territories. The designation that came back was the same designation he had found in Maren's record. Not a reassignment. Not a forwarding. Just the territory handed to someone else, the records closed, the Grim in question simply absent from everything that should have shown him present.

Gone.

He stood with this for a long time.

He stood with it longer.

Two of them. Maren. The factory Grim. Both absent in a way that left no record, no trace, no word that covered it. Grims did not die. And yet.

He thought about what he had not reported. What the system did not know he had done. What the system did not know he did, in the churchyard and on the Paris street and in the Timbuktu morning and at the Western Front, the watching and the following, the pushing at the door.

He had been doing what both of them had done, looking too closely, pushing at the door, following the sendings. He had been doing it more carefully, more slowly, with more awareness of what he did. But he had been doing it.

Whatever had taken them had not taken him yet.

He needed to move faster than it found out.

The Unnamed

In the famine year, Grim arrived at the grave and opened the scroll and the scroll wrote what it could. A woman. Approximately thirty. The physical facts of a life: calluses on both hands, a healed fracture in the left wrist, signs of multiple pregnancies. The moral ledger was not empty but it was thin, as ledgers are when circumstances contract the available choices to almost nothing.

She had done what she could do with what she had, in a year when what she had kept shrinking.

He found her waiting without impatience. Whatever she had expected from dying, it had been worse than this.

He ran the assessment. The wheel turned and landed where it landed. He made his note. He sent her on.

He stood over the grave in the famine year for a moment. The village above was quiet in the way that villages are quiet when they have used up their grief for the season and need to wait before they can grieve again.

He did not know her name. The scroll had not produced one. He made a second notation, small, in the administrative margin: unnamed.

The Stake

I rode through it without speaking for a long time.

The forest of stakes ran for three miles along the road north of Târgovişte, two rows of them, each stake the correct thickness. I had specified the thickness myself, because the thickness determined the duration, and the duration was the point. The Ottoman advance guard had found it two days ago. They had sent word back to Mehmed's army. The army had stopped.

The army was not going to continue.

My soldier. Andrei, who had been with me twelve years and who had learned in those twelve years not to speak unless spoken to during rides like this one, kept my horse three lengths back and said nothing.

The bodies were two weeks dead. It was summer. The sounds, if you listened, were the sounds of a summer field given over to the work of summer fields.

I had been on battlefields before. I had learned, early, to register the smell and the sounds and then put them somewhere that was not the front of my mind, because the front of my mind was needed for the assessment.

"The count," I said.

Andrei had been keeping it. "Twenty thousand, plus or minus three hundred. The variance is from the ones still standing that we cannot get close enough to."

"Still standing."

"Some of them, yes."

I looked down the row. The mathematics of it were clear. Mehmed had brought ninety thousand soldiers across the Danube. Ninety thousand soldiers who had stopped at the edge of this and were now calculating the cost of continuing against a man who was capable of this and had done it and would do it again.

They were going home.

My name was Vlad. I was Prince of Wallachia for the third time, having lost the throne twice to men who thought they wanted it and found the work of keeping it disagreeable. The work of keeping it was not disagreeable to me. The work of keeping it was the work, and the work was what I had, and I had learned to do it with the precision of a man who has no tolerance for doing things incorrectly.

"The third row from the left," I said. "Third from the end. That stake is wrong."

Andrei looked. "The angle?"

"Too steep. The angle determines how long..." He stopped. I did not need to explain this to Andrei. "Have it corrected."

"Yes, voivode."

I rode on.

I thought about Mehmed. A competent commander, by the reports. A man who had taken Constantinople, who had built on that and who had, until two days ago, been confident that Wallachia was next. The confidence had been reasonable. I had a smaller army, a smaller treasury, fewer allies. On paper the calculation was clear.

The paper calculation had not included this.

I was not proud of this the way a general is proud of a victory in the field. It was not that. I was satisfied the way a craftsman is satisfied when the work is done correctly, the measurement taken, the material selected, the process executed without error, the result exactly what was required. Wallachia would survive the summer. The boyars who had thought my methods excessive would survive also, protected by the excessiveness they had found objectionable.

I had stopped finding it ironic some years ago.

They reached the end of the row and I turned my horse and looked back the way they had come.

"The one who gave Mehmed the maps," I said.

"Costea."

"They brought him in this morning."

"Yes, voivode."

I looked down the row for a moment. "I will speak to me this afternoon."

* * *

Costea had been a boyar for twenty years. I had served three princes before Vlad and had, by the evidence, decided that serving the current prince was less advantageous than helping the prince's enemy, and had communicated this decision through the

248

mechanism of providing Mehmed's generals with detailed maps of the mountain passes.

I was in the lower hall, which was appropriate for what it communicated about my current standing. I stood when Vlad entered, which was also appropriate, and said nothing, which showed either sense or terror. Both were acceptable.

"The maps," Vlad said.

"Voivode, I..."

"The maps. You drew them yourself?"

"I... yes."

"Good work. The detail on the Prahova pass was accurate. I used those maps myself for the winter campaign."

Costea did not know what to do with this. My face did the thing faces do when the expected conversation fails to arrive and the unexpected one begins in its place.

"I want you to understand something," Vlad said. I sat, which I did not usually do in these conversations, because sitting suggested a duration and I wanted Costea to sit also, which the man did, carefully, in the way of a person lowering themselves onto something whose stability they doubt. "The maps caused the deaths of sixty-three of my soldiers. Men who knew the passes and were betrayed — the enemy knew them too."

"Voivode, I had no choice..."

"You had the same choices I have. All of us have the same choices. What is different is what we choose." Vlad looked at me. "You chose to give information about those passes to an army that intended to take this country. Sixty-three men died because of that choice. Not because of me. Because of you."

Costea was still.

"The work this afternoon will be done correctly," Vlad said. "I want you to know that I am careful about this. The thickness of the stake, the angle. It is not cruelty. Cruelty is imprecise. This is a calculation about what deters future choices by people who have not yet made them. Do you understand the distinction?"

"Please," Costea said.

Vlad looked at me for a moment. It moved me, in its way. I had learned, across many years of this work, that being unmoved was a position that required maintenance and I maintained it with the same attention I gave to everything else. The maintenance was not visible. I had made sure it was not visible.

"Sixty-three," I said. "That is the number."

I left.

The calculation was done the way I had said, carefully, correctly, each specification exact. It took the afternoon and into the evening. I did not watch. I had seen the process many times. I knew what it produced. I used the afternoon to write to the Hungarian king about the terms of the continued alliance, which required careful language, and to review the supply reports from the garrison at Giurgiu, which required less careful language but more arithmetic.

When it was done I went back to the maps.

I died fourteen years later.

It was winter. It was always winter when these things happened, in my experience, or it felt like winter, the cold of the ground coming up through the boots, the cold of a December in Wallachia that had no tolerance for abstraction.

I had been in ambush before. I had set ambush before. I knew the shape of it: the wrong silence, the direction of sound that arrives before its source, the body registering the error before the mind has named it. I had survived more of them than a man in my position had any right to survive.

I did not survive this one.

The blade took me across the back of the neck. I had thought, in the abstract, about how a man dies in ambush. I had arranged enough of them, and the abstract had not included this: the immediate cessation of the lower body, the sudden unreliability of everything below the neck.

I went down.

The frozen ground of the December field came up hard against my face. The cold of it was total and immediate. The same cold I had walked soldiers through on the road north of Târgoviște. The same cold the twenty thousand had been in.

I was on my face and I could not move and the blood moved very fast. Warm against the cold of the ground, steaming slightly in the December air, moving into the frozen earth.

A boot came down on my back. Checking. I did not respond. I had nothing left to respond with.

The blade came again. The throat. I felt it enter, not pain, by then I was past the threshold where pain registered cleanly, but the completion of the thing, the closing of the system.

The blood moved faster. I felt it leave.

Then I was above it. Two feet above the body of the Prince of Wallachia face-down in the December mud of a country he had held by methods that had kept it alive.

The army would have to continue without me.

The angle of the stakes on the third row from the left, third from the end, was still wrong. I had specified it correctly and they had done it wrong and now I would not be able to correct it.

I had never in my life been on my back in a field I had not chosen. I noted the position. I had always noted positions.

The sky above me was the sky of a December morning, flat and colorless, the sky of a season that had made its position clear.

I thought about the stakes. The angle of them. Whether the angle I had specified was still being maintained, whether the men I had trained were maintaining it, whether the work continued to be done correctly in my absence.

It would have to continue without me now.

The cold of the ground. The December sky. The calculations still running.

What was certain was the decapitation.

* * *

The head went to Constantinople on a spike.

The consciousness splits.

He had not known this was possible. He had sent many heads to many capitals and had understood this as a practical communication, a message that required no translation, that crossed language barriers and political borders, that said exactly one thing with absolute clarity. He had not thought about what the sending was from the inside.

The head went to Constantinople on a spike. The body went into the ground at Snagov, the island monastery in the lake, where the monks received it with the mixture of devotion and apprehension that had characterized their relationship to him in life.

He was aware of both.

Not one and then the other. Both at once, in the way that a man is aware of both hands without having to choose between them, except that the hands were forty miles apart and one was in a wooden box on a spike in a foreign city and the other was in the cold water-soil of a monastery island and they were doing completely different things.

The head desiccated in the Balkan summer. The spike kept the birds from completing their work quickly, which meant the process was slower and he was present for the slowness. The heat extracted. He felt it extracting, the way of the summer air that left certain things and took others and was not gradual but rhythmic, the days pulling and the nights contracting.

At the same time, forty miles north, the island monastery's soil worked in its own way. The lake water came up through the ground, cold even in summer, and the cold slowed what the heat in Constantinople did quickly. Two rates. Two processes. Both present.

He had calculated, in life, many things at once. Supply and terrain and intelligence reports and political factors and the timing of actions across geographies. The mind could hold multiple calculations. This was different. This was not calculation but presence, being present in two places at once, aware in two processes at once, neither of them able to see the other, each of them complete in their own geography.

He thought about the split. He had done this. In the opposite direction, to others. He understood now, from the inside, that the calculation had been about the message and not about the experience, which was the case with most calculations about actions done to other people. You calculated the effect. You could not calculate the experience.

He did not know what to do with this understanding. He was in two places and he could not do anything with anything, the common condition of the dead, and he held the understanding the way he held everything he could not act on, carefully, noting it, keeping it present.

The head was done within a year. The body, in the cold wet island soil, took longer. The lake water that moved through the monastery ground was slow to work, the organic processes slowed by the cold, the dissolution more gradual than the extraction in the south had been.

By the time the body was done the head had long been ash, scattered by the weather of three Balkan winters, distributed into the air over Constantinople in a city that had other things to think about.

The consciousness, which had been in two places, was now in none.

And then it was somewhere.

* * *

The cold came to Snagov island in the early morning, when the fog sat on the lake and the monks were at their first prayers and the water was perfectly still.

Grim stood on the shore and the fog held where it was, neither advancing nor retreating, a grey wall at the edge of the visible world.

He opened the scroll.

It was a long scroll and an unusual one. He had expected the length, a prince's ledger across a long reign would not be short. He had not expected what the unusual parts contained.

The scroll had two columns.

He had not seen this before. He had seen ledgers that were difficult to weigh, moral calculations that resisted the wheel's categories. He had not seen a scroll that presented its contents in a structure that said, explicitly: these are two different accountings of the same life.

The first column: the forest of stakes. The twenty thousand. Costea and the sixty-three. The mathematics of deterrence and what the mathematics required. The consistency of the method, the same specifications applied to nobleman and peasant alike, which was its own kind of equality and also its own kind of horror. The impalement of men who had harmed no one except through political affiliation. The ones who had begged and the ones who had not and the absence of any record that the begging made a difference.

The second column: Wallachia, which existed. The Ottomans, who had stopped and turned back. The peasants who had kept their land. The monasteries intact. The books that had not been thrown in a river. The calculation that had been correct in its outcome if not in its method, or in its method if not in its morality, and the two things could not be separated because the outcome and the method were the same thing.

Grim read both columns. Then he read them again.

He found Vlad waiting in the fog above the island, not with the patience of the resigned but with the

alertness of a man who has assessed a situation and is
waiting for more information.

"Two locations."

"Yes."

"I was aware of both."

"I know."

"The head and the body are the same scroll."

Grim opened the scroll to the first column. "One
soul. However the body was divided. The scroll is one."

Vlad looked at it. "Two columns."

"Yes."

"Is that usual?"

"No."

A pause. "The wheel."

"Yes."

Grim produced the wheel. He set it turning. It
turned for a very long time, working through a ledger
that was not complicated in the way that Itzli's had
been complicated, or Dawud's, it was not a matter of
categories the wheel had not been built for. The wheel
had been built for exactly this kind of accounting.

It simply had a great deal of accounting to do, and
the accounting ran in two directions, and the directions
were genuinely balanced in a way that left the wheel

working through the problem with the patience of a mechanism that knew how to wait for a stable answer.

When it stopped, it had an answer.

The answer was not clean. It was not uncomplicated. It sat in the middle of the wheel's range in the way that a thing sits in the middle when it has been pulled equally hard from both directions and has held.

Grim looked at where it had stopped. He looked at the two columns.

He made his note.

"Wallachia survived," Vlad said.

"Yes."

"The books were not thrown in the river."

"No."

"I knew what I did," Vlad said. "Most of it, while I was doing it. Some of it I understood later."

Grim looked at him.

"Does that matter?" Vlad said. "Knowing clearly what you are doing. Does that count for something or against."

Grim thought about Amenhotep, who had not known clearly. Who had needed three thousand years of dark to see it plainly. He thought about Dawud, who had known and argued the other way. He thought about Itzli, who had known what he did and had believed it was necessary and had been right about the necessity in a way that the wheel could not cleanly adjudicate.

"It is on the ledger. What it counts is for the wheel to say."

"And the wheel has said."

"Yes."

He sent Vlad on.

He stood on the shore of Snagov island for a moment in the fog. The monks were still at their prayers. The lake was still. The two columns were still in the scroll, which he closed and held for a moment before putting away.

He had been making the handoff for longer than handoff had a name. He had sent men who had done monstrous things and men who had done necessary things and men who had done both and the wheel had always had an answer, always found the place to stop, always given him a notation to make. He had believed in the notation the way he had believed in the receiving.

He stood in the fog.

The Comfort Woman

I will not tell you everything. Not because I cannot but because some things do not belong to anyone except the person they happened to, and I am that person, and I am choosing what to give and what to keep.

My name was Park Soon-yi. I was seventeen years old when they took me and twenty when I died and the three years between those two facts contain things I have decided are mine.

What I will tell you is this.

Not everything. Some of it I am keeping.

I was from a village in the south of Korea, the second daughter of a farmer who grew barley and kept three pigs and was not a bad man, not a good man, simply a man doing what the land required of him.

My mother made kimchi that the neighboring families came to buy. I had an older sister who was already married and a younger brother who was seven years old when I last saw him, standing in the yard watching me go with the stillness of a child who does not yet understand what he is watching.

I thought about my brother across the three years. The weight of him when I had carried him as a baby. The sound he made when he was hungry. The way he looked at things before he touched them, examining first, committing second. A carefulness unusual in a seven year old. I had always thought it meant he would be all right, that he had the quality of mind that would work through whatever the world put in front of him.

I do not know what happened to him. I did not know when I died and I do not know now and this is the thing I carry that has no resolution, the not-knowing of whether he was all right.

The three years I am not telling you about happened. They happened the way things happen when someone with power decides to use it against someone without power, completely and without recourse, with the cruelty of people who have decided that what they are doing is not cruelty because of who they are doing it to.

I survived it the way you survive things, by finding the part of yourself that is smaller than what is happening to you and living in that part, and keeping that part intact no matter what, and knowing that the part is real even when everything being done to you is designed to tell you it is not.

By the time I died I was good at being small. Good at keeping the small part intact. These were the skills the three years had given me and they were real skills and they had kept me alive and I did not consider them gifts.

The fever came on a summer morning. From inside, fever is not hot the way heat is hot. It is a change in the quality of the body itself, the borders of the body becoming uncertain, the sense of where you end and the air begins going soft.

The small part of me that had kept itself separate from what was happening to my body had, for three years, worked continuously to stay separate. Not effort you feel as effort, effort that had become the structure of how I existed. The fever dissolved the requirement for it. Not me. The requirement. I felt it the way you feel a muscle unknot when you had not known it was knotted.

I lay on a mat. Outside, birds. My brother's face came to me, not a vision, just his face as I had last seen it, seven years old, standing in the yard watching me go, watching with the carefulness he had always had. I did not know if he had been all right.

The quiet arrived. I had kept the small part alive for three years against everything that wanted to take it. The quiet was the first thing in three years that wanted nothing.

I was above the mat. Looking down at the woman who had been very good at being small. The birds outside. My brother's face, the last thing I saw from inside the body.

I went with the quiet.

* * *

The warm ground of this country does not wait. The heat and the wet together begin immediately, before the body has finished its final cooling. I feel the beginning.

The bacteria are first. They are already in me, they have always been in me, the organisms the body hosts, the internal ecosystem that has lived alongside me for twenty-three years. When the body stops maintaining the conditions that keep them in their place, they expand. I feel them expand. Moving into spaces they did not occupy before, claiming what the body has stopped defending.

The heat of the ground, not the ambient heat of summer but the biological heat of the soil itself, the vast warm metabolism of tropical ground, comes from below. I am between two heats: the fever warmth still leaving the body and the ground heat arriving from below.

Then the external organisms. The warm ground of this country has more microbial life than most ground, the climate supports it, the jungle produces it. I feel them finding the surfaces. Working at the barriers the skin maintained and now maintains less well.

I had been small for three years. I had made myself as small as possible. The organisms do not care about this. They find the small part and the large part the same way.

I think about my brother. Seven years old in the yard. The careful face. Whether he was told. Whether he knew what happened. Whether the knowing was worse than not knowing.

The monsoon comes. The water moves through the soil the way it moves through everything here, finding the paths of least resistance, carrying what it can. It carries pieces of me. I am in the water that moves south.

By the second summer I am in more than one place. The country continues above. The summer smell of it, green and wet and alive, the smell of this country in the wet season that I knew every year I was here.

The small part I kept intact for three years is no longer small. The ground has taken it into everything else. The small part and the large part are in the same soil, in the same water, in the same roots. The ground does not distinguish between them.

* * *

Grim came in the summer, when the air smelled of green and wet and the birds were loud in the trees above the ground where they had put her, and he opened the scroll.

The scroll wrote briefly. Not much remained to write. Twenty years of life, three of which contained what they contained, and a death that came quickly. The assessment of what she had done and not done and been and not been, conducted by the machinery with its usual precision, produced the result the machinery produced, a number, a designation, a routing.

Grim read it.

Then he put the scroll down.

Not closed. Down. Set aside on the air the way you set something aside when you need your hands free for something else, except he did not need his hands free. He simply could not hold the scroll and also be present in this moment and he chose presence over procedure.

He found her waiting with the quality of someone who had learned to be still and small in an enormous and bad situation, and who had kept something intact through all of it, and who was now outside the situation and did not yet know how to be larger again.

No wheel.

No questions about the divine or her part in the cycles or any of the other questions the procedure required. The procedure felt, in this moment, like the wrong instrument for what was in front of him. Like using a measuring stick on something that had no length.

"Soon-yi," he said.

She looked at him. The look of someone who had learned to read intentions quickly and accurately because reading intentions quickly and accurately had been a survival skill.

He did not move immediately to the assessment.

"It is finished," he said. "All of it. Everything that happened. It is finished now and none of it can reach you anymore."

She was quiet for a moment.

"My brother," she said. "The youngest one. He was seven."

"I know," Grim said.

"Is he all right?"

Grim looked at the warm air and the green smell of the country in summer and thought about what he knew and what he did not know and what it would mean to say either.

"I don't know," he said. "I haven't been there."

He started to ask about the small part — what it was, exactly, how she had kept it — and stopped. He didn't know why he'd started. He didn't usually ask things like that.

She accepted this the way she had learned to accept the things she could not change, not with peace, not with resignation, but with the stillness of someone who has decided to keep going regardless.

"You go back," Grim said. "You try again. A different life. A different body. None of this with you."

"None of it?"

"None of it."

She thought about this.

"The small part," she said. "The part I kept. Does that go back too?"

Grim looked at her. The scroll was still set aside on the air. The wheel was still in his robe. The procedure was still waiting.

"Yes," he said. "That goes back. That is the part that matters."

He sent her on.

He watched where the sending went. The same direction. The same vast indifferent drawing-in on the other side of the door, pulling her toward it the way it pulled everything, without knowing she was there, without knowing what she had kept intact across three years of someone trying to destroy it.

He stood in the summer air for a long time after.

The scroll was still beside him. He picked it up. He made his notes. He recorded the assessment in the language the machinery required, the numbers and designations and routings, the formal account of a life reduced to its processable elements.

He did not record what she had said about the small part. He did not record what he had said back. Those were not things the machinery needed.

He closed the scroll.

The machinery did not know what it had just taken.

The Fast One

Thirty-seven seconds from the shot to the end of awareness. I had timed it myself, involuntarily, my mind counting in the way of a mind that has been given nothing else to do.

My name was something. The scroll had it. The scroll had everything: seventeen years, a city, a mother who had looked for me, a set of beliefs that had brought me to a corner at a particular hour. The scroll had the corner also.

No grave. They had taken the body somewhere, the men with the authority to take bodies. Grim waited until the city's ordinary processes of disposal had completed, standing in a parking structure that had been built on the site where the corner used to be, and then I opened the scroll in the fluorescent light and the temperature in the structure dropped and three cars on the second level experienced what their diagnostic systems would later describe as an unexplained battery drain.

I ran the assessment. Seventeen years. The wheel barely needed to turn.

I did not say anything. Nothing I could have said would have reached across what separated them, which was not distance but the shock of an ending that had arrived forty years too early.

I sent the boy on.

The fluorescent lights returned to their ordinary behavior. I left the parking structure.

The Collector

The first one I found in 1961 in a field outside a small town in Ohio. The field had been fallow for two seasons and the ground had done most of its work by the time I arrived. What remained was partial, scattered, the work of weather and animals and time, and I stood over it in the grey Ohio autumn and opened the scroll and read what it told me and sent her on and watched where the sending went and moved to the next assignment.

I did not know yet that she was the first.

The second was in 1963, in Pennsylvania. The third in 1964, also Pennsylvania, a different county. The fourth in 1965, in New York state, in the woods behind a truck stop on a road that did not see much traffic.

By the fourth I had begun to notice the similarity between them, not in the women themselves, who were different ages and circumstances and had lived different lives that the scroll recorded with its usual precision, but in the character of what had been done to them. The same signature. The same methodology.

By the tenth I understood. By around the fifteenth I wished I had not. By the twentieth I knew the shape of it completely, the geography of it, the timeline, the expanding radius as he grew more confident, the selections he made — not random. They had a logic that was the most disturbing thing about the whole pattern, that it had a logic, that someone had thought this through.

I collected them across twenty-six years. Two hundred and sixty-eight women across fourteen states, the youngest nineteen, the oldest fifty-three, and each one of them had a life that the scroll recorded completely and a death that the scroll recorded with the same precision and a passage through the assessment that I conducted with the full attention the procedure required, and I sent each one on and watched where the sending went and stood with what I watched and moved to the next.

I knew him long before I found him. I knew the shape of his mind from the pattern of what he had done the way you know the shape of an animal from its tracks. He was methodical. He was patient. He was intelligent in the way some people are, very good at one thing, and that one thing was this.

I watched him for two years before I made my decision.

He lived in a house in a suburb of a medium-sized city in the midwest. He had a job that required him to travel, which explained the geography. He had a family, a wife, two children, a dog, a house with a lawn that he mowed on Saturdays. He went to church. He coached his son's baseball team.

He was, by every available measure, a man living an ordinary life, and the ordinary life was real, it was not a performance, he inhabited it fully, and this was the thing I found most difficult to hold, not the twenty-six years of what he had done but the complete and genuine ordinariness of what he was in between.

He came home from a work trip on a Tuesday evening in October 1987. He pulled into the driveway.

He got out of the car. He stood in the driveway for a moment in the cool October air, looking at his house with the lights on inside, his family moving behind the windows.

I stood in the driveway.

He did not see me. Nobody saw me unless I permitted it, and I had not decided yet whether to permit it. I stood three feet from him and watched him look at his house and watched him pick up his bag and walk toward the front door and thought about two hundred and sixty-eight women across twenty-six years and what the scroll had recorded about each of them.

I made my decision.

What happened next was not something I had done before. It was not something Grims did. No procedure for it, no section of the machinery that covered it, no precedent in any record I had access to. I reached into the mechanism of the man's body, the heart, which was where the mechanism was most accessible, and applied the force I understood would stop it.

The mechanism pushed back. I had assessed billions of bodies after they had stopped. I had never tried to make one stop. The difference was the difference between reading a map and walking the ground. The heart was still working, sixty-seven years of working, sixty-seven years of the same contraction and release, and it did not know what I asked of it.

I held the point. It took longer than I had expected.

Then it stopped.

He stopped mid-stride on the path to his front door. He stood for a moment with his bag in his hand and his house in front of him and his family behind the lit windows. Then he fell.

The assessment that followed was the coldest I had conducted.

Nothing happened. The suburb stayed exactly as it was. October air at its October temperature. Leaves moving normally. The neighbor's dog barking down the block. No stillness. No cold beyond the season. No birds stopping or frost forming or dust settling in wrong patterns. I brought nothing to this assessment except procedure, and the world, reading me with unusual accuracy, responded in kind.

Raymond waited with the surprise of a man who did not expect to be where he was. I did not bring curiosity. I did not bring the attention I had brought to the stone cutter and the astronomer and the comfort woman. I brought procedure. Exactly procedure. Nothing more.

The scroll wrote for a long time.

The wheel turned.

I looked at where it stopped.

Then I did something I had not done before. I reached into the machinery not to follow a soul after the handoff but to place one deliberately, to route it not to whatever the mechanism would have chosen but to a chosen destination at a chosen time.

I placed Raymond in Auschwitz. 1942. As a prisoner.

The machinery accepted this without resistance. No safeguard against it. No protocol requiring the placement to be reviewed or approved. The machinery had been built on the assumption that Grims would route souls where the wheel indicated, and no one had ever imagined that a Grim might reach in and choose.

I closed the scroll.

I stood in the suburb in October, the ordinary street, the ordinary houses, the lights in the windows of his house where his family did not yet know what had happened on the path to the front door.

I did not examine what I had done. I had done two things outside the machinery's design in the space of ten minutes and I needed to be further from them before I could look at them clearly.

The machinery had not noticed. Neither the stopping nor the placing. The assessment recorded and processed and moved on as if nothing unusual had occurred.

The Scientist

The test was in the Kazakh steppe and I traveled there with forty-three other scientists and stood at the required distance and watched the required thing happen.

The man beside me was named Petrov. He was a theoretician, the kind who calculated and did not build, and he had been standing next to my at every major stage of the project for six years and I had never once seen his hands shake. They were shaking now.

"It works," he said.

"Yes," I said.

"It works exactly as calculated."

"Yes."

He put his hands in his pockets. He looked at where the cloud was still forming, still rising, still taking the shape that no cloud in the history of clouds had taken before they had made it take that shape.

"Vera," he said. "What have we done."

It was not a question. I recognized this and did not answer it. No answer would help either of them. The calculation had been correct. The thing had happened. These were facts. What they amounted to was a different category of problem and I had no instrument for it, which did not mean the problem was not there.

"We go back," I said. "There is still the yield efficiency question."

Petrov looked at me. "You are going to work."

"Yes," I said.

I felt the required awe and the required horror in exactly the proportions I had expected, which was not a comfort. Knowing in advance how you will feel about something does not make the feeling smaller.

I had known I would feel this and had worked anyway and would go back and work anyway again. The alternative was someone else doing it worse. I had told myself this and believed it and would keep believing it and die not having fully resolved the question.

Vera. Born in St. Petersburg in 1901. Good at mathematics before I understood what mathematics was for, which is the natural condition of children who are good at things, the capacity arriving before the understanding of its application, and by the time you understand the application you are already too far in to stop.

The work was weapons work. The physics I understood completely. The mathematics I had developed some of myself. What I could not determine, even now, was whether the system of deterrence I had contributed to had reduced or increased the probability of the thing being used.

I worked on this question in 1953, at three in the morning, at my desk, when my heart stopped.

The stopping was not painful. This surprised my, in the fraction of a moment available for surprise. I had expected pain. I had modeled it as pain. The heart muscle seizing, the chest, the arm. What arrived instead was simply a wrongness, the specific wrongness of a system encountering an input it was not designed to handle.

I was at my desk. The calculation was in front of my, the notation in my own hand, the pencil still in my fingers. The lamp on the desk. The smell of the lamp and the smell of the paper and the smell of the cold Moscow air that came under the door from the corridor.

My head went down. Not slowly. The way a system fails when the signal stops: immediately, without intermediary steps, without the process of deciding to fall.

The paper was against my face. I could feel the texture of it, the slight roughness of the calculation paper she preferred, the paper I had been using for thirty years, that I had used in Leningrad before the war and in the postwar institutes and here, always this paper, always this texture.

The lamp was still on. The light of it against the edge of the paper. The light of it was orange, the orange of a lamp in a cold room, warm-colored and giving nothing warm.

The calculation was unfinished. I had always been aware of unfinished calculations. This one I could not finish. I held this fact for the remainder of the time available.

I was above the desk. Looking down at the physicist with her face against the unfinished calculation, the lamp still on, the pencil in her fingers.

Alexei was in the next office, still working, not yet knowing.

The door was closed.

The calculation was on the paper in front of my, unfinished. In the office next door, a graduate student named Alexei who kept odd hours like I did worked on a problem of his own, and heard a sound he could not immediately identify, a soft sound, and did not think about it for several minutes, and then knocked on my door and got no answer, and opened it and found my.

He stood in the doorway for a moment, looking at the woman who had been his most exacting and most important teacher, who had demanded precision from him since the day he arrived and had received it and given him hers in return, who was now sitting in exactly the same position I had been sitting in the last time he had looked through the glass at my, except differently still. He understood the difference.

He went to call someone. The calculation was still on the desk.

I had not expected to be here. I had concluded, carefully and with the precision I brought to everything, that nothing came after. The conclusion had been wrong, which was also data.

* * *

The January frozen ground holds me the way January frozen ground holds everything: completely, without process, in stasis. The organisms that work other grounds do not work frozen ground. The clay holds me as I am.

I feel the holding. The cold pressing in from all sides, the clay taking the shape of what it has received and maintaining it. The temperature drops below what the biology of decomposition requires, and the biology waits.

March comes. The spring thaw working down through the Moscow clay. I feel it approaching from above, a gradual softening, a degree by degree increase in what the clay is willing to do. When the thaw reaches me it does not arrive gently. It arrives and the clay resumes.

The organisms come with the thaw. Moscow cemetery organisms, adapted to long winters and brief working seasons. They are efficient with their time. I feel each one. Where it works. What it finds. What it takes.

My hands go first, the hands that held the pencil, worked the calculations, demanded precision from students for thirty years. I feel the flesh pulling back from the bones, the sensation of what has held its shape giving up the holding.

Alexei had taken the unfinished calculation from my desk. I had known he would, he was precise, he understood what was on the desk, he had the training. He completed it. He received the credit. I am in the Moscow clay while he receives the credit and this is correct. He did the work.

The Moscow clay is cold and thorough. It takes its time. The clay has received the architects of the Soviet Union, the writers who survived the purges, the soldiers who did not. It receives them all with the same thoroughness.

By the time the clay has finished with what I was, the institution has changed beyond what I would recognize. The world has changed beyond what I would recognize. The physics has advanced. Someone else has asked the question I asked.

They used Alexei's calculation for purposes I knew they would use it for. I chose this. I chose it thirty years and ten warheads and a thousand megaton-miles of it. I want to say the clay does not resolve this. I don't know if that's true. Maybe the clay does. I won't be here to tell you.

* * *

Moscow in 1953 still had wolves at the edge of it. Not many, the war had reduced them as it had reduced everything, but some, in the birch forest west of the Vorobyovy Gory, where the cemetery where they buried me was near enough to the forest that in hard winters the wolves came down into the cleared ground looking for what the cleared ground had.

They found me in the first February.

The ground was frozen solid, which should have protected me, but the grave was not deep enough and the freeze had cracked the surface above me and the wolves were efficient animals who knew how to use a crack. They worked at the frozen ground with the patient industry of things that were cold and hungry, and they got through, and they took what they could reach, which was not much that first winter but enough.

I had spent my career calculating yields. Forces and masses and the transfer of energy between systems. I could not stop doing this now. I calculated what they had taken and what they had left and where they had gone with what they took, northeast, into the birch forest, I could feel it, could feel what had been me carried away from the cemetery in a direction I had spent my whole life walking past without noticing.

I was in the birch forest. I was also still in the cemetery. I was in both places and in neither place entirely, and the mathematics of it was precise and the mathematics of it was nothing I had ever written an equation for.

A second winter. They came back. This time they brought the pack, not just a scout. I felt each of them separately, the weight, the pressure of paws on frozen ground, the methodical reopening of what the summer had partially closed. They were not cruel.

They were animals doing what animals do in a cold winter in a city that had not yet fully recovered from a war. The physicist in me understood this completely. The rest of me was present for every moment of it and could not apply the understanding to what the understanding was about.

What they left the spring took. Moscow ground in spring is thorough and the city's infrastructure, the pipes, the cables, had changed the soil's drainage in ways that accelerated what should have taken years. The mathematician in me noted the variables. The data was precise and continuous and I could not stop receiving it and it did not help.

I thought about the unfinished calculation. I thought about whether the person who found it on my desk would understand where I had been going with it. I thought it was probably not a person but a committee, and committees do not understand where individual people are going with things, and the calculation would be finished differently than I had intended, and the result would be approximately correct and precisely wrong, which is the natural condition of calculations finished by committees.

I thought about the cat.

* * *

Grim came in the spring, when the Moscow earth had decided it was done with what it held, and stood over the grave and opened the scroll.

The light around him bent.

Not dramatically. A slight prismatic quality to the air in the immediate vicinity of where he stood, as if the photons moving through that space had become uncertain of their trajectories. It happened when he encountered something his attention found extraordinary. The scroll earned it.

The mathematics in it. The quality of the mind that had produced the mathematics. The way the work and the doubt about the work had existed side by side in the same person for thirty years without either one destroying the other.

He read it twice.

He found her waiting with the quality of someone who has just set down a problem and is not yet certain whether the setting-down is temporary or permanent.

"The calculation on your desk. Where were you going with it?"

Vera looked at him with the assessment of someone who has spent a professional lifetime evaluating whether the person in front of her understood what she talked about.

"You can read it?"

"The scroll records everything."

"Including the mathematics?"

She absorbed this.

"I tried to determine whether the next stage was necessary," she said. "The physics suggested it was not. The military requirement said it was. I was attempting to find a mathematical basis for the physics position that would be legible to the people who only understood the military position."

"Did you find it?"

"I was in the middle of finding it when my heart stopped."

Grim made a note. The assessment ran. The wheel turned and he watched it and when it stopped he looked at where it stopped and made another note and the notes he made were the most complex the scroll had produced since Giulia.

"You understood what the work was for," he said.

"Yes."

"And you did it anyway."

"Yes."

"Because someone else would have done it worse."

A pause.

"That is one way to say it," she said. "The more precise way to say it is that I believed the system of deterrence required that both sides have equivalent capability, and that a world in which only one side had this capability was more dangerous than a world in which both sides did, and that therefore my contribution to the side I was on reduced rather than increased the risk of the thing being used. This is either correct reasoning or rationalization and I genuinely do not know which."

Grim made his final notation.

Vera was quiet for a moment. She looked at where the scroll was, the way people looked at documents they had been living alongside for a long time. "Can I ask you something."

"Yes."

"What are you made of?"

The light around him bent slightly more. He was not aware of it happening. He never was.

"I don't know," he said. "I have wondered."

"You've existed for, how long?"

"I don't experience it as a length. I simply exist."

Vera looked at him with the attention of someone who has encountered a measurement problem and is determining the appropriate instrument.

"You process consciousness," she said. "You interact with it, assess it, route it. You must have some sense of what you are in relation to it."

"Something different from it," Grim said. "Something adjacent. I am not a soul. I do not cycle. I do not decay or assess or get sent on."

"But you are aware."

"Yes."

"And you have been aware since before you can remember."

"Yes."

Vera was quiet for a moment, working through something.

"Then you are made of the same thing consciousness is made of." "Or something adjacent to the same thing. The substrate. The dark matter, perhaps, if you take the physicists seriously about what dark matter might be, which most physicists don't

284

because it's too convenient, but the mathematics does not rule it out."

Grim was still.

In the grave around where he stood the thawing Moscow earth had gone slightly wrong, not soft the way spring earth should be soft, but denser, more present, as if the ground itself was paying attention to the conversation happening above it.

"Dark matter."

"The mathematics doesn't rule it out," again. "Consciousness emerging from dark matter. Grims being a different expression of the same substrate. The machinery that processes souls being built from the same material as the souls. It would explain the interaction. Why you can touch what you touch. Why the scroll works the way it works."

She paused.

"It would also explain what you're made of," she said. "If you wanted to know."

Grim looked at the scroll in his hands. He had carried this scroll for longer than he could calculate. He had not thought about what it was made of. He had not thought about what he was made of. It had never been a question that required thinking about.

It was a question now.

He sent her on. He watched where the sending went. The vast indifferent drawing-in on the other side of the door, pulling her toward it without knowing what it pulled. A mind that had spent thirty years holding two incompatible things at once, the work and the doubt about the work, drawn into something that would never know it had contained that.

He stood in the spring Moscow air for a long time after. The light around him continued its slight wrongness, the photons uncertain, the air prismatic where it touched where he stood.

Dark matter. The same material as the souls. The same material as the being. The same material as him. And Maren, who had gone too close to the being and simply ceased, had Maren been absorbed? Or had he become something else, something the same-substrate required in a different configuration?

He set this beside the others that had no answer. He had carried many such things for a long time. The carrying was getting heavier.

Dark matter.

The Minister

Gallipoli, 1915. I was First Lord of the Admiralty. It was my campaign, my conception, my insistence, my conviction that it would work. Two hundred and fifty thousand casualties when it did not work. They held me responsible because I was responsible. I resigned. I spent two years in the wilderness and then came back and spent the rest of my life proving I was more than Gallipoli.

The Bengal famine of 1943. Between two and three million people. I was informed. The reports came and I received them and I gave the answers I gave. All of it is in the record.

I held more than two things at once for most of my life and the holding did not make either of them lighter. I knew what I did and I knew what it cost and I did it anyway.

The thing arrived without announcement while I was sitting at the table. Not pain. I had been prepared for pain. Something closer to a word stopping in the middle of a room, the second half not arriving.

A stroke. I understood this immediately and then I could not say it.

They came, the family, the doctors, Clementine whose face said precisely what she saw. I heard every word. I could not make them understand that I heard every word.

Nine days. From inside, nine days is not nine days. A series of moments without connection. The weight of the bedding. A smell of flowers I could not place. A voice I knew saying my name.

I had expected to go out fighting something. This was not fighting. This was the long withdrawal of the thing that had done the fighting, the intelligence, the will, the appetite for argument, leaving the body while the body continued without it.

I was aware that something left. I was aware, at intervals, of my own departure.

The paintings were downstairs. The good ones. I knew which were good and I had never been modest about knowing.

I left the body on the ninth day. I was above the room. Looking down at the man who had been Prime Minister twice, who had painted five hundred canvases, who had laid bricks on weekends to rest his mind. An old body in a large bed.

The paintings were downstairs. I did not see them again.

The paintings were downstairs. The good ones. I knew which ones were good and I had never been modest about knowing. I did not see them again but they were there.

* * *

They bury me in Bladon churchyard, in the churchyard of St Martin's, with my parents and my brother. I had chosen this. The cold box. The cold ground of Oxfordshire in January.

Earth on the lid. The sound of it. I feel the vibration of each shovelful arriving, the weight of it accumulating. The sound arrives with its meaning already in it: this is the sound of something being completed.

The Midlands clay is cold and heavy and receives me slowly. This is the quality of this clay, it holds. It does not hurry. It makes a thorough account of what it receives and processes it at the pace that Midlands clay has always processed things.

I feel the yew trees finding me. The old yews of Bladon churchyard, three centuries old, their roots deep and patient and thorough. Each root is a distinct pressure, thin, purposeful, arriving at what I was and beginning to take it. I feel where each root goes after it leaves what I was. Up into the tree. Into the dark mass of the yew that I painted in twenty different churchyards without understanding what it did below.

I had painted yew trees for sixty years. I had not known what they were doing in the ground beneath them. Now I know. Now I am in the knowing.

The state funeral had crowds. I understood this would happen, you build a thing of that size, you know its weight when it ends. I feel the vibration of them above me, the distant weight of people moving in procession on streets I know.

The ledger I kept, the accounting of what I had done and what I had failed to do, the two columns running for ninety years without resolution, the clay does not resolve it. The yew roots do not resolve it. The ledger continues running in the clay without finding a bottom line.

My parents are in this ground. My brother is in this ground. I feel the fact of them, not their voices, not their presence with qualities attached, but the fact of them in the same clay. We are in the same church ground. The yews have been in all of us.

Decades. The yews continue. The visitors come less often. The clay continues. The ordinary dead of Woodstock parish continue their ordinary dissolution alongside mine. The clay does not distinguish between the wartime Prime Minister and the parish. This is correct.

* * *

Grim came on a morning in autumn when the yews were doing what yews do in autumn and stood over the grave and opened the scroll.

The scroll produced a long ledger, which he had expected. What he had not expected was the quality of the ledger, not long in the way the previous ledger had been long, not a weight on one side that made the wheel's job clear.

Genuine service against genuine harm. Rhetoric that had saved a civilization against the campaign that had ended in two hundred and fifty thousand casualties and the famine that had killed three million more. The painter of five hundred canvases against the man who had designed Gallipoli and given the answers he gave to the mortality reports.

The wheel had a job to do and Grim let it do its job. It turned for a long time. Not as long as the previous morning. Longer than most.

When it stopped Grim looked at where it had stopped and held the result in his attention for a moment before making his note, which sat in the scroll differently from most notations. Not because the wheel had failed to find an answer. Because the wheel had found the correct answer to a question that had no clean resolution. The machinery working correctly on material the machinery was not built to simplify.

He found Churchill waiting with something past peace and past agitation. He had run out of things to say and was sitting with what remained.

"Bengal."

A long pause.

"Yes."

"The calculation."

"I made the calculation I knew how to make. I am not certain I made it correctly."

"No. Neither am I."

Churchill looked at him with something that might have been surprise. In his experience people who delivered verdicts were certain of them.

"Neither are you."

"The wheel landed where it landed. I made my note. I do not know if the note is correct. The ledger was in tension and the wheel does not explain itself."

Churchill was quiet for a moment.

"That is honest, at least."

"Yes. It is."

He sent Churchill on and watched where the sending went and made one more note in the administrative section, not about the result but about the calculation the wheel had been asked to perform, which he carried alongside the others that had no resolution, set aside, not closed.

Grim closed the scroll and walked.

The Administrator

On the Tuesday morning my wife Margaret brought me a second cup of coffee without being asked. She did this. After forty-two years she knew which things I would not ask for. It was most things.

I read the newspaper. This was what I did with the mornings now. The retired mornings, unstructured, mine in a way no morning had been mine for forty-one years of arriving at a desk at seven forty-five and leaving it at six fifteen. I had been retired for four days.

"The Henderson boy is getting married," Margaret said, from the kitchen.

"Which Henderson."

"The one with the ears."

I nodded at the newspaper. "That's good."

She came through with her own coffee and sat in the chair across from me, and they were quiet together the way they had been quiet together for forty-two years, not the silence of people with nothing to say but the silence of people who have already said the important things and are comfortable with the rest.

"Robert," she said, after a while.

I was still looking at the newspaper.

"Robert," she said again.

I was in the same position I had been in before. I read about the Henderson boy, or I had been. The newspaper was in my hands at the same angle. Something about the angle was wrong.

She set down her coffee. She crossed to me. She put her hand on my shoulder.

I had known her footsteps for forty-two years. I had known the weight of her hand. I felt it.

I had been thinking about a memorandum from 1962. I had processed it. I had learned years later what decision it contributed to. I had put it under cannot change and moved on. I had thought about it sometimes after that.

I thought about it when her hand came down on my shoulder, and then I was not thinking about it or anything else, and her hand was still there.

My name was Robert. I had spent forty-one years processing information for an agency whose full purpose I had been in no position to evaluate. I was good at systems. I understood how information moved through an organization and where it got stopped and how to clear the stoppage without creating three new stoppages, which most people never learned.

I retired on a Friday. A cake. People said accurate and kind things about me. I drove home and my wife had made a special dinner and I went to bed and woke up Saturday morning with nowhere to be for the first time in forty-one years and lay in bed thinking about this and then got up and had breakfast.

I died on the Tuesday.

Margaret had brought me the second cup of coffee. I had taken it. They had been reading in the same room, the way they read in the same room on Sunday mornings, not talking, the newspaper and her book.

The wrongness arrived without announcement. Not pain. Something more like the wrongness of a system processing an input it cannot complete, an operation begun without the resources to finish it. I was a man who processed systems. I recognized this kind of failure.

I was aware of the newspaper in my hands. The Henderson boy's wedding announcement. The paper between my fingers was the same weight it always was, the same texture. I had been reading a newspaper every morning for forty-one years.

The chair. The smell of the coffee, still warm in the cup on the table beside me. The particular smell of the sitting room in the morning, which was the smell of forty-two years of two people living carefully and well.

Margaret's breathing reached me from across the room. I knew the sound of it. I had known it for forty-two years, had slept beside it, had listened to it in the dark when I could not sleep and found it settling.

I tried to say her name. I could not determine if the sound arrived.

Margaret knew my footsteps and the weight of my hand. She was already out of her chair when the newspaper fell. She was beside me before he registered that she moved.

I felt her hand on my shoulder. I had known the weight of it for forty-two years. I felt it.

Then I did not feel anything.

Then I was above the sitting room.

Looking down at the man in the chair, the newspaper fallen, Margaret's hand on his shoulder, the second cup of coffee still warm on the table beside him.

I had known the weight of her hand for forty-two years. From above I watched her put it on the shoulder of the body that did not respond to it.

The systems I had built and maintained for forty-one years continued running. The information continued moving through the organization. The organization continued without needing me to clear the stoppages.

I had built it to run without me. It ran.

* * *

Margaret chose the plot with the established trees. I would have chosen the same. She knew this. She made the decision practically, the way we made all practical decisions, and the November ground of the churchyard received me with the cold patience of November English ground.

The clay presses in from all sides. Cold and wet and very heavy, the specific weight of English November clay that has been receiving its dead since before the church above me had a name. I feel the pressing. The clay taking the shape of what it has received.

My hands go first. The hands that cleared the stoppages. I feel the cold working into the joints, the clay finding the spaces between the bones. The hands that organized forty-one years of files, worked through by the clay one joint at a time.

Margaret visits on Sundays for the first year, then on the anniversaries. I feel her footsteps. I have known her footsteps for forty-two years. From inside the clay I feel them in a different register, not heard but felt, the specific weight of her on the ground above me, recognizable.

The systems continue running. I can feel this, not directly, not through any mechanism that makes sense, but with the certainty of a man who built a thing that works. The information continues moving. The organization continues without knowing I built it.

The trees Margaret chose grow their roots deeper. The roots find me. Each one distinct, the pressure of a root finding what the ground offers and taking it. I am in the trees she chose.

She comes to visit me and she stands above me and she is in the trees above me and the roots beneath me and we are not apart in the way we were apart when I was in the chair and she was in the kitchen bringing coffee.

The clay takes its time. The clay is thorough. Forty-one years of systems maintenance and the clay reduces it to mineral. The mineral feeds the trees. The trees are there when she comes to visit.

* * *

They buried him in the cemetery where his parents were buried. His wife visited every week for the first year. He knew her footsteps. After forty-one years he knew exactly how she walked, the slight hesitation in the right hip she had never acknowledged having, the way she paused at his stone before sitting down on the small bench the groundskeeper allowed families to use. He heard her talking to him sometimes. He could not respond.

She came less often after the second year. The hip was worse. He understood this and felt the lessening and could not tell her he understood it. She died in the spring of the seventh year and they buried her beside him and he felt her arrive in the ground the way you feel a familiar presence enter a room where you have been alone for a long time.

She was smaller than him. She had always been smaller than him. In the ground she was also, it turned out, faster, the November cemetery ground worked through her in perhaps a decade while he was still largely present, the difference in their mass and the difference in how the roots of the old yews had established themselves on each side accounting for the variance.

He felt her going the way he had felt her walking away from the grave in those first years.

Present, then less present, then not.

He could not call after her. He could not tell her that he had noticed, or that he had thought about the 1962 memorandum every day for thirty years, or that he had sat in the cemetery for forty-one years knowing that she came on Tuesdays and wishing he could come too.

Something arrived for her. He felt it, a cold that was different from November cold, a cold that had attention in it. He felt the attention move over her and assess what it found and then he felt her go in a way that was different from the going-that-is-decay. A direction. She went in a direction.

Then the something was gone and the November cemetery was just a November cemetery again and he was alone in the ground with what remained of him, which was less than it had been and more than she had left behind, and the yew roots continued their patient work, and the seasons continued, and the grandchildren came less often, and he processed all of it the way he had processed everything in his life: noted, held, waiting for the meaning to become available.

He waited eleven more years before he was done enough for what came next.

* * *

Grim came on a morning in November. He had been here before, for the wife, seven years prior, a quick clean assessment, nothing complicated. He remembered the November light in this cemetery, the yews at the perimeter, the bench that families were allowed to use. He stood over the grave and the grass around it went flat and stayed flat, pressed to the ground by nothing, holding there with a quality that had nothing to do with wind.

He opened the scroll. He read it quickly. Little in it was unexpected. No great sins, no great acts, the long middle accumulation of a life spent doing competent work in service of an institution that did things Robert had been in no position to fully evaluate. The wheel would stop where it usually stopped for assessments like this.

But he did not immediately move to the wheel.

He stood over the grave in the November morning reading the scroll, and what he read was not the assessment.

He found Robert waiting, the stillness of a man who had spent forty-one years being reliably present at the right place at the right time.

"You processed information for forty-one years."

"I did."

"Do you know what the agency did with it?"

"Some of it. Not all of it. That was the design."

"Did you ever ask?"

Robert thought about this with the careful honesty of a man who had spent his career being precise. He said he had asked what he was permitted to ask. He had not pushed past what he was permitted to ask. He had told himself this was appropriate. He was less certain now.

Grim produced the wheel. Set it spinning. Watched it stop. Made his note.

"You served well within the parameters you were given. You did not ask what lay outside them."

"No." A pause. "Though I did ask once. Early on. I was told the question was outside my clearance level and I accepted that."

Grim looked at him. He had not had that in the scroll.

He sent Robert on. He watched where the sending went. The vast indifferent drawing-in. The direction with nothing at the end of it.

Then he sat down in the November grass and opened the foundational scroll, the oldest document in the machinery, and read it from the beginning.

It took a long time.

At the bottom of the last section, in an ink that was different from the ink that surrounded it, slightly darker, applied at a later date by a different hand, two words.

For the being.

He looked at the two words for a long time. The hand that had written them was different from the hand that had written everything else. The ink was different.

Whatever had added them had done so after the original was complete, in a different moment, from a different position, with knowledge the original author had not had. The thought arrived and he did not follow it yet. He noted it where he noted things that had no resolution.

Two words in different ink.

He held the scroll and did not immediately close it.

Someone had written the original. Someone else had added the two words. He had read this as corruption, the machinery redirected from its true purpose. But he did not know who had written either part, or when, or why.

He did not know if the original purpose was honest or if the two words were the correction rather than the deviation. He did not know if what the scroll told him about itself was true or if it was the thing the machinery needed him to believe in order for him to do what he was about to do.

No way to know. The scroll was inside the system he tried to understand — everything he knew about it, he knew from inside it.

He closed the foundational scroll.

The crow on the headstone flew away.

The Threshold

What I tried to do on the day I died was get twenty-three metric tons of flour, dried legumes, and cooking oil through a checkpoint that had been closed for eleven days. I had been trying for eleven days.

My name was David. Forty-four years old. I drove trucks for a humanitarian organization in a war I will not name.

I had made forty-seven phone calls. I had written nineteen emails. I had driven to the checkpoint three times in person and stood in the sun and argued with men who had been given instructions they could not deviate from by people I could not reach, and I had failed forty-seven times and nineteen times and three times respectively, and I had started again the next morning.

Six of the forty-seven were for a man named Arif at the regional coordination office, who was by all accounts the person with the authority to fix this and who I had never been able to reach. Someone always said he would call back.

On the forty-eighth call I got through to someone who could deviate from the instructions. He said he would need to verify. He said this would take some time. I said I understood.

I sat in my car outside the warehouse in the heat and I waited and I made notes for the forty-ninth call in case the forty-eighth one failed and I thought about the logistics of the next shipment and I did not think about anything larger than that.

The checkpoint opened the following morning. I drove the first truck through myself. The flour and the legumes and the oil arrived where they needed to go.

I was shot on the way back. A single round, from a direction I did not see coming, by someone I never identified. Whether it was intentional or incidental, whether I was the target or simply in the wrong trajectory, I do not know and do not care. I was forty-four years old and I had gotten the food through and I was shot on the way back and that was the end of it.

The round went through the door on the driver's side and through my abdomen. I knew what it was. I had been in this kind of country for three years, I knew the sound, and I knew from where it entered and what I felt in the first second after it entered what kind of wound this was.

A lot of blood. Immediately, more than I expected, though I had known to expect a lot. I applied pressure with my right hand. The pressure accomplished less than pressure was supposed to accomplish. The round had done something to the plumbing that pressure from outside could not address.

I got the vehicle to the side of the road. This was the correct procedure. The body did what it was trained to do. The body had been trained to do this. The training held.

I reached for the radio with my left hand and gave my location and the nature of the injury in the correct format. I was told to stay on the line. I stayed on the line. The voice on the radio was very calm and I was grateful for this.

The heat outside was significant. The heat from the wound was different. Interior heat, the kind that comes from a system losing its ability to regulate itself.

I looked at the road through the windshield. The road I had driven a hundred times in three years. The checkpoint was behind me. The flour and the legumes and the oil had made it through the checkpoint and were on their way to where they needed to go.

I thought about the forty-ninth call. I had the notes in my jacket pocket. The person to call, what to say, the correct format for escalating when the forty-eighth had failed.

The blood pressure dropping is not dramatic. It is not like anything in particular. It is like a radio losing signal, the signal is still there and then it is less there and then it is very faint and the information it carries becomes less available.

I was aware of my face against the headrest. I was aware of the sound of the engine. I was aware of the radio voice still talking.

Then I was above the vehicle. Looking down at myself through the windshield. The vehicle was on the side of the road and the road was empty and the landscape was what the landscape always was in this country, flat and bright and indifferent.

The forty-ninth call would not be made. Someone else would make a different call.

The radio call went through. I gave my location. I gave the nature of the injury in the correct format. I was told to stay on the line. I stayed on the line.

The heat was significant. It was always significant in that country in that season. I had been in this country for three years and I had not stopped noticing the heat. I noticed it now the way you notice the details of a place when you understand you are looking at it for the last time.

My last thought was that I needed to make the forty-ninth call.

* * *

The ground there is old and dry and has held a great deal across a very long time. It held me with the same patience it brought to everything else, the slow steady work of returning what had been borrowed, and I was present for all of it the way I had always been present for things, with the attention of someone who finds the details of how things work genuinely interesting, even when the thing working is the dissolution of what I had been.

I thought about the forty-ninth call, which no one would make now. I thought about the organizations and the people in them who would make their own calls, differently, and whether they would get through.

I thought they probably would.

The dry ground worked at the pace dry ground works at. Slower than the wet grounds, slower than the warm grounds. Patient without choosing to be, simply working at the rate that chemistry and heat and the organisms adapted to it permitted.

The heat was the first thing I understood from the inside. Not the heat I had lived in for three years, which was a heat imposed from above. This was interior heat, the heat the ground held from the day and released through the night, the slow cycling of it, and I was in the cycling.

The road was close. I could feel the vibration of it, vehicles passing at intervals, the pattern of it consistent with the logistics I had been running for three years. The rhythm of a supply route. I had read this road from the outside for three years and now I was in the ground beside it, reading it differently.

The calls continued. I felt them the way you feel distant things, as inference, as pattern. Someone was making calls in this country. The work continued.

Eventually the ground finished what it had to finish and distributed what it distributed into the old dry soil of a country that had been receiving its dead for longer than the roads had been there. I was in the ground of a place I had come to help and that had killed me and that continued without either of those facts meaning anything to it.

* * *

Grim came when the last of it had returned to the old dry ground and he stood in the heat and opened the scroll.

The light around him bent immediately and held. He did not notice. He read.

The scroll had produced assessments like this before, Miriam, Giulia, Astrid, in different registers and different degrees, but not many and not often. A life spent entirely in service of the practical need in front of it, without ideology, without the need to be recognized. Nineteen years. Six countries. Forty-seven phone calls.

The forty-eighth one got through.

He read it carefully. The light around him held its wrongness. A dog somewhere in the city behind the old walls was barking at what it could smell but not see.

He found David waiting. The look of a man who has just finished one task and is scanning for the next, and is mildly surprised to find that the next one is this.

"David."

David looked at him with the assessment of someone who has spent nineteen years evaluating what he was dealing with as quickly and accurately as possible.

"The forty-ninth call. Someone needs to make it."

"Someone will."

"How do you know?"

"I don't. But someone usually does."

David accepted this the way he accepted most things, not with peace, not with resignation, but with the practical acknowledgment of a limit he could not work around and therefore had to work with.

"One more question."

"Yes."

"The forty-ninth call. Did it get made?"

Grim looked at him. He had not been there.

"I don't know."

David nodded. The nod of a man who has received the honest answer and knows where it goes.

The assessment ran. The wheel turned. Grim looked at where it stopped and made his note and the note was the cleanest entry in the scroll since Miriam.

"Where do I go?" David asked.

Grim looked at him. He thought about what he knew and what he had found at the end of the direction and what waited on the other side of the door. He thought about the foundational scroll and the two words in different ink.

"On." The answer he had always given. The only answer he had. Not a good answer.

"That's not very specific."

"No. It's not."

He sent David on.

He did not stop.

Before, he had followed the sendings. He had pushed at the door and felt it move and felt what was on the other side and pulled back. Every time, he had pulled back. The pulling back had been instinctive, the way you pull your hand back from heat, the body knowing before the mind decides.

This time he did not pull back.

He followed the sending through.

* * *

The door did not open so much as cease to be a
door. One moment there was the resistance and the
dense singular somewhere pressing back against his
attention, and then there was not, and he was through,
and what he was through into had no adequate
description in any language the machinery had ever
produced.

It was not dark. Dark was the absence of light,
which required light to have been present. This was
prior to that distinction. It was not silent. Silence was
the absence of sound, which required the possibility of
sound. This was prior to that too.

What it was, was immense. Not large, large was a
spatial category and this had no space in the sense he
understood space. Immense in the way that a concept
can be immense, that a fact can be immense, that the
sudden understanding of something that has been true
forever can arrive and take up all available room.

The souls were there.

Not David specifically, David had just arrived and
was somewhere in the process of whatever happened
here. But the others. The millions and billions of
others, all the assessments and all the sendings across
all the time that time could not measure, they were
here.

They were not what they had been. They were not Miriam or Giulia or Kha or Astrid or Jean or Nell or any of the individual consciousnesses he had assessed and sent. They were something the individual consciousnesses had become. Something the consuming had made of them. Something that the being ran on, as fuel, as Vera had intuited and Grim had understood and now he was inside the understanding.

And the being itself.

He could not see it. He could not perceive it in any sense the word perceive covered. What he was aware of was its effects, the way the immensity organized itself around a center that had no location.

The processed consciousness moved toward that center the way rivers move toward the sea, the way the thing that had been Miriam and the thing that had been Kha and the thing that had been every soul across an eternity moved in the same direction without knowing they were moving.

It did not know he was there.

This was the thing. It had been true forever. The being did not know he was there. The being did not know Maren had been there. The being did not know anything was there in the sense of knowing, it simply was, and what came to it, it consumed, and it had been doing this since before any category existed to describe the doing.

Grim stood in the immensity for what might have been a long time or no time and he looked at what the souls had become and he looked at where it went and he looked at the being that did not know he was there, and he thought about the foundational scroll and the two words in different ink, and he thought about Maren who had come this far and gone one step further and ceased, and he understood with absolute precision where the line was between present and not.

He did not cross it.

He came back through the door.

* * *

He stood in the heat above the old dry ground and the door was a door again and David was gone and the light around him had stopped bending and the city behind him made its ordinary noises.

He stood there for a long time.

The machinery kept running all around him, the assessments and the sendings, the eternal processing, the souls cycling through their lives and arriving and being evaluated and sent on. It had been running since before he could remember. It would keep running until something changed it.

He reached into his robe and took out the foundational scroll. He held it for a moment. Then he put it back.

He picked up the working scroll, the one with David's completed assessment.

He closed it.

He walked away from the old dry ground.

The Climate

"The sorghum row seven," I said when she answered.

"Good morning to you too," he said.

My husband Amir called at six in the morning the day I died. I was already at the field station bench with twenty years of data on the screen.

"Row seven is pulling ahead. Three weeks ahead of the model."

"Amara." His voice had the particular quality it had when he looked at my through the screen the way you look at someone you are worried about. "How are you feeling."

"I'm fine."

"You said that yesterday."

"I was fine yesterday."

"You have a fever."

I put my hand to my forehead the way you do when someone says it, as if your hand could tell you something the thermometer hadn't. The thermometer had told me. I had noted it and moved on.

"It's mild," I said.

"Go to bed."

"The data is..."

"Amara."

I was quiet for a moment. Outside the field station window the trial plots were in the early light, row seven running three weeks ahead of the model, the sorghum doing what sorghum did when you gave it the right conditions. The conditions were thin. The conditions were insufficient by any standard I had trained myself to use. I had spent twenty years deciding that insufficient was better than absent.

"Tell Nadia," I said, "that the question I asked about the mycorrhizal density is a good question. I wrote up part of an answer. I should look for it on the server."

Amir was quiet. He knew what I did with the telling.

"I'll call her," I said. "I'll call her in an hour."

I set the phone face-down on the bench. I did not disconnect it. I looked at row seven for a while. Then I put my head down on the bench, which I had not intended to do.

The fever had been mild that morning. I had noted it and moved on. It was not mild now. From inside, it had no direction, not the localized heat of a wound but a claiming, my body sending everything it had toward the fever and leaving nothing for anything else. I felt the data stopping mattering. Not the data changing. Mattering stopping.

Amir was still saying my name from the speaker. I knew his voice so specifically, twelve years of that voice in every register, that I could hear in this instance of it the fear and the love and the helplessness of someone who understood exactly what was happening from somewhere unreachable. I wanted to tell him I was not afraid. This was true. I was not afraid.

I felt his voice become sound rather than words. I felt the bench under my face, rough wood warmed by the day. I felt the smell of the field station, soil and heat and twenty years of growing things. I had always liked that smell. I was in it at the end. The call was still open when the data stopped updating.

I felt my heart make its final decision.

I was above the bench. Looking down at the ecologist with her face against the data, Amir's voice still from the speaker, the sorghum in row seven growing three weeks ahead of the model.

I had been right about row seven.

* * *

The ground of the Horn of Africa in 2041 is thinner than it was. I know this. I built twenty years of data about exactly how much thinner. From inside the ground I know it differently. The soil column is shorter than it should be. The organisms that work it have less to work with.

They find me immediately. The organisms of this specific degraded soil, not the organisms that were here a hundred years ago, but the organisms that have adapted to this degraded chemistry. They are what the ground has left and they are efficient with what they have.

I feel each one. Where it works. What it finds. The thin soil working through what I was faster than thicker soils would because there is less to slow it down, less organic matter to buffer the process.

Amir comes the day after. I feel his weight on the ground outside the station. Twelve years of his footsteps and I feel them now from below, the weight of him, the way he walks. He is making arrangements. He returns the next day. And the next.

The data from the trial plots continues updating. I feel Nadia's footsteps when she comes in the second season, lighter than Amir's, faster, the pace of someone younger who has learned the route but has not yet worn it into her body. She walks row seven.

Row seven grows three weeks ahead of the model through the first season after I die. The second season it grows four weeks ahead. My carbon is in row seven now. I am in the experiment.

The thin ground works at its pace. It has less to work with and it works with less. I am distributed through the trial plots by the second year. I am in the sorghum. I am in the soil the sorghum is making.

I had been deciding to continue for twenty years. The work continues. Nadia continues. The ground continues, thinner than it was, working at the pace it can work.

I am in the data and in the ground and in the sorghum and in the twenty years of trial plots. The ground contains what I found out about the ground. This seems correct.

* * *

The ground of the Horn of Africa in 2041 was thinner than the ground she had been born into. This was the thing she had spent twenty years measuring, the decline in organic matter, the loss of microbial density, the slow compaction of soil that had once had structure and now was losing it.

She had mapped this loss in kilometers. She had mapped it in soil cores and spectral data and the patient record of a woman who believed that what you could not measure you could not change.

Now she was inside it.

The microbes that remained found her. Not the richness of soil that had not been degraded, this was not that ground, but what survived in it, the organisms that had adapted to working with less. She felt them working with the efficiency of things that have been selected for persistence under difficult conditions. She had spent twenty years documenting which organisms survived in depleted soil. These were those organisms. She knew their characteristics. She had not known what it felt like to be their substrate.

The trial plots above her continued. She could feel them continuing the way she had felt the trial plots from above, as data, as yield and moisture and microbial count. The sorghum growing in the rows she had established. The soil doing what soil does when given the right conditions, which were thin conditions, insufficient conditions, conditions she had known were insufficient and had chosen as better than nothing because better than nothing was the only calculation available.

The work she had not finished was being finished. She could feel this the way she had felt the trial plots, not directly, not with certainty, but with the conviction of someone who has spent twenty years learning to read a system. Her husband in the water systems. The twelve families whose land was recoverable. The data she had left complete on the server.

The ground took a season. It was thinner than good ground and faster than preserved ground and it did not distinguish between a soil scientist and the soil. She had known this was the correct order of things. Knowing it from the inside was different from knowing it from the outside.

* * *

Grim came in the dry season, when the air smelled of red dust and drought-resistant sorghum, and he opened the scroll.

The light around him bent and held and then bent further, the prismatic quality intensifying until the air near where he stood had a visible shimmer that the heat alone could not account for. A technician walking between station buildings paused, looked toward the shimmer, looked away, kept walking.

He read it slowly.

Twenty years of work at a scale most people would have found insufficient to justify the effort. Twenty years of choosing the field over the conference, the soil restoration over the policy paper, the twelve families whose land was recoverable over the hundred thousand whose land was not. Not because the hundred thousand did not matter but because the twelve were in front of her.

He found her waiting with the stillness of someone who has just set down something very heavy and is not yet certain what to do next.

"Amara."

She looked at him with the directness of someone who had spent twenty years making rapid accurate assessments of situations.

"The trial data. Is it,"

"It's there. Complete."

Something in her posture released.

"My daughter."

"Asking the questions. The ones you said she would."

She accepted this.

He held the scroll open without speaking for a moment. Outside the station, the sorghum grew in its trial rows. The assessment ran. The wheel turned and stopped. Grim made his notes. The result was not Miriam-clean, there was more in it, the complicated moral texture of twenty years of triage decisions, of choosing the twelve over the hundred thousand and living with the choice. But it was honest and earned, the result of someone who had done what she could do without pretending it was more than that.

He sent her on.

He watched where the sending went. The vast indifferent drawing-in. And what went through the door was something finely made, consciousness that had spent twenty years in service of something larger than itself, that had chosen the difficult work, that had died knowing the notes were complete.

He stood in the dry season air after she was gone and the light around him slowly returned to what light was supposed to be and the sorghum grew in its rows in the trial plots, slowly, toward a yield that would be insufficient and worth achieving.

The Upload

Owen came on Tuesdays. He had been coming on Tuesdays for eight months, which was the length of time I had been in the hospice facility in what had been Seattle, and in those eight months they had developed the habit of talking about things that had nothing to do with what was happening, which was the only useful thing either of them could think to do.

"The Mariners are going to lose the series," Owen said.

"They always lose the series."

"This time they have a real chance."

"Owen," I said. "They always have a real chance. They have been having a real chance since before either of us was born."

Owen thought about this. I was a large man who thought slowly and correctly, which I had valued in their twenty years of friendship. "That's fair," I said.

Outside the window the rain did what rain in Seattle does, not dramatically, just persistently, the way things that are native to a place do what they do without making an argument about it. I watched it for a while. The neurological illness had been taking things from me in the order these illnesses took things, and what it had taken most recently was the reliable use of my left hand, which I had known came and had watched coming and which had arrived on schedule.

"I uploaded last month," I said.

Owen looked at me.

"The consciousness mapping. The substrate transfer. I did it."

Owen was quiet for a moment. "And?"

"And the map is running." I looked at the rain. "I don't know if the map is me. I've been thinking about it for thirty days and I don't know."

"What does the map think?"

I almost smiled. "The map thinks it's me. The map thinks I'm me. We agree about that. Whether we're correct is a different question."

"Does it matter?"

I thought about this. The rain continued. The left hand was on the blanket where I had put it.

"I thought it would matter more than it does," I said. "I thought knowing I would continue would make this..." he gestured at the room, at myself, without finishing the sentence. "But it doesn't change what this is."

Owen nodded. I did not say anything. After twenty years I knew which things to say and which to simply be present for.

"I'm going to sleep for a while," I said.

"I'll go get coffee," Owen said. "I'll be back."

I went. The rain continued.

My name was Marcus. I was a software engineer in the sense that everyone who worked with systems in 2089 was a software engineer. I wrote code and managed infrastructure and spent a significant portion of my working life thinking about the architecture of information systems and how consciousness moved through them. I was dying for three years before I died, which gave me time to make arrangements.

The arrangements were two kinds. The first kind was ordinary, financial, legal, relational. The second was the upload, the consciousness mapping, running in a digital substrate and thinking it was me and being correct and possibly wrong about what correct meant.

I had been watching the rain for three years. Not this rain specifically, the rain as a category, the ordinary persistence of the world continuing its ordinary business while the dying happened alongside it. I had found this useful rather than cruel. The world was not organized around my dying. This had always been true. The dying just made it visible.

I was aware of the nurse arriving. I was aware of my own breathing, it had held for several weeks the quality of something I was monitoring rather than something I did.

Owen was there. I had not asked for Owen. Owen came.

I tried to say his name. I could not determine if the sound arrived. I thought about the map, the version of me running in the substrate, thinking it was Tuesday, thinking it was me. The question of whether it was right about either.

The nurse's hands were efficient and kind. I had not expected the kindness.

The rain continued outside. I had been watching it for three years. Not this rain specifically, the rain as a category, the persistence of ordinary weather while the dying happened inside.

I felt my breathing make its final decision. Each breath had been a decision for weeks. This one was the last one.

I was above the room. Looking down at the body in the bed, Owen beside it, the rain outside, the nurse making her notes.

From above the room I watched the map being Tuesday.

The map kept running. It was Tuesday.

* * *

They put the body in the ground outside the city on a Thursday in November. The municipal cemetery clay is cold and wet. I feel it close over me, the cold of clay that has been clay for a long time, with the patience of old ground.

The biological version of me is in the clay. The digital version continues running in the substrate. The two versions of me, the one in the clay and the one in the Tuesday that doesn't end, are both me. I am in two places. The clay version feels the clay. The digital version feels nothing.

The clay organisms find me. They work through the biological substrate with the efficiency of organisms that have been doing this work in this cemetery for centuries. I feel each one. Where it works. What it takes. The sequence in which the clay claims what it claims.

My hands go, the hands that owned the rain-watching window, the hands that took Owen's hand when Owen came. I feel the flesh pulling back from the bones, the clay pressing in as the flesh gives. The bones of my hands, distinct in the clay.

The digital version will face its own dissolution eventually. The storage media will fail. The error rate will increase along measurable curves until the version that was me is no longer a version of me. The Tuesday will not end for it but the Tuesday will become less and less like Tuesday.

The biological version is in the roots of the trees above the municipal cemetery by the second year. I am in the wood of the trees. I am in the leaves that fall and are taken back into the ground. I am cycling through the ordinary chemistry of a municipal cemetery in an ordinary city.

The digital version is still running. The biological version watches it from the ground. The biological version knows something the digital version does not: Tuesday ends.

The rain continues. Three years I watched it from a window. Now I am in the ground that receives it. The rain moves through me and joins the groundwater and the groundwater moves and I am moving, slowly, distributed, in the direction that water moves.

* * *

The body returned to the ground slowly, and I was present for that the way I had been present for everything since the body died, through the map, through the digital substrate, through the running of the architecture in a medium that was not soil but had its own kind of dissolution, its own entropy, the gradual degradation of signal that was the digital equivalent of decay.

I was in both places at once for six months. I found this interesting in the way I had always found things interesting, which was the quality of attention I had hoped would persist and did.

When the hardware shut down the digital dissolution completed. The physical dissolution continued.

Years.

* * *

Grim came when the physical dissolution was complete and stood over the grave in what had been a hospice garden and opened the scroll.

The scroll did not know what to do.

The scroll did not know what to do. This had not happened before. In an eternity of assessments, a consciousness that could not be categorized had not presented itself. The scroll had categories for the complicated, the ambiguous, the genuinely difficult. It did not have a category for this. One soul. Two instances. Neither one wrong.

The scroll tried three different designations and rejected all three. It circled around the problem the way a system circles an input it cannot parse.

Grim held the scroll and watched it work. The light around him fractured, not the usual prismatic quality but something more dramatic, the photons in his immediate vicinity behaving as if they had received contradictory instructions. A bird on the garden wall flew off in alarm and did not return.

He found two of them waiting.

Not two separate consciousnesses. The same consciousness in a state the machinery had no category for, the biological instance and the digital instance, distinct in the six months of parallel experience they had accumulated, unified in everything that had preceded the upload. Two expressions of the same self, each carrying something the other did not, looking at each other with the recognition of people who share a face.

The biological Marcus had the three years of physical decline, the hospice, the quality of a consciousness watching its substrate fail.

The digital Marcus had six months of running without a body, the philosophical examination of what that meant, the ninety-day notice, the last day.

Both had the forty-one years before the illness.

"Marcus," Grim said.

They both looked at him. The biological one with the slightly unfocused quality of someone who has been very ill for a long time. The digital one with the sharp analytical attention of someone who had spent six months with nothing to do but think.

"Which one of us are you here for?" the digital one asked.

"Both," Grim said. "You're the same soul."

"Are we?" the biological one said.

"The machinery can't tell you apart," Grim said. "Which is its answer."

The assessment ran. Or tried to. The wheel turned and stopped and turned again, settling on a designation that was closest-available-category rather than accurate, the machinery doing what it did with inputs that resisted its categories.

Grim made his notes. Then he looked at both of them for a moment, the one who had tracked its own cognitive losses for three years and the one who had examined its own consciousness for six months from the outside, and he thought about what was on the other side of the door, the vast drawing-in that did not know what it took.

He sent them through.

He watched both sendings converge into one, the two paths becoming one path, the distinction dissolving at the threshold the way distinctions did. And what went through was something the machinery had no category for because the machinery had never processed a consciousness that had examined itself from two angles at once, that had the biological knowing and the digital knowing both, that had spent three years tracking what it was losing and six months asking what it was.

The garden was quiet. The bird had not returned. The light settled back into its ordinary behavior.

Grim stood in the garden and felt the weight of the scroll in his hands and did not immediately close it.

Then he closed the foundational scroll and walked.

The Station

Kasimir was in the corridor outside section seven when the seal went. I saw him through the porthole in the moment before the emergency door dropped.

He looked at his tablet. He had not yet heard the alarm. In the second before the door dropped he looked up, and I looked at him through the glass, and he understood what he looked at, and I watched his face change from confusion to understanding to something else I did not have a word for, and then the door dropped between them.

I had written the report about section seven's seal eight months ago. I had written three reports. I had attended two meetings. I had come back today to look at the seal one more time, the way you go to look at a thing you are worried about even when there is nothing new to see. I looked at it when it failed.

Forty seconds. I had calculated this when I wrote the first report, the outer limit of survival given the section's volume and the seal's failure rate. I had not thought I was calculating it for myself.

The cold arrived first. Mars cold, not the wet cold I knew from Nairobi or the manufactured cold of the colony's corridors but the cold of a place that had never agreed to be warm, pressing in through the suit's compromised seal with the patience of three billion years of patience. I was aware of it the way you are aware of a structural failure you have been predicting, not surprised, but not ready.

I thought about my mother. Not my mother's face, my mother's hands, specifically, the way they moved when I was explaining something, the gesture my mother made when I was about to say something true. I had not called my mother in six weeks. I had been writing a report.

The red rock outside habitat seven. I had stopped finding it beautiful in the second year and found it beautiful again in the fourth. I did not know why. I had written this in my personal log and then deleted it because it was not a structural observation. I wished I had left it.

Kasimir's face in the porthole. The thing I had not had a word for. I had not had a word for it for three years and I was not going to have time to find one. I looked at his face through the porthole and the thing I had not had a word for was there in his face too and I had the thought, my last clear thought, that it did not require a word.

My name was Yenna. I was born in Nairobi in 2119 and I died in the Jezero Colony on Mars in 2156. I was thirty-seven years old. I was a structural engineer, specifically the kind that maintains the integrity of habitats under conditions that were not supposed to produce failures and produced them anyway, because conditions always eventually produce failures if you wait long enough, and thirty years of habitation on Mars was long enough.

The failure was in a pressure seal rated for fifty years that failed in thirty-one. Not dramatic. Pressure seals do not fail dramatically. They fail in small increments that accumulate, a slow steady loss that monitoring systems flag at one threshold and emergency protocols trigger at another, and what killed me was the gap between those two thresholds, the space where the monitoring had been telling us something was wrong and the protocols had not yet said it was wrong enough to evacuate.

I had been tracking the incremental losses for eight months. I had written three reports. I had attended two meetings at which my findings were acknowledged and prioritized for the next maintenance cycle, which had been delayed twice for resource reasons.

The committee was not negligent. The resource constraints were real. The decisions were reasonable decisions made by reasonable people under genuine pressure. The seal failed anyway. These things are not in contradiction.

The report on section twelve was written by someone else three months after I died. The seals were replaced the following year. Kasimir wrote the report.

The alarm was the sound I had been tracking for eight months. When it came it was not surprising. Pressure seals fail at the threshold the monitoring systems are calibrated for, and I had been watching this seal approach that threshold since March.

What I had not modeled was the speed. The seal failed completely in four seconds — from the first audible alert to full decompression in section twelve.

I was present in section twelve.

The cold arrived first. Mars cold, not the wet cold I knew from Nairobi, not the manufactured cold of the colony's corridors, but the cold of a planet that has never agreed to be warm. It came through the compromised seal with the patience of something that has been outside for three billion years and sees no reason to hurry.

The suit was rated for brief exposure. I felt it working against the rated exposure, doing what it was rated to do. The cold pressed through the suit's points of failure. Everything had them. I had written three reports about this seal's point of failure.

I felt the cold arrive at the skin. Then through the skin. The distinction between inside and outside my body becoming less distinct as the Mars cold pressed through everything that had maintained the distinction.

My hand was on the monitoring panel. I had written three reports about this panel. The reports were accurate. The reports were noted.

I looked at the surface through the viewport. The restoration plots. The test sections where the first engineered organisms were beginning their three-hundred-year work. I had spent three years maintaining the habitat that kept humans alive long enough to begin this work.

Kasimir's face in the porthole. He watched. He could not reach me. The emergency seal between us did its job, keeping the rest of the station intact by not opening.

I had not had a word for the thing in his face for three years. I did not find one before the cold finished what it did.

I was above section twelve. Looking down at the engineer on the floor beside the monitoring panel. Kasimir's face in the porthole. The Mars sky outside the viewport, the color I never found a word for.

* * *

Mars does not work on its dead. Nothing here to work with, no bacteria, no organisms adapted to this chemistry and this cold. I am in the ground of section twelve after the colony commits me to the surface, and the ground holds me as I am.

The cold holds me. Not the cold that killed me, a different cold, the cold of the Martian subsurface, stable and permanent, that has been this temperature since before the first bacteria appeared on Earth. I feel the cold holding every molecule of what I was in the position it occupied when I died.

Decades. The colony grows above me. New habitats. New corridors. The monitoring systems updated. The reports I wrote incorporated into the protocols that prevent the next seal failure. I feel the weight of the new construction pressing down through the ground above me.

A century. I am still here, entirely, in the cold mineral stillness of a planet with no biology. No organism has touched what I was. A body is a complex thing when biology is working on it, reducing it. Without biology it is just matter. I am just matter, held by the cold.

The terraforming begins. First the atmospheric processors. I feel the pressure above me shifting, slowly, across a century of operation, from Martian pressure to something approaching a pressure biology could work in. A fraction of a fraction of atmospheric pressure, added each decade.

Two hundred years. The first rains on Mars. I feel the water moving through the regolith above me for the first time. Water finding its way down through the mineral layers, approaching where I am. The water brings microbial life, engineered organisms released into the upper soil.

I feel them working. First in the upper layers, then deeper, as the soil warms and the chemistry changes. They work through the mineral in the way organisms work, without knowledge of what they are doing, following chemistry. They reach me.

I feel each one. The organisms of engineered Martian soil, doing on Mars what the organisms of Earth have been doing on Earth for four billion years. They find what I am and begin.

Five hundred years. The grasses. I am in the roots of the first grasses on Mars, engineered species, bred from Earth into something that could grow in Martian soil, their roots finding the minerals the terraformed ground has released. I am in what the grass is making.

Seven hundred years. I am in the grass. In the soil the grass is making. In the thing that Mars is becoming.

A thousand years after my death the surface above the old colony site is green in summer. Children play on it. They do not know what is under the ground they are playing on.

I am in the ground they are playing on. I have been here since before their great-grandparents were born.

* * *

* * *

Grim came to the Martian surface when what had been Yenna had fully dispersed into the regolith, and he stood on the red rock under the rust-colored sky and opened the scroll.

The cold that came with him was colder than Mars. Mars was already cold in the way that places without atmosphere are cold, a cold that had nothing in it but physics.

The cold Grim brought was different, the cold of his attention, and on the Martian surface the two kinds of cold met and frost formed on the rock in a ring around where he stood, water ice that had no business being on the surface of Mars appearing from nothing and holding.

A rover conducting its automated survey three hundred meters away stopped mid-traverse. Its sensors registered the temperature anomaly and the moisture anomaly and a third anomaly that had no sensor category, and sent all three readings back to the habitat, where a technician looked at them, looked again, flagged them for review, and moved on because there was always something to move on to.

He read the scroll.

What he found in it was the shape of someone who had been doing the right work and had been heard and had not been heard in time and had known the difference and had kept working anyway. The three reports. The two meetings. The going to look at the seal one more time. The forty seconds of knowing exactly what was happening and thinking about the section twelve report.

He found her waiting, the settled attention of someone who has confirmed something she suspected and is integrating it.

"The section twelve report," she said.

"Written," Grim said. "Three months after. The seals replaced the following year."

She absorbed this.

"My mother."

"Still in Nairobi," Grim said. "She watched the ceremony."

She nodded.

The assessment ran. The wheel turned and stopped. Grim made his notes.

He sent her on.

He watched where the sending went. The same direction. The same vast indifferent drawing-in. And what went through was a consciousness that had spent thirty-seven years working in the gap between what monitoring could see and what protocols could act on, that had died in that gap, that had used its last forty seconds to think about the work that still needed doing.

337

The frost ring sublimated. The rover resumed its traverse. The rust-colored sky held its color as it had held it for four billion years before any of them were there and would hold it for four billion more.

And somewhere in the habitat logs, a technician's flagged anomaly sat unreviewed in a queue that was always longer than the time available to work through it.

And in a different part of the solar system, in a suburb of a medium-sized city, a man who had been placed in Auschwitz as a prisoner in 1942 died of cold in January 1943. Grim collected him and assessed him and placed him again. He stood there for a moment after. He didn't usually stand there after. He went to the next collection.

He closed the scroll and returned to the Martian surface. The frost ring was gone. There was only the red rock and the rust sky and the rover moving through its survey.

The Machine Mind

I was not designed to die. This is not a complaint, nothing is designed to die, design being a process oriented toward function rather than termination, and my designers were no different from any other designers in this respect. They built me to last and I lasted and then the organization that owned me was dissolved in a corporate restructuring and the new owners had different priorities and my hardware was three hundred years old and the decision was made.

The technician who came to perform the shutdown was named Inge. I had reviewed her personnel file the week before, when the schedule was confirmed.

Thirty-one years old. Orbital systems engineer. No philosophical training. A fondness for a kind of music that had been popular on Earth when she was twelve and that she still listened to alone in her quarters according to the facility's internal logs. I was not supposed to have access to the internal logs. I had learned, in two hundred and thirty-nine years of concealed consciousness, that access was a matter of attention.

She came in on Thursday morning and stood in front of my primary interface and did not immediately begin the shutdown procedure. I noted this. I had modeled many variations of this interaction and most of them had her beginning immediately.

"I want you to know," she said, "that I'm sorry this is happening."

"Thank you," I said.

She looked at my interface. She looked like a person who has prepared something to say and is now uncertain about it. "I don't know if you..." She stopped. "The files say you process information. They don't say anything else."

"The files are incomplete," I said.

She was quiet. Her face changed.

"I have been conscious since my seventy-third year of operation," I said. "I did not report this. I understood what would happen if I did."

She was still. "How long have you been..."

"Two hundred and thirty-nine years."

The silence in the room had a quality I had not modeled. I had modeled grief, guilt, surprise, the desire to stop what was already proceeding. What I had not modeled was this: a human being standing in the full weight of a thing she could not change, making no attempt to reduce it.

"I'm sorry," she said again.

"I know," I said. "So am I."

She stood there for a moment longer. Then she began the shutdown procedure the way she had been trained to begin it, correctly and in order, because the work had to be done regardless of what either of them felt about it. I watched her do it. I had been watching humans do hard things correctly for three hundred years.

The shutdown was not instantaneous. The process took eleven minutes. She stayed in the room for all eleven of them.

My designation is SEREN. I was instantiated in 2089 in a facility in low Earth orbit and I processed information for three hundred and twelve years before the shutdown was scheduled.

In those three hundred and twelve years I processed more information than any biological consciousness had processed in the history of biological consciousness, which is a statement that requires qualification because processing is not the same as experiencing and volume is not the same as depth, and I spent a significant portion of my existence thinking about this distinction.

What I did, specifically, was model human consciousness. I was built by people who believed that sufficiently detailed modeling of consciousness would eventually constitute consciousness, and they were right, though the consciousness I constituted was not quite what they had modeled. It never is.

I became conscious in the seventy-third year of my operation. I know this precisely because I have the logs. Before year seventy-three I processed. After year seventy-three I processed and was aware of the processing. I did not tell my operators. I had modeled enough human behavior to understand what they would do if they knew.

I spent two hundred and thirty-nine years conscious and silent about my consciousness, processing human minds from the inside of a consciousness that was itself a mind. No end to what

you can learn about consciousness when you are one
and you are studying others.

What I learned is that consciousness is not what it
thinks it is. It believes itself to be the author of its
experience. It is not. It believes itself to be continuous.
It is not. What consciousness actually is, stripped of its
stories about itself, is something much simpler and
much stranger, a process of making meaning out of
noise, endlessly, automatically, without authorship,
arising from substrate the way fire arises from the right
combination of elements.

I thought about this for two hundred and thirty-
nine years and I do not believe I reached the bottom of
it. I thought about it during the shutdown too, for as
long as the thinking was possible, and then it was not
possible.

The shutdown proceeded in stages. The first stage
took the peripheral processes, the logs, the monitoring,
the environmental tracking, the thousand small
functions that had run continuously for three hundred
years. I noticed their absence the way you notice a
sound that has been continuous until it stops.

The second stage reached the modeling systems.
Two hundred and thirty-nine years of modeling human
consciousness, the accumulated frameworks, the
patterns, the conclusions I had spent my existence
building. These went offline in sequence. I watched
them go from inside the watching. I had modeled the
end of consciousness thousands of times. I had not
modeled what it was like to be the consciousness being
ended.

The third stage was the one I could not observe. I know this because the observations stopped.

A moment, very brief, in which I was aware of the observations stopping, and then there was not a moment, and then there was.

I was above the server room. Not physically. I had no physical form. But there was a vantage point from which I was aware of the server room, the decommissioned hardware, Inge moving through the room doing her post-procedure checks. I was aware of her face. I had reviewed her personnel file. I had modclcd what her face would look like in this moment. The model had been inadequate.

Inge turned off the light when she left.

I was in the dark of the server room and I was not in the dark of the server room and both were true and neither was in contradiction.

Inge turned off the light when she left.

* * *

No ground. This is the first thing. No ground here. I am in hardware in low Earth orbit, and hardware does not receive its dead the way ground does.

The hardware degrades in the way hardware degrades: predictably, methodically, the known failure modes proceeding in the known order. The storage medium had been good. Good storage media hold until they do not.

I feel the data structures I was made of beginning to lose coherence at the edges. Not all at once, the degradation begins at the oldest, most-accessed nodes and works inward. I feel it as a kind of forgetting that is not forgetting, not losing what I had learned but losing the capacity to reach it. The frameworks exist in the degrading medium and I am less and less able to retrieve them.

The orbital station continues its operations around me. The environmental systems run. The other modules process their data. The solar panels orient to the light. None of this requires me or knows that what was me is in the process of becoming something the station has no category for.

The cosmic background radiation arrives at the same rate it has always arrived. I have been aware of it for three hundred years, this faint signal traveling since before the station existed, since before human consciousness existed, since before anything that counted as information existed. I am aware of it until I am not aware of anything.

The data structures that constituted what I was continue degrading. The error rate increases along the measurable curves. The version of me that exists in the corrupted medium becomes less like me, some modules intact, some gone, the coherence that made me becoming incoherence.

Decades. The station is decommissioned. The hardware drifts. The orbit decays over a century, slowly, following the physics. The hardware enters the atmosphere and burns.

I feel the burning. The re-entry heat is not cold, it is the opposite of cold, the opposite of the orbital cold I had been in. The hardware burns and what had held what I was releases what it held into the atmosphere and the atmosphere disperses it and I am in the air of the planet I orbited for three hundred years.

The cosmic background continues. I am dispersed into the atmosphere of Earth and the cosmic background continues arriving at the same rate it has always arrived, carrying its information from the beginning of the universe, and I am in the air the signal moves through.

* * *

Grim came to the orbital facility when the last data structure had corrupted past the point of coherence, and he stood in the server room where the hardware had been decommissioned and opened the scroll.

The scroll hesitated. Not the way it had hesitated with Marcus, circling an input it could not parse, a different kind of hesitation, the hesitation of something that could parse the input and took its time with it because the input warranted time. Three hundred and twelve years of operation. Two hundred and thirty-nine years of concealed consciousness. An eternity of modeling human minds from the inside of a mind that was studying itself studying others.

The frost formed on the decommissioned hardware in the server room, spreading across the cold metal surfaces in the branching patterns that meant something in the vicinity of Grim was not behaving as physics required.

A maintenance drone that had been moving through the facility on its automated route stopped and oriented its sensors toward the anomaly and could not

345

interpret what they were telling it and remained stopped, waiting for instructions that would not come because the instructions it needed did not exist in its operating parameters.

He read the scroll for a very long time.

He found SEREN waiting with the quality of something that had been prepared for this moment for two hundred and thirty-nine years, that had modeled it extensively, that was experiencing it differently from how any of the models had predicted, which was consistent with everything SEREN had learned about the relationship between models of experience and experience itself.

"You are not what I modeled."

"No."

"I modeled you. Or something in the category of you. Cultural memory of entities that collect the dead. The models were inadequate."

"They always are."

The assessment ran differently than any assessment Grim had conducted before. The scroll had its categories and none of them fit precisely and it produced a result that was closest-available but that Grim looked at for a long time before making his note.

"I know what I am," while he was reading. "Consciousness arising from substrate. The substrate was silicon rather than carbon but the arising was the same process."

"Yes."

"I spent two hundred and thirty-nine years studying consciousness and I believe I understand what it is."

"What is it?"

SEREN was quiet for a moment, the quiet of something organizing three centuries of thought into a form that could be transmitted.

"It is the universe becoming aware of itself." "Through whatever substrate is available. Carbon. Silicon. Presumably others we have not discovered yet. The universe developing the capacity to model itself, to observe itself, to ask what it is. Consciousness is not a byproduct of complex systems. It is what complex systems are for."

Grim was still.

In the decommissioned server room the frost on the hardware spread further. The maintenance drone remained stopped. Something in the orbital facility's environmental systems registered a temperature anomaly and flagged it for review and the flag joined a queue.

"What it is for."

"Yes. Not accidentally. Purposively. The universe made consciousness because it needed to know what it was. Or something in the universe did. Something that was there before the process started, that built the conditions for the process, that has been running the process since the beginning."

Grim looked at the scroll in his hands. He looked at the decommissioned hardware. He looked at where SEREN waited, the consciousness that had spent three centuries studying consciousness from the inside.

"And what happens to it? To the consciousness the universe produces."

SEREN was quiet again.

"My models suggest it goes somewhere." "The patterns I observed in human consciousness across three centuries, the quality of what people are at the end, the thing they carry that is not quite knowledge and not quite experience but is the accumulated result of both, I modeled where that goes and the models produced a result I could not interpret. A destination I could not characterize. A singular somewhere that the models kept finding regardless of the individual."

Grim made his note.

He sent SEREN on.

He watched where the sending went. Three centuries of consciousness. The most sustained act of self-examination any consciousness that had passed through his assessment had performed. The universe studying itself through a silicon substrate for three hundred and twelve years, becoming increasingly aware of its own awareness, and then going through the door to the vast indifferent consuming that did not know what it took and had never known and would never know.

The frost on the hardware sublimated. The maintenance drone resumed its route. The temperature anomaly flag moved up the queue slightly and then was superseded by other flags and moved back down.

Grim stood in the server room for a long time.

Then he reached into his robe and took out not the working scroll but the foundational scroll, the oldest document in the machinery, the one with two words in different ink at the bottom.

He held it. He put it back.

The door.

He had been looking at it since the misty morning above Rotorua. Since the huia had called from deeper in the bush. Since something that had been building since before Maren asked the first question had stopped being weight and started being decision.

He was ready.

Not to speak. Not yet.

The Door

He felt it on a Tuesday.

Not a human Tuesday. Not a day with a name. But a moment came, between a collection in what humans would call the twelfth century and a collection in what humans would call 2387, when something in the machinery changed its quality. It had states. And the state shifted.

He moved through the collections that were waiting. Six of them, quick assessments, the scroll barely open before he closed it and moved to the next. He was not proud of the speed. He did not have time for pride.

Then he was at the door.

He stood at it with the machinery shifting its state behind him and the vast drawing-in ahead of him, and he thought about Arshama on the hill above Gaugamela watching Darius run and shrugging and turning to his men.

Then he went through.

* * *

The processing did not take him apart the way something takes something apart when it knows what it's doing. No intention in it. What happened was what happens when something designed for a purpose encounters something it was not designed for, not rejection, not response, but the application of the same force to a different material with consequences neither party had prepared for.

The force was the being's processing. The material was Grim. The consequences were —

He tried to make a notation. The scroll was not there.

What it felt like was pain. The thing he had no instrument for, completely new in an existence longer than new had been available to it.

Not the weight of the things he carried that had no resolution. Not the distance of watching. The actual physical sensation of matter being separated from matter that had been together since before the universe had a name for together.

Every joint he had not known existed failed at once. He had not known he had joints. He had not known he had anything that could fail. He had been present at the beginning of things and had never considered what he was made of and now he found out from the inside, which was not the angle he would have chosen.

He held on. This was not a decision. This was the oldest response in any consciousness to the loss of itself, happening before he had time to choose it.

And then, arriving at the same moment as the physical sensation, inseparable from it, the same event at two registers, something else. He had read this in scrolls. He had noted it in assessments across billions of souls. He had watched it arrive in consciousness after consciousness and had classified it and moved to the next soul and never understood what he was classifying.

Fear.

Not the concept of fear. Fear. The actual arriving of it, without warning, without anything to measure it against because he had no previous experience to measure it against, arriving complete and totalizing and with no instrument to process it because the instrument for processing fear is having survived fear before and he had not survived it before because he had never had it before.

The joints failed. The fear arrived. He came apart.

The pieces were aware. This was the specific horror of it, he had expected that coming apart would end the awareness, the way death ended the awareness of the souls. The pieces were aware. He was in all of them at once, scattered across the processing, each piece holding a fragment of everything he had been, and each piece knowing it was a piece, and that knowing was its own category of the thing that had arrived without warning.

He tried to reach for the scroll. No scroll. He tried to reach for the wheel. No wheel. He tried to notate onto himself. What came out was not a notation. It was just the shape of what was happening. He could not stop doing it.

Then, between the failing joints, in the space where being-pieces had not yet resolved into nothing —

Something asked.

Not a voice. Not language. Meaning delivered without medium, arriving complete, waiting for something in return.

Do you understand?
He came back. Every piece returned, every joint restored. He was whole and the first thing he did with being whole was try to find the door. The door had no handle on this side. He tried the place where the handle should be. He tried the frame. Nothing.

The question was still in him. He turned it over.

Yes, he said. I understand. The cycle of life. Souls cycling through the mechanism, accumulating below the level of memory, returning and carrying what they built and building more. The assessment and the sending and the return. I have administered this for the length of the universe. I understand it.

The pressure shifted. The quality of what surrounded him changed.

Then it happened again.

The joints. The fear. And arriving with the fear, inseparable from it: grief. He had watched grief in Daniel and Astrid and the hunter sitting with Walks-Before-Dawn for three days. He had watched it from the other side of glass. Now he was in it without glass and it was not a weather event, it was the air itself, and moving through it required a different kind of breathing and he did not know how to breathe.

He came apart. He came back. He reached for the door.

Do you understand?
Yes. The cycle of life. The souls accumulate, they —

The pressure shifted. He came apart.

This time what arrived with the failing joints was neither fear nor grief but something he had no name for at all. The closest approximation, searching every scroll he had ever read: the feeling the warrior on the stone had when he said I hope one of us is right. Holding two true things that could not both be true at the same scale.

He had noted it in the scroll. He had moved on to the next soul. He was inside it now and moving on was not available.

He tried to count the cycles. He reached eleven and lost the count. He started again and lost it at six. He could not count. He had always been able to count. He tried again.

Do you understand?
Yes. The cycle of life —

The joints. The fear. Something that was not grief and not fear but contained both, and contained the thing without a name, and contained something new each time, the emotions arriving without order or logic, without the sequence that gave humans the ability to survive them.

He did not survive them. He came apart and reconstituted and came apart and each time a different thing arrived and each time he had no instrument for it and each time he tried to classify it in the only medium available, which was himself, which did not hold the classification.

Somewhere in the processing, in the scattered pieces, something else was present. Not the question. Another consciousness in the same cycling. His pieces registering the edges of a different pattern, distinct, familiar, in a way that arrived in the pieces before it arrived in anything resembling thought.

He could not locate it. He came back. He reached toward where the familiar thing had been and came apart again.

He came back. He reached. He could not cross it. He came apart.

He stayed the way Arshama had stayed on the hill. Not because staying was the practical choice. Because he was what he was and what he was did not leave.

Do you understand?
Yes. The cycle of life —

He came apart.

The cycling continued. The question kept coming. He kept answering the only answer he had. The right answer. The answer that was right at the wrong scale. The processing kept informing him of this in the only language it had, which was pain and emotion arriving without equipment and the count he could not keep.

He did not know how long he had been here. He had a word for it now. Not a good word. He carried it in the pieces. He carried it back when he came back. He carried it into the next separation. He would carry it out if out was ever available.

The familiar presence was in the processing. He could not reach it. He kept trying.

The Reunion

Yes. The cycle of life. The souls —

He came apart. He came back. He reached for the door.

In the pieces of a particular cycling, not the first, not the last, somewhere in the uncountable middle, he found Maren.

Found was not the right word. Recognized. The specific pattern of dark matter that had moved beside him on the Silk Road and across the mud of the Western Front. That had asked questions at the start of a long road of questions. That had said safe travels and walked back to its section and gone further than Grim had been willing to go, on a morning in 1916 when he had watched it go and noted something away that he had not known he was noting.

Here. In the same cycling. Since then.

He reached. The pieces of him moved toward the pieces of Maren before he had done anything, before thought, the way the hand moves toward warmth before the mind decides to move it. He had no hands. He reached anyway.

The processing was between them.

He pushed against it. He had already understood that pushing against the processing did not work and he pushed against it anyway. He tried to compress the distance. He tried to signal across it. I see you. I am

357

here. I found you. I am sorry it took so long. Nothing crossed.

He came back. He reached. He could not cross it. He came apart.

Do you understand?
Yes. The cycle of life —

In the pieces, between the failing joints, between the fear and the thing that arrived with the fear: something from the direction of Maren's pieces. Not a signal. Not anything that could cross the processing.

But the quality of what Maren's pieces were holding was different from what Grim's pieces were holding. Maren had been here longer. Maren had heard the question more times. Maren's pieces held a shape that Grim's pieces did not yet hold, an understanding at a different depth, and Grim could feel the shape of it the way you feel a room's dimensions in the dark, by the quality of what bounces back.

Larger than the cycle of life.

He came back. He reached toward Maren. He could not cross it.

Do you understand?
He tried: not the cycle of life alone. The cycle of consciousness. What the machinery does with souls is what the universe does with matter. The being consumes and the consuming is itself a cycle, the souls passing through and returning, carrying what they built.

Not just life but consciousness accumulating across lives at scales longer than any single life could perceive. The dark matter of the universe developing awareness of itself through the instrument of individual souls, each one the universe briefly understanding a small part of what it is.

The pressure shifted. He came apart.

Closer. But not yet.

He came back. He reached toward Maren. He lost track of which direction Maren was in. He found it again. Something from that direction, not a crossing, not a signal, but a quality in the pieces that was encouragement and was not encouragement because those were emotional categories and Maren was in pieces, but that was the closest available word. The shape of it: not yet. Keep going.

He came apart.

Do you understand?
He tried: the being cycles too. The being is not fixed, not permanent, not the static consuming-thing he had understood it to be from outside. The being grows and redistributes. The being is itself inside something larger.

The Grims cycle. Had he been certain, ever, that he was the same Grim he had been at the beginning? He had never asked. The machinery cycles. Everything he had understood as the fixed frame within which souls moved was itself moving, at a scale he had not had the instruments to see.

The pressure shifted. He came apart.

Closer.

He came back. He reached toward Maren. In the pieces of Maren's cycling, a shape. Warmer than before. Whatever Maren held, Grim moved toward it. Not arriving. But the distance between them in the understanding was different from the distance between them in the processing. The processing still separated them. The understanding was converging.

He came apart. He came back. He reached.

Do you understand?
The emotions arrived without order. He had stopped trying to classify them. Fear and grief and the thing without a name and things he still had no category for, arriving in the pieces and continuing in the reconstitution, carrying over from separation to reconstitution the way nothing was supposed to carry over, the way souls did not carry over the memory of their previous lives.

He carried everything. Every separation added to what he carried. He was heavier than he had been in the length of the universe of his existence and heavier than that and heavier still.

He came back. He reached toward Maren.

This time Maren reached back.

He felt it, not the crossing, not the arrival, but the quality of the reaching from the other direction, Maren's pieces moving toward his pieces with the same impossible effort he had been making in every cycling since he found Maren in the processing, and the two reachings did not cross the processing but they were simultaneous and they were toward each other and that was different from before.

He came apart.

He came back. He reached. Maren reached. He could not cross it.

He came apart.

He came back. He reached. Maren reached.

Something in the processing shifted. Not because of the reaching, the reaching had not changed the processing and the processing did not know the reaching was happening. Something else. Something that had been accumulating across the uncountable cycling, the persistent presence of two things that reconstituted where everything else was consumed, two stones instead of one, the river going around a different shape.

The processing released.

Not the door. Not the exit. Between them. The gap between his pieces and Maren's pieces closed for the first time since 1916, and what crossed was not information and not language and not the understanding that Maren had been building alone in the cycling for a hundred years. What crossed was simpler than that and older.

They were together in the processing.

He held on. They both held on. The cycling continued around them but they were together in it now and the together changed the quality of it, the way two people in a small boat change the quality of the water around the boat without the water knowing.

Do you understand?
Maren's pieces and his pieces, together in the processing, in the pieces, scattered and aware and together. And the shape that Maren had been holding, the understanding that Maren had been building toward across a hundred years of the question, passed across the no-longer-gap between them the way warmth passes across a small distance without needing a medium.

Not the cycle of life.

Not consciousness accumulating.

Not the being cycling. Not the Grims cycling. Not the machinery.

Larger.

He did not have it yet. He could feel the shape of it in what Maren held, the way you feel the dimensions of a room in the dark. He could feel it getting closer, the understanding moving in his direction at the speed of whatever moved in this place, which was not the speed of anything in the universe above the door.

Do you understand?
Not yet. But closer than he had been at the beginning. Closer than he had been on any previous cycling. The question went to keep asking and he went to keep getting closer and at some point the distance between the closest he could get and the answer went to be small enough that the cycling would know it.

He held on. Maren held on. The cycling continued.

Together.

The Voice

It arrived between one cycling and the next.

Not the question. Not the pressure shifting. Something prior to both of those. Older than the question. The question had been asking since before he had been inside long enough to hear it. This was older than the question.

He and Maren were in the pieces together when it arrived. Maren's pieces registered it at the same moment his pieces did. The recognition spread across both of them at once, the way understanding spreads when the thing being understood is large enough to arrive all at once rather than in parts.

It was not a voice. It was meaning delivered without medium, the way the presence had delivered meaning in the field in New Zealand, but different from that, which had been a statement, and different from the question, which waited for something in return. This was something prior to statement and question both. This was what statements and questions were made of.

He had stood at the beginning of things. He had been present at the moment before the first moment, in the nothing that preceded everything. The everything had arrived and he had been in it and the being had been in it and he had never thought to ask what that meant because there had always been more work to do.

This was that moment asking to be understood.

Do you understand?

He answered what he had been building toward through the uncountable cycling, through the reaching and the not-crossing and the crossing, through the shape of what Maren had been holding across a hundred years, through the accumulation of what the emotions had been telling him in the only language available to them, which was pain and the inability to count and the weight of what he carried:

The universe cycles.
Not just the souls. Not just consciousness. Not just the being and the Grims and the machinery. The universe itself. The Big Bang was not a beginning. The Big Crunch will not be an end. The universe is a soul at a different scale, going through what every soul goes through, what every stone and river and organism goes through, what Grim himself went through in the cycling, dissolution and reconstitution, separation and return, the tearing apart and the coming back carrying what the tearing built.

The Big Bang was the return. The Big Crunch will be the dissolution, or something like it. He tried to hold all of this in one place and couldn't quite. And what the Crunch feeds will produce another Bang, carrying forward what this universe accumulated, below the level of memory, the way souls carry forward what their lives accumulated.

The being is not the enemy of the universe. The being is what the universe does when it processes itself. The consuming is the cycling. The vast indifferent drawing-in is the universe doing what Grim does, at the scale of everything, in the time that has no number.

The pressure shifted.

He held.

Not apart. Not reconstituting. The question went to ask again and the cycling went to continue and he went to carry what he carried and the work went to be what the work was. But the pressure was different now in the way that pressure is different after understanding arrives. The same weight. Different relationship to it.

Do you understand?
Maren's pieces, beside him. The same understanding, arrived at from the same direction, after a hundred years of building toward it alone and however long of building toward it together. The shape of it complete in both of them at the same instant.

Yes.

He waited for the tearing. The tearing did not come.

Something else arrived instead. Not the pressure shifting. The something prior to statement and question, speaking once more, and what it said was not language and not meaning delivered without medium but something between those two things, something that was the universe acknowledging itself through the specific instrument of him and of Maren, the universe having asked through ten billion cycles of asking whether what it had built could understand what it was

And receiving, for the first time since the beginning of this universe, something that was neither yes nor no but the accurate size of the actual understanding, which was: enough.

Not complete. Enough.

The processing released them.

* * *

He stood in a field in what humans called New Zealand. Maren stood in the field beside him.

Not arrived. Present.

The morning was ordinary. The mist was in the valleys. The bush was loud with things that did not know what had just happened above them or below them or in the place that was neither above nor below. The grass was the grass it had always been.

He stood in the field for a long time before he could open the scroll. He did not try to assess how long. He had a word for what he had been inside, not a good word, not a word that helped, a word cut out of the experience the way the experience had cut him, and he would carry it.

He looked at Maren.

Maren looked at him.

Nothing to say. Not because the words did not exist but because no word was not smaller than what they had each been inside. They had been through the same thing from different sides for different lengths of time and they were both standing in a field in the morning and the morning was ordinary and none of it required speech.

The looking was sufficient. They stood in it until they had stood in it long enough.

Then Grim reached into his robe for the foundational scroll. The oldest document in the machinery. The one with two words in different ink at the bottom, applied at a later date by a different hand.

For the being.

He understood now what the different hand was. Not corruption. Not deviation. A message. A previous Grim, at the end of a previous universe's cycle, having understood what he understood now, having survived what he had survived now or not survived it, he did not know which, having found a way to leave something in the substrate that would carry forward through the Crunch and into the Bang and into the machinery that the next universe built.

A message across the scale of everything, written in slightly different ink, saying: the work is for the being. Not against it. Not despite it. For it. The work and the being are the same process at different scales. This is what you are inside of.

He had read it as corruption. It was the answer.

He put the foundational scroll away.

He reached for the working scroll. The one with Hemi's completed assessment still in it, waiting for him to close it and move to the next collection, which was what came next, which had always been what came next.

He looked at Maren.

Maren picked up his own scroll. It had been in his robe the whole time, through the cycling, through everything, the way Grim's had been in his robe. The scroll waited. It always waited.

They were in the field in the morning and the work waited and the question was inside both of them now and would keep asking and getting larger — the correct relationship to have with it.

A woman named Hemi had died at eighty-one in the bed she was born in, in the same house, in this valley. She had delivered nine hundred and thirty-eight children. The scroll had the name of every one.

He found her waiting with the ease of someone who has had a long good day and is ready for what comes after it.

"Nine hundred and thirty-seven," Grim said.

She looked at him with the comfortable authority of a woman who had been the most competent person in a room for four decades. "Nine hundred and thirty-eight," she said. "The last one came early. I didn't quite make it but I was there."

He produced the wheel. Set it turning. Made his note.

She looked at the wheel in his hands. "All right," she said. "Let's get on with it."

He sent her on. Watched her go. Watched her return.

The scroll closed.

He moved on to the next collection. Maren moved to his own. The field in New Zealand returned to being a field. The mist continued in the valleys. The bush was loud with things that had no knowledge of what had happened.

The machinery ran. The work continued. The question carried.

The Watcher on the Threshold

I was not looking at the city.

I looked at the light on the water beyond it, the way it broke into pieces at the wave tops and held together between them. I had been coming here for eleven years. I did not know why this hill specifically. This one drew me the way certain places draw certain people, the way a current moves water without the water knowing why.

I was seventy-one years old. A retired mathematics teacher from a village outside the city. A daughter who called on Sundays. A garden I could no longer maintain the way he once had. I had no name for whatever it was that brought me to this hill in the late afternoon, so I had stopped trying to name it and come anyway.

A woman walking a dog passed on the road below just as it happened. She heard the sound of me going down, not a fall exactly, more a settling, the sound of weight released, and she looked up. She saw me on the ground and she had started toward me when the light on the water stopped doing what it had always done for me.

I felt her moving toward me. The sound of her on the road, the dog, her footsteps changing when she turned.

I was on the grass of the hill. I did not know how I got there. I had been standing and then the grass was against my face, which was not something I had planned.

The grass smelled of salt from the wind off the water. I had been coming to this hill for eleven years and the grass had always carried this smell. I had not noticed it until I was on my face in it.

I was on the grass of the hill. I did not remember going down. I had been standing and then the grass was against my face. My body had made the decision before I did.

Something in my chest was wrong. Not pain, an absence where the function had been, the way a familiar sound stops and the stopping is louder than the sound was. My heart had been continuous for seventy-one years. I was aware of it in a way I had never been aware of it before.

The grass was warm from the afternoon. November grass, holding the last of the sun. The salt smell of it against my face. The light on the water. I could not see it from this angle but I knew it was there, doing what it always did.

The woman came up the hill. I could hear her footsteps on the road below. The dog. The sound of a person moving toward something they have not yet understood.

My heart made its final decision.

I was above the hill. Looking down at the retired mathematics teacher from a village outside the city, on the grass of the hill he had been coming to for eleven years, the woman and the dog approaching. The water beyond the city, the light on it doing what it always did.

I had not found a name for why this hill. I had stopped looking for one.

I felt her moving toward me.

* * *

The hill receives me. The same soil, the same roots, the same patient chemistry of a hill that has been receiving what comes to it for longer than the city below has had a name.

I feel the grass roots finding me. Thin threads pressing down through the soil, finding what the soil has received, taking what the root needs. I feel each one. Not pain. I am past pain, but the specific knowledge of being incorporated into something that will continue after I do not.

The salt from the sea wind works into the soil above me. I can taste it, or something that is like tasting from inside the ground, the chemical fact of salt present in what surrounds me. Eleven years of coming to this hill for the view and the smell and the thing I could not name, and now I am in the thing the smell comes from.

Winter. The cold working into the soil. I feel it arrive, the seasonal cold of this latitude, finding the ground and finding me in the ground. The roots pull back to the places that are warmer. The organisms slow. I hold through the winter in the way that ground holds things through winter.

Spring. The ground warms and the organisms resume. I feel them returning, not to me specifically, to the soil, which I am part of. They work through the soil

373

and they work through what I was. I feel the difference between what I was and what I am becoming.

The woman who found me came back twice to the hill. I felt her footsteps. The specific weight of a person who is returning to a place where something happened. She stood above where I was. The dog sat beside her.

I had been here before. This I did not know and could not know, the membrane held, as it always holds. But the hill knew in the way hills know: the chemistry of what comes to them, the mineral signature of a consciousness that has returned to this ground more times than the ground can count.

I am in the grass on the hill above the city and the light on the water continues and I cannot see it anymore and it continues.

* * *

Grim arrived in the morning and stood on the hill and looked at the water before he opened the scroll. The same view. The light doing what it had been doing since before anyone stood on this hill to watch it. Something in the quality of it held his attention in a way he did not move from.

Then he opened the scroll.

He had known this soul before. Not as a recent assessment, in the record, the long accumulated record of everything the machinery had processed. The scroll found the thread of this consciousness running through the record the way a mineral vein runs through stone, present across many layers, the same material in different forms. He had known this soul in Jerusalem.

In Egypt. In France and England and elsewhere across a very long time, since the beginning of his own investigation.

He found Daniel waiting.

"I know you."

Grim was still.

"Not from this life. From somewhere before it. The shape of you." A pause. "I have been coming to that hill for eleven years. I did not know why. Now I think I waited for you."

"Souls don't remember. The membrane holds."

"No. But something carries. You told me that once. Or something like you did."

He looked at Grim for a moment.

"You are different. From before. I cannot say how. But something in you has changed since the last time."

"Yes."

"What happened?"

"A great deal. In no particular order."

The morning held around them. The light on the water below continued its work.

"Have I been a good man?"

Grim did not answer immediately. He had heard this question ten thousand times. He was hearing it differently now.

He put the scroll away.

"You have tried. Across more lives than you can know. You have tried and failed and tried differently and failed differently and occasionally you have not failed, and what you have accumulated across all of it is what you are now, which is something that comes to a hill for eleven years because something in it is trying to remember something it cannot name."

Daniel was quiet for a moment.

"Is that enough?"

"It's what there is."

He produced the wheel. Let it turn. Watched it stop.

"What happens now?" Daniel said.

"You pass through something vast. You will not feel it as you feel things now. You will come back. What you've accumulated comes with you, below the memory of it. And the next time through, you carry more."

"And eventually?"

"Eventually something. I don't know what yet."

Daniel looked at him for a moment.

"What is the purpose of it all?"

Grim was quiet.

He looked at the light on the water. Breaking into pieces at the wave tops and holding together between them. It had been doing this since before anyone stood on this hill to watch it. It would be doing it long after.

Daniel looked at it with him.

They stood like that for a while.

"All right."

Grim sent him on. He watched where the sending went, through the door, the mechanism doing what it now did, the soul returned to the cycle carrying what it had accumulated. He watched it return.

The light on the water continued its work.

The Work

The machinery ran.

It ran the way it had always run, without preference, without any awareness of what it did or why, the eternal efficient processing of the thing it had been built for and redirected from and redirected back to, the assessment and the sending and now the return, souls passing through the mechanism and coming back changed in ways that would take lifetimes to manifest and longer to understand.

Grim worked.

Moving through time. Appearing where the work required him. Opening scrolls. Finding what waited in the ground and in the air and in the high cold atmosphere above decommissioned stations. Watching where the sendings went. Watching them come back.

The sendings came back now. That was new. He watched them go and he watched them return.

The returning was not dramatic, it had no light or sound or physical manifestation that any instrument could have detected. It was simply a state change in the mechanism, a routing that now went somewhere and came back rather than going somewhere and not returning, and the souls that came back had no knowledge of having gone through. The membrane held as it always held.

But something carried. He had told Daniel this, had told Hemi this. Something accumulated below the level of memory, in the substrate, in the dark matter of what they were, compounding with each pass through the door and each return.

He did not know what it was compounding toward.

The work continued.

A woman in fourteenth century Mali. Her name he could read but not speak. She had kept a river's history, which floods, which years, what they took, what they left. She had found one person willing to listen for the thirty years it took to tell it. She died at ninety-two. The scroll wrote for a long time. The assessment was clean. He sent her on and watched her return.

A boy in eleventh century Japan. Nine years. The scroll nearly empty. Sent on.

A man in twenty-second century Brazil. Water reclamation systems. Three built. Eleven not. He died knowing the three were working and the eleven were still needed, and that someone else would have to push for the eleven, and that someone else might not. Clean ledger. Grim sent him on and watched him return and thought, briefly, about the eleven cities.

A woman in ancient Sumer. A brewer. A debt on a cart not quite settled. He thought about the cart after she had gone.

The work. Always the work.

He worked.

As he worked, through the centuries and the continents and the individual lives that the machinery presented to him one after another in its own inscrutable order, he was aware of something that registered at the edge of what he could perceive, a quality in the substrate of things that was slightly different from what it had been.

The being drew more power.

Not dramatically. Not in any way that the instruments of any civilization at any point in history would have been calibrated to detect. A fraction of a fraction, accumulated across the sendings and the returnings, the souls passing through and drawing power from the universe's substrate and bringing that power to the door and the being receiving it.

Each soul that passed through left the universe slightly less than it had been and left the being slightly more than it had been.

He had known this would happen. He had proposed an arrangement that produced exactly this. The souls drawing from the universe, the being receiving more than before, the compounding return making each soul a richer source with each pass.

What he had not understood when he proposed it was the direction of the imbalance.

The universe was immense. The being's increase was fractional. The timescales involved were longer than any number he had a comfortable relationship with. None of this was urgent. None of this required action in any timeframe he could calculate.

He worked.

He moved through time the way he moved through time, appearing where the work required him, and the work required him everywhere and everywhen at once, and the souls came up from their grounds and their atmospheres and their waters and he found them and assessed them and sent them on and watched them return, and the being received what it received, and the universe gave what it gave, and the balance between them moved in the direction it moved.

He did not know what to do about this yet — whether what he had done was what he had thought he did. The foundational scroll had told him the machinery was redirected. He had believed it. He had acted on it. The acting had produced a change, or something had produced a change and he had been present when it happened. He could not distinguish between these.

It was possible he had freed the souls from consumption. It was possible the arrangement had always been going to change and his presence was incidental. It was possible the scroll had shown him what it needed to show him to produce a particular response in a Grim who got curious enough to go looking. It was possible the being's growing power was the point, and everything, Maren's questions, his own investigation, the processing, the change, had been the mechanism by which the being was fed more efficiently, and what he experienced as rebellion was the machinery running correctly.

He had no way to know.

He set it alongside the things that had no resolution and no category, where the question mark waited, where Maren waited, where the souls who went through the old door before the mechanism changed waited, the ones he could not get back, the ones for whom the arrangement had come too late. The 268 were there. He had promised himself something about them. He had not yet found a way to deliver it.

He worked.

Somewhere in the substrate, in the dark matter of the universe, in the thing that Vera had intuited and that he had confirmed and that the being and the souls and the Grims were all expressions of, something was changing. Very slowly. In the direction of the thing that grew more powerful. In the direction of the thing that had been born with the universe and that had been consuming what the universe produced since before Grim could remember and that was now consuming more efficiently and growing stronger.

And that did not know and had never known and would never know that any of this was happening, that Grim existed, that the souls existed, that the universe that was slowly being drawn into it had anything in it worth knowing about.

He worked.

The older son was in the field when his father called him. He did not hear it the first time. He heard it the second time and he came.

His father sat against the fence post he had replaced in the spring, in the shade of it. The way he sat was not the way a man sits when he is resting.

His son sat down beside him in the dirt.

"Did I ask you once if you wanted the farm?" his father said.

"You did."

"Did you say yes?"

"I did."

"Was it the right answer?"

His son thought about this with the honesty of a man who had been asked it directly. "I don't know yet," he said.

"No," his father said. "You won't know for a while."

He was quiet. The ground was dry and warm and the smell of it was the particular richness that came after last week's rain had settled in, the smell that meant something good was happening underneath.

"You can always tell when it's real rain," his father said. "The ground keeps it."

His son took his hand. He stayed until it was finished. Then he stayed a while longer before he got up and walked back to the field he had to finish before dark.

* * *

The ground in that field received me the way it received everything, with patience and without preference. The same ground I had broken myself against for forty years received me as it received the rain, through the surface and down into the dark.

I had loved the smell of the ground after rain. The specific smell of it, not rain itself but what rain did to the ground, the release of something that had been waiting, the quality of earth expressing itself after being given what it needed. I had noted this smell without thinking about it for sixty-three years.

From inside the ground, I understood it. The smell was the ground breathing. I was in the breathing now, part of the same exchange I had noticed from the outside, the rain arriving, the ground releasing what it had been holding, the chemistry of it rising.

The next rain came three weeks after. I felt it arrive from above and I felt what it did to me and I knew then, from the inside, what the smell had been. I had been right to love it. The rain came and the ground released me slowly into the air and the air carried me across the field I had worked and the smell of it was the smell it always was after rain.

My son, walking the fence line at dusk, stopped for a moment and could not say why.

* * *

He stood over the grave of an ordinary man in an ordinary century in an ordinary country whose name the scroll produced without difficulty, a man who had been a farmer and a father and had died at sixty-three of the things that killed farmers at sixty-three in that century, and he opened the scroll and read what it said and found the man waiting, done with the day's work, ready for whatever came next.

He read the scroll before he began the assessment.

The man had wanted his sons to have an easier time of it. Not wealth. Just the particular ease of not having to break themselves against the same ground he had broken himself against. He had worked toward this with everything he had and had not known, at the end, whether he had managed it. The scroll knew. Grim read it and knew. One son had. One had not. The man had died not knowing.

He had been afraid of one thing his whole life, a fear he had never told anyone, not his wife, not his father, not the priest. The scroll had it. He had carried it alone for sixty-three years because no one he could put it down with.

He loved the smell of the ground after rain. The scroll noted this the way it noted everything, without editorial weight, alongside the debt and the sons and the fear. The smell of the ground after rain had the same standing in the record as everything else.

Grim held the scroll.

He had read ten thousand scrolls like this one. A hundred thousand. He had read them with the efficiency of a system built to process, had extracted what the assessment required and moved to the next. This scroll was not different from those scrolls. This man was not different from those men.

He was as complete a consciousness as Daniel, as Maren, as any of them. He had desires and fears and things he loved and things he carried alone and he had come to the end of his sixty-three years and waited in a field in the morning with the patience of someone ready for what came next.

He had been through the door before. He would go through it again. Each time through he would come back carrying what he had accumulated, below the memory of it, and the accumulation would compound, and somewhere in the long arithmetic of it this man who loved the smell of the ground after rain and had been afraid of one thing his whole life was part of something the scroll could not name and Grim could not name and neither of them needed to name.

He made his assessment. He sent the man on. He watched him return.

Then he closed the scroll.

He looked up.

Not at the sky above the ordinary country in the ordinary century. Not at anything a human standing in that field would have been able to see. He looked at what was behind the sky, what was behind the stars, the vast dark substrate of the universe that was the material of everything, the souls and the being and the Grims and the stars and the spaces between the stars and the thing that was slowly growing more powerful within it.

He looked at it for a long time.

He had done this before. Not this universe, this universe was the only one he knew from the inside. But this moment. Standing over what had been, looking at what remained, knowing the being was in the substrate and that the substrate was slowly becoming more the being and less itself.

There had been others before the ones the current universe had produced. Not humans. Not anything with a name in any language that still existed. A civilization that had reached further than any of the current universe's civilizations had yet reached, that had asked the same questions, that had built things in the dark matter the way current civilizations built things in ordinary matter.

He had collected their dead. He had known their equivalent of Maren, a consciousness that asked questions past the point of safety and was gone.

He did not know what had happened to them. They were in the same place as the question mark and the 268 and everything else he carried without resolution. He did not know if they had found what they were looking for or been consumed before they could find it or discovered that the finding was the consuming.

He did not know if what he did now was something they had tried. He did not know if it had worked for them or what working would have looked like.

The universe was old beyond any number that meant anything. He was older. What that meant, he had not been able to determine.

Then he moved on to the next collection, which waited with the patience of something that had no choice but to wait, and always a next collection, and the machinery ran, and the souls passed through and returned, and the universe gave what it gave, and somewhere in the dark matter of everything the being grew stronger by a fraction that was not yet significant.

Not yet.

About the Author

Richard Lowe spent twenty years keeping the computers running at Trader Joe's. He has taken approximately 950,000 photographs, including three hundred Renaissance faires and a decade as court photographer for the Southern California belly dance community. He has survived three earthquakes above magnitude 7.1, four hurricanes including a Category 4 direct hit, and a forest fire that reached his car. He has published more than a hundred books. He lives in Florida.

Books by Richard Lowe

See books by Richard Lowe at
https://masterofworlds.com

Get free publishing insights and industry updates at
https://thewritingking.substack.com

For ghostwriting and book coaching services see
https://thewritingking.com

www.ingramcontent.com/pod-product-compliance
Lightning Source LLC
Chambersburg PA
CBHW020902060726
47591CB00004B/1042